Ammie, Come Home

Barbara Michaels

"Michaels has a fine downright way with the supernatural. Good firm style and many picturesque twists."

—*San Francisco Chronicle*

"This author never fails to entertain."

—*Cleveland Plain Dealer*

"Miss Michaels has a fine sense of atmosphere and storytelling."

—*New York Times*

"A master of the modern Gothic novel."

—*Library Journal*

"With Barbara Michaels, you always get a great story."

—*Ocala Star-Banner*

"We are not normally disposed to read Gothic novels . . . but when Michaels turns her talents to the genre, we admit to being hooked!"

—*Denver Post*

Berkley books by Barbara Michaels

AMMIE, COME HOME
BE BURIED IN THE RAIN

BARBARA MICHAELS
AMMIE, COME HOME

BERKLEY BOOKS, NEW YORK

AMMIE, COME HOME

A Berkley Book/published by arrangement with
the author

PRINTING HISTORY
Meredith Press edition published 1968
Berkley edition/May 1987

ISBN: 0-425-09949-0

A BERKLEY BOOK ® TM 757,375
Berkley Books are published by The Berkley Publishing Group,
200 Madison Avenue, New York, NY 10016.
The name "BERKLEY" and the stylized "B" with design are trademarks
belonging to Berkley Publishing Corporation.

PRINTED IN THE UNITED STATES OF AMERICA

Chapter One

By five o'clock it was almost dark, which was not surprising, since the month was November; but Ruth kept glancing uneasily toward the windows at the far end of the room. It was a warm, handsome room, furnished in the style of a past century, with furniture whose present value would have astonished the original owners. Only the big overstuffed sofas, which faced one another before the fireplace, were relatively modern. Their ivory brocade upholstery fitted the blue-and-white color scheme, which had been based upon the delicate Wedgwood plaques set in the mantel. A cheerful fire burned on the hearth, sending sparks dancing from the crystal glasses on the coffee table and turning the sherry in the cut-glass decanter the color of melted copper. Since her niece had come to stay with her, Ruth had set out glasses and wine every evening. It was a pleasant ritual, which they both enjoyed even when it was followed by nothing more elegant than hamburgers. But tonight Sara was late.

The darkening windows blossomed yellow as the streetlights went on; and Ruth rose to draw the curtains. She lingered at the window, one hand absently stroking the pale blue satin. Sara's class had been over at three thirty. . . .

And, Ruth reminded herself sternly, Sara was twenty years old. When she agreed to board her niece while the girl attended the Foreign Service Institute at a local university, she had not guaranteed full-time baby-sitting. Sara, of course, considered herself an adult. However, to Ruth her niece still had the touching, terrifying illusion of personal invulnerability which is an unmistakable attribute of youth. And the streets of Washington—even of this ultrafashionable section—were not completely safe after dark.

Even at the dying time of year, with a bleak dusk lowering, the view from Ruth's window retained some of the famous charm of Georgetown, a charm based on formal architecture and the awareness of age. Nowadays that antique grace was rather self-conscious; after decades of neglect, the eighteenth-century houses of the old town had become fashionable again, and now they had the sleek, smug look born of painstaking restoration and a lot of money.

The houses across the street had been built in the early 1800's. The dignified Georgian facades, ornamented by well-proportioned dormers and handsome fanlights, abutted directly on the street, with little or no yard area in front. Behind them were the gardens for which the town was famous, hidden from passersby and walled off from the sight of near neighbors. Now only the tops of leafless trees could be seen.

The atmosphere was somewhat marred by the line of cars, parked bumper to bumper and, for the most part, illegally. Parking was one of Georgetown's most acrimoniously debated problems, not unusual in a city which had grown like Topsy before the advent of the automobile. The vehicles that moved along the street had turned on their headlights, and Ruth peered nervously toward the corner, and the bus stop. Still no sign of Sara. Ruth muttered something mildly profane under her breath and then shook her head with a self-conscious smile. The mother-hen instinct was all the stronger for having been delayed.

II

Ruth was in her mid-forties. She had always been small, and still kept her trim figure, but since she refused to "do things" to her graying hair, or indulge in any of the other fads demanded of women by an age which makes such a fetish of youth, her more modish friends referred to her pityingly as "well-preserved." She bought her clothes at the same elegant little Georgetown boutique which she had patronized for fifteen years, and wore precisely the same size she had worn at the first. The suit she was wearing was a new purchase: a soft tweedy mixture of pink and blue, with a shell-pink, high-necked sweater. As a business-woman she clung to the tradition of suits, but as a feminine person she liked the pastels which set off her blue eyes and gilt hair, now fading pleasantly from gold to silver.

Standing at the tall window, she shivered despite the suit jacket. This part of the room was always too cold; even the heavy, lined drapes did not seem to keep out tendrils of chilly air, and the room was too long and narrow for the single fireplace halfway along its long wall. Ruth wondered idly how her ancestors had stood the cold in the days before central heating. They were tougher in the good old days, she thought—tougher in every way, less sentimental and more realistic. None of them would have stood jittering and biting their nails over a child who was a few minutes late.

Of course, in those days a well-bred young woman wouldn't be out at dusk without a chaperone.

As Ruth was about to abandon her vigil a car slowed. It hovered uncertainly for a few minutes and then darted, like the strange insect it resembled, into a narrow space by a fireplug. Ruth leaned forward, forgetting that she could be seen quite clearly in the lighted window so near the street. Since there was hardly any subject which interested her less than that of automobiles, she was unable to identify the make of this one, except that she thought it "foreign."

The near door opened; and a tangle of arms and legs emerged and resolved itself into the tall figure of her niece. Ruth smiled, partly in relief and partly because the sight of Sara trying to get her long legs and miniskirts out of a very small car always amused her. Her smile broadened as she got a good look at Sara's costume. Usually the girl was still in bed when Ruth left for work in the morning; Sara was a junior and had learned the fine art of arranging classes so that they did not interfere unduly with social activities or sleep; and every evening Ruth awaited her niece's appearance with anticipation and mild alarm. Every new outfit seemed to her the absolute end, the extreme beyond which it would be impossible to go. And each time she found she was mistaken.

Sara had one arm filled with books. With the other hand she swept the long black hair out of her face in a gesture that had proved the biggest single irritant to her long-suffering but silent aunt. The hair was absolutely straight. Ruth had never caught Sara ironing it, but she suspected the worst. At least the hair covered the girl's ears and throat and shoulders, serving some of the functions of the hat and scarf which Sara refused to wear; part of the time it also kept her nose and chin warm.

The flowing locks presumably compensated for the lack of covering on Sara's lower extremities. This evening she was wearing the long black boots which had been her most recent acquisition, but there was a gap of some six inches between their tops and the bottom of Sara's skirt. The gap was filled, but not covered, by black mesh stockings, which displayed a good deal of Sara between the half-inch meshes.

Sara's present costume was especially amusing when Ruth recalled her first sight of the girl, that morning in early September. Sara had stepped out of the taxi wearing a neat linen suit, nylon stockings, alligator pumps, and—incredibly—a hat and gloves. Ruth hadn't seen the suit or the hat or the gloves since. In retrospect Ruth couldn't help feeling a bit flattered, not so much by Sara's effort to be conventional for her—since she suspected that Sara's mother had had a good deal to do with that—but by Sara's assumption that she need not continue to be conventional.

Sara leaned down to address the driver through the window. The hair fell over her face again. Ruth forgot her twitching fingers in her curiosity. This was not one of her niece's usual escorts. Sara was apparently inviting him to come in, for the car door opened and a man stepped into the street. He narrowly missed being annihilated by a Volkswagen which skidded by him, but he seemed to be accustomed to this, as, indeed, are most Washingtonians.

Ruth's first impression was neutral. He was a big man, tall and broad-shouldered, but his most outstanding feature, visible even in the dimmish streetlight, was his hair. Its brilliant carroty red seemed untouched by gray. Yet Ruth knew he was not young; there was something about the way he stood and moved. . . .

He turned, in a brusque, sudden movement, and stared at the house. Ruth dropped the drape and stepped back. The sudden lift and turn of his head had been as direct as a touch. And what a fool she was, to stand gaping out at the street like a gossipy suburban housewife—or a Victorian guardian, checking up on her ward. She was blushing—an endearing habit which even fifteen years in the civil service had not eliminated—when she went to open the door. She had been told that she looked charming when she blushed; the rosy color gave vivacity to her pallor and delicate bone structure. Therefore she was slightly annoyed when the eyes of the man who stood outside her door slid blankly over her and focused on something beyond.

"Good God Almighty," he said.

Ruth's first, neutral impression was succeeded by one of profound distaste.

She glanced over her shoulder.

"I'm so glad you like it," she said frostily. "Won't you come in and have a better look? The wind is a bit chilly."

"This is Professor MacDougal, Ruth," Sara said, with the familiar sweep of hand across brow. "He was nice enough to drive me home. My aunt, Mrs. Bennett, Professor."

"Putting his worst foot forward, as usual," said Professor MacDougal, displaying a set of predatory looking teeth. His attention was now fully upon her, and Ruth wasn't sure she liked it. He was much bigger than she had realized—well over six feet and bulkily, thickly built. His national ancestry was written across his face, but it was not the Irish stereotype, which is more caricature than actuality; it was the sort of face one sees in old Irish portraits, combining dreamer and soldier. The hair was not pure red after all. It had plenty of gray, iron-colored rather than silver. The skin of his cheeks and chin was just beginning to loosen. He must be fifty, Ruth thought, but he does have rather a nice smile. . . .

"I'm sorry, Mrs. Bennett," he went on. "That was a hell of a way to address a strange lady, wasn't it? Particularly when you have just returned the lady's young niece. But I like good architecture, and that's a remarkable staircase. Smaller than the one at Octagon House, but equally fine."

"Come in," Ruth said.

"I am in. Want me to go back out and start all over?"

For a moment Ruth gaped at him, feeling as if she were on a boat in bad weather, with the deck slipping out from under her feet. Then something came to her rescue—for days she mistakenly identified it as her sense of humor. She said smilingly, "Never mind, the damage is done. What on earth do you teach, Professor?"

"Anthropology."

"Of course."

"Of course," he repeated gravely. "The abrupt, uncivilized manners, the profane speech, the weatherbeaten look. . . ."

"Not at all," Ruth said, trying to keep some grasp of the conversation. "Sara has mentioned you often. She enjoys your course so much. It was good of you to bring her home."

"She stayed to help me sort some papers. But it wasn't out of my way. I had nothing in particular to do this evening."

"Then you must have a glass of sherry—or something else, if you'd rather—before you go back out into that wind."

He accepted sherry, somewhat to Ruth's surprise; it seemed an inadequate beverage for someone so boisterously masculine, and a beer stein was more suited to his big hand than the fragile, fine-stemmed glass. He sat down on the sofa and relaxed, with a sigh which was an unconscious tribute to the restful charm of the room.

"Nice. Very nice. . . . The hanging stair is the *pièce de résistance,* though. Was the designer old Thornton himself?"

"The man who did the Capitol? So tradition says, but it can't be proved."

"In my salad days—about four wars back—I thought I

wanted to be an architect. I took the Georgetown House
tour, along with the social climbers and the gushing old
ladies, but I never saw this house. I'd have remembered the
stairs."

"Oh, then you're a native? They are rare in Washington,
and rarer in Georgetown."

"I don't live here anymore," he said briefly.

"But you may recall why this house wasn't on display.
The previous owner was an eccentric old lady, a genuine
Georgetown personality. She used to say she didn't want the
vulgar rabble tracking dust on her rugs and gaping at her
possessions."

"That's right, I remember now—though I never heard her
reasons expressed quite so forcibly and unflatteringly. Am I
right in assuming that you bought the house furnished? You
couldn't have collected this furniture and all the bric-a-brac,
in your short lifetime."

"Your general assumption is correct," Ruth said, ignoring the blatant attempt at flattery. "But I didn't buy the
house. Old Miss Campbell was my second cousin. She left
it to me."

"I didn't know she had any living relatives. It's beginning
to come back to me now—wasn't she the last of the
descendants of the original builder?"

"Yes, she was. This is one of the few houses which has
never been restored because it was never neglected; much of
the furniture has stood in its present location for a hundred
and fifty years. I'm a member of a collateral line. Actually,
Miss Campbell's father disowned my grandmother, about a
thousand years ago."

"How did you ever captivate the old lady?" MacDougal
ran one finger along the scalloped rim of the table beside
him. He had big, brown hands with thick fingers, but his
touch was as delicate as a musician's.

"Darned if I know. When I came to Washington years

ago I called on her, just as a matter of courtesy. I wasn't even interested in the house, as I was going through my Swedish modern phase at the time. But I knew that all her near relatives were dead, and I thought the poor old soul might be lonely. I couldn't have been more wrong! She had a tongue like an adder, and she employed it freely, believe me. If I hadn't been so well brought up I'd have walked out after the first five minutes. But I did adore the house; it was the first time I'd ever seen a place like this. Even now my interest is completely uneducated; I don't have time to study architecture or antiques, I just enjoy them. I was absolutely astounded last year, when Cousin Hattie's lawyer wrote to tell me that she had left the house to me."

"Maybe you were the only relative she knew personally. And she probably had a strong sense of family, like so many of these vinegary old virgins."

"I suppose so. I always felt guilty, because I didn't even know she had died. Her lawyer said she insisted on a private funeral, but if I had only read the newspapers. . . ."

"People our age haven't yet taken to studying the obituaries," MacDougal said dryly. "Why should you feel guilty? She wanted it that way. She isn't going to haunt you. Or does she?"

"Does who do what?" asked Sara, coming in with a tray. Ruth blinked, and managed to keep her face straight. Professor MacDougal was getting what she and Sara, in their sillier moments, referred to as "the full treatment"— smoked oysters, nuts (without peanuts), and hot cheese puffs (frozen).

"Does old Miss Campbell haunt your aunt. Thanks, Sara, that looks good." MacDougal helped himself liberally to oysters; and cast a disparaging eye over Sara's costume. "But I must say that, while I am generally in favor of the clothes you girls are wearing of late, in this room you look as incongruous as a headhunter in Versailles."

"I share your aesthetic reaction," Ruth said with a smile. "But I can't picture Sara in ruffles and crinolines."

"People just aren't impressed by this sort of thing any more," Sara said scornfully. "In fact it's terrible—sherry, antiques and all that junk—while only a few blocks away . . ."

"That sort of contrast is the most banal cliché of them all," MacDougal said; and to Ruth's surprise Sara took the reprimand meekly.

"Yes, sir. But a cliché isn't necessarily untrue, is it?"

"No, dear, and I'd like to have everybody happy and equal too. In the meantime, I'm just going to go on wallowing in my sinful bourgeois pleasures, such as sherry and antiques. Aren't you at all susceptible to the charm of this place? It's your family too, isn't it?"

"I suppose so," Sara said indifferently. "My mother is Ruth's sister, so that makes me Cousin Hattie's—what? Fourteenth cousin once removed? See how silly it sounds? Why should I have any more feeling for Cousin Hattie than I do for Hairy Joe, who plays a great guitar down at Dupont Circle?"

"All men are brothers," said MacDougal sweetly.

"Yes, damn it!"

"Sara—" Ruth began.

"That's okay," MacDougal said calmly. "I shouldn't bait the girl. I can't help it, though. I get a sadistic thrill out of poking the right buttons and seeing them jump. They equate squalor and soulfulness; but, as a matter of fact, Joe plays lousy guitar."

"Oh, I'm not defending the Flower Children," Sara said, in a worldly voice. "Some of them are pretty silly. But at least they're thinking about the important problems, even if what they think is wrong. Whereas the Georgetown mentality—I'll tell you what typifies it for me. The story about the governess who used to make her charges blow out their candles at ten o'clock sharp, and then, after she died, all the lights in her former room would go out at that hour, by themselves. Empty traditions, pointless sentimentality—"

"You did read a book about Georgetown, I see," Ruth said, refilling glasses.

"The one and only. Honest to God, it turned my stomach! So much sweetness and light, and such big fat lies."

"Come now," MacDougal said, grinning.

"You know what I mean. According to that book all the gentlemen and ladies of Old Georgetown were kind, noble philanthropists. Just look at their pictures! Tight-lipped, hawk-nosed, grim old holy terrors! Never a mention of scandal, crime, disgrace—why, you know that in two hundred years this town must have seen a lot of violence. But the books never mention it—dear me, no!"

"One of the things I hate about the younger generation," said MacDougal sadly, "is its bitter cynicism."

"I expect you see a good deal of it, don't you?" Ruth said.

"God, yes; they depress me utterly. You wouldn't consider cheering me after a hard day of late adolescents by having dinner with me, I suppose?"

"We'd love to," Sara said enthusiastically.

"Not you," MacDougal told her. "Just your aunt. You're old enough to scramble an egg for yourself." He added parenthetically, "You have to be blunt with them, they don't understand subtlety."

Ruth studied the topaz shimmer of the wine in her glass. She had only had three small glasses of sherry, not nearly enough to account for the pleasant glow that warmed her. And, after all, he was a professor—such a respectable occupation, she mocked herself silently.

"Thank you," she said aloud, keeping it deliberately formal. "I'd enjoy that. But I've got to be in early."

She knew (and how odd that she should know) that this

last qualification would amuse him. It did; his mouth quirked and his eyebrows went up. Sara's reaction was worse. After the first start of surprise she beamed at Ruth like a fond mother sending a daughter out on her first date.

III

They dined at a French restaurant in Georgetown, not far from the house. The decor was self-consciously and expensively provincial, with brass warming pans festooning the walls, two giant fireplaces, and capped and aproned waitresses. The gloom was almost impenetrable. According to MacDougal this was an unsuccessful attempt to conceal the inadequacy of the cooking.

"I'm no gourmet," he explained, eating with calm satisfaction. "I know enough to know when cooking is bad, but I don't really care. But I'm sorry, for your sake, that I made a poor choice. I don't know my way around town too well."

"I suppose you're gone a great deal," Ruth said, abandoning the onion soup as a lost cause. "And Washington does change a lot, in a short space of time."

"True, to both. I spent last year in Africa, just got back this fall. Maybe that's why I can't afford to be critical about cooking. Compared to what I ate for ten months, this is *cordon bleu* quality."

"What do you do in Africa?" Ruth studied, in some dismay, the omelette which had been placed before her—her usual order when she wasn't sure of the chef. Bad as the light was, it was obvious that the brownish roll on her plate had been sadly mistreated.

"Study Black Magic."

"Oh, really. What is that you're eating?"

"Stew. On the menu it goes by the name of *boeuf bourguignon*, but it's stew. Don't eat the omelette, if it offends you that much. Fill up on bread, and let me regale you with tales of raising the devil."

"I thought you were joking."

"No, no. Turns out I'm one of the world's foremost authorities on magic and superstition. Don't tell me you've never heard of me?"

He grinned at her and took an enormous bite of stew.

"I'm sorry . . ."

"Can't you tell when someone is kidding you? Have more wine; that's one thing that infernal chef can't mangle."

"Thanks. But how did you ever get interested in such a . . . such a—"

"Crazy subject? Well, you might say I walked into it—on my first field trip, to a village in central Africa where the natives were dying of a curse."

His voice was matter-of-fact, but Ruth saw him cock an eye at her over his wineglass. She decided perversely that she, for one, was not going to jump when he pushed the right buttons.

"Really?" she said politely.

"Terrible woman! Are you robbing me of my sensation?" MacDougal beamed at her. "I'm serious, though. They were, literally and actually, dying because their witch doctor had gotten annoyed and put a curse on them." His face was sober now, his eyes darkened. "They were amiable savages," he said. "Shy and timid as rabbits. I used up all my little stock of first-aid supplies trying to cure them, before the truth dawned on me."

"What did you do when you did learn the truth?" Ruth asked.

"What? Why, I—er—persuaded the shaman not to interfere with my activities. Then I took the curse off."

"Now you are joking."

"No, I'm not. In my youth, in addition to wanting to be an architect—and a fireman, a cowboy, a spy, and a garbage man—I aspired, for a brief period, to be a stage magician. I produced a few snakes out of people's ears, sang songs, did a dance . . ."

He shrugged. Ruth studied him thoughtfully and decided that, despite his bland smile, he was perfectly serious.

"I didn't know such things could happen," she said.

" 'Sticks and stones may break my bones, but names will never hurt me'? That's false, even in our so-called rational society. Names do hurt. The wrong names, applied to a disturbed child, may lead to murder years later. And in a culture where the power of the word is accepted, a curse can kill. It killed eight people in that Rhodesian village."

"I think they want to close," Ruth said, with an uneasy glance at the waiter, who stood in an attitude of conspicuous patience against the wall. "Shall we . . ."

"All right." His smile broadened as he looked at her across the candle flame. "You don't like to talk about it, do you? Why not?"

"Why, because it violates . . ."

"Reason and logic? No, that's not why it bugs you."

"What are you, some kind of psychologist too?"

"In my business I have to be. The phenomena we label 'supernatural' are products of the crazy, mixed-up human mind, and that's all they are."

He held her coat for her, and Ruth put on her gloves. As they went to the door she said, "You're right, the subject does distress me. Silly. . . . But I'm darned if I intend to let you dig into my subconscious to explain why I feel that way." Through his chuckle she added, more lightly, "Anyhow, if poor old Cousin Hattie's ghost does appear, I'll know who to send for."

"Damn it, you're missing the point! I don't believe in

ghosts any more than you do; if Cousin Hattie turns up, you'll have to call in a priest or a medium. The things I study are perfectly natural—"

"All right, all right. Sorry."

It took only five minutes to reach the house. They were both silent as the car passed smoothly along the empty streets. MacDougal stopped in front of the house. Instead of getting out and opening her door he shifted sideways and faced her. Ruth was not aware of having moved in any significant manner, but after a moment MacDougal's expression changed and he leaned back, away from her.

"I won't ask if I may come in," he said casually. "I might be tempted. . . . And I wouldn't want to shock Sara."

"She wouldn't be shocked," Ruth said; her smile was only slightly forced. "Only sweetly amused."

"That would be worse. Good night, Ruth."

Chapter Two

The kitchen was warm and bright, and filled with the smell of perking coffee. Ruth was buttering toast when the sound of footsteps made her drop the knife.

"Goodness, you startled me," she exclaimed, as her niece entered. "What are you doing up at this hour? It isn't even light outside."

"I couldn't get back to sleep." Sara yawned till Ruth's jaws ached in sympathy. "Here, let me do that."

"You're still half asleep. Sit down and have some coffee. Unless you want to go back to bed. . . ."

Sara shook her head and slumped into a chair by the table. Her green velvet robe brushed the floor and had full sleeves trimmed with lace. It was obviously one of the contributions of her doting mother, but instead of making her look young and innocent, the rich dark sheen of the material and the medieval sweep of the style gave her a magnificently anachronistic appearance, like something produced by a Spanish court painter of the sixteenth century. The girl's skin was smoothly olive; her black hair, braided into a thick tail for bed, gleamed like polished metal.

With a glance at the clock Ruth poured herself another cup of coffee. It was still early. She always allowed herself ample time in the morning.

"Want some toast?"

"No, thanks." The phrase was broken by another gigantic yawn.

"Come now; you don't need to diet, and if you haven't had enough sleep you must eat." Without waiting for a reply Ruth put two slices of bread into the toaster and gave Sara the plate she had prepared for herself. By the time she got back to the table with fresh toast, Sara was biting appreciatively into the golden triangles.

"Good," she said, and gave her aunt a smile. "Sorry, Ruth. I've got a nerve, I ought to be getting your breakfast."

"I don't know why you should." Ruth returned the smile. What a pretty child she was! The long dark lashes were so thick that they made her eyes look enormous, even when they were heavy with sleep; they had the smudgy sultriness which expensive eye-makeup kits are supposed to produce, and seldom do.

The toast and coffee revived Sara to such an extent that she got up and began scrambling eggs.

"I love this kitchen," she said, stirring.

Ruth cast a complacent glance over her shining kitchen. It looked charming, particularly in contrast to the bleak gray dawn that was breaking outside. The stainless steel of the counter stove, wall oven, and double sinks was as modern as the spotless white door of the refrigerator; but the cabinets had been done in maple, with hammered iron hinges and handles, and the one papered wall had an old-fashioned print of peasants haying, which had been copied from an old French original. The bright red of the workers' shirts and the golden sheaves of grain gave the kitchen a gaiety which was augmented by warm red-brown tile on the floor. Ruth's inherited collection of teapots, in all materials and colors, occupied shelves in a glass-fronted corner cupboard.

"The refrigerator ought to be brown, though," Sara said.

"I don't like colored refrigerators," Ruth said absently. They had been through this dialogue several times; it had the pleasant monotony of routine now. "They're decadent."

"Like colored toilet paper," Sara agreed, and they both laughed.

"I could tell just by looking at this room that you chose the decorations," Sara went on. "Was it so bad when you inherited the house?"

"You should have seen it! I suppose Cousin Hattie had been living on boiled eggs for forty years. She didn't care for new-fangled inventions."

"It must have been ghastly."

"Some of the furnishings were museum pieces. One of those enormous, black, wood-burning ranges—I don't suppose you've ever seen them. Of course, hers hadn't been used for years, since there was no point in firing up such a monster for one person. She cooked on a kerosene stove with a single burner—terribly dangerous, those things are. It's a wonder she didn't burn the house down."

"How about an egg?" Sara brought the pan, copper-bottomed and steaming, to the table and waved it invitingly under Ruth's nose.

"Dear child, I've had one breakfast!"

"It's cold outside. And you don't need to worry about getting fat." Sara put a puffy yellow spoonful on Ruth's plate. "You aren't going to be late, are you?"

"No, that's all right. How about you? When is your first class?"

"Not till eleven. That dull diplomatic history course. But I think I'll go in early and work at the library."

"Or have coffee with what's-his-name," Ruth said dryly.

"Bruce. You know perfectly well what his name is; you're just trying to deny the fact that he exists."

"You sound like your friend Dr. MacDougal," Ruth said.

"What time *did* you get in last night?"

"None of your business. As for Bruce, I don't have any mental blocks about him. He simply doesn't interest me, one way or the other. But you know what your mother would say about him."

"He's not as bad as Alan was," Sara said wickedly.

"Never having seen Alan, I can't say. Your mother's description was pretty ghastly, but I'm willing to allow for exaggeration. People do exaggerate," she added, realizing that she had just violated the united front of the older generation, "when they are worried about someone they love."

"That was just Mother being silly. I hadn't the faintest intention of marrying Alan."

"Maybe that's what she was worried about."

Sara chuckled; she had a delicious laugh, soft and throaty and contagious, which brought out dimples in both cheeks.

"Ruth, you're marvelous, you really are. I admire your loyalty to Mother—after all, she is your sister. But don't you think her attitude toward sex is positively medieval?"

"That's a subject on which I am not an authority."

"What, sex?"

"Your mother's attitude toward it. Don't be impertinent."

Her tone was light, but Sara had a sensitivity for nuances which was rare, Ruth thought, in a girl of her age. She changed the subject.

"Alan was just a temporary aberration," she explained airily. "A manifestation of adolescent rebellion on my part. If Mother hadn't howled about him so constantly I would have dropped him long before."

And that, Ruth suspected, was probably true. How many times had she had to bite back the words of advice that popped into her mind when she heard Helen make some maddeningly wrong statement to Sara or one of the boys, some red flag to their bullish emotions. Yes, she reminded herself sardonically, spinster aunts always did know better than parents. And, whatever her mother's minor errors, Sara was a credit to the family—charming, bright, well-mannered, pretty. Then Ruth's smile faded slightly as she studied the girl's face. Pretty, yes, healthy. . . . This morning there was a change. Something was wrong. What?

". . . the fact that he never washed," Sara was saying. "It wasn't that he couldn't, you know; he lived at home and his parents had an absolutely gorgeous mansion in Shaker Heights, five bathrooms, no less. It was a matter of principle."

"I never could understand the principle which is expressed by a cultivated filth," Ruth murmured, only half following the conversation. She was still trying to pin down that elusive sense of wrongness in Sara's face.

"Well, you know, protesting how terrible the world is."

"Adding one more stench to the world doesn't improve it, surely?"

"Ruth, you're hopeless," Sara said, with a burst of laughter. "At least you must admit Bruce is immaculate. It's the beard you can't accept."

"It's not so much the beard as my suspicion that he pastes it on. He isn't old enough to have a beard like Philip of Spain's. Sara, do you feel all right?"

"Sure, I feel fine. A little tired, that's all."

"You said you couldn't get back to sleep. What woke you?"

Sara's eyes dropped. She picked up her fork and began pushing golden fragments of egg around her plate.

"My conscience, probably. I do have to go to the library. There are midterms coming up."

"Well, all right. . . . There is some flu going around, and you look a little shadowy under the eyes."

"After all those eggs can you suspect me of flu? No, dear, leave those dishes, you know that's my job. I don't have to go for another hour. Want me to make spaghetti tonight?"

"Fine. You make good spaghetti."

"I should, it's the only thing I can cook, besides eggs." And then, as Ruth collected purse and gloves and started toward the door, she said, "Ruth."

"What?"

"Don't those people behind us have a dog, or cat, or something?"

"The Owens have a Weimaraner, and someone in back owns a Siamese cat. I've seen the dog exploring the shrubbery once or twice."

"Weimaraner? Oh, that ghosty-looking gray dog with the red eyes. What's its name?"

"I haven't the faintest idea. Why do you ask?"

"Oh, no reason." The hesitation, the sidelong look, were so unlike Sara that Ruth felt a resurgence of her concern. The girl sensed this; she smiled, and said quickly,

"It sounds so silly. But that was what woke me, someone out in back calling, in the middle of the night. I assumed some cherished pet didn't come home for dinner."

"Calling what?" Ruth said sharply.

"Oh, damn, that's why I didn't want to tell you; I knew you'd start thinking about homicidal maniacs and peeping toms." Her tone added, "All 'grown-ups' do." Aloud she continued, "It wasn't like that at all, it was just someone calling an animal, or a child. I couldn't imagine that children would be wandering around at four A.M., so I figured it must have been a missing pet. I used to yell that way for our old tomkitty when his mating instinct got too much for him."

"I hope you didn't make enough noise to wake up all the neighbors. I'll have to speak to Mr. Owens."

"No, don't do that; it was a soft, sort of crooning voice, really. I hope they find poor Sam," she added. "He's a spooky-looking beast, but he was very friendly last time I talked to him through the fence."

Halfway out the door, Ruth turned.

"Sam? The dog's name is Wolfgang von Eschenbach, or some such absurdity."

"It must have been the missing cat, then," Sara said calmly. "I didn't absolutely catch the name, but it surely wasn't Wolfgang etcetera. It was Sammie, or something like that. 'Come home, come home'—that's what the voice kept saying—'Sammie, come home.'"

II

"The name," said the voice at the other end of the wire, "is Pat MacDougal."

"Impossible," Ruth said involuntarily.

"I admit it's a funny name. Sounds like a cartoon character. But it happens to be my name."

"You silly fool," said Ruth; and blushed scarlet as her secretary looked up in surprise. "I meant, how did you find me?"

"Called Sara and asked her where you worked. The Department of Agriculture has a very efficient information service. What the hell are you doing at the Department of Agriculture—counting apples?"

"Something like that."

"Sounds like a dull occupation for a woman of your talents."

"How do you know—" Ruth began, and stopped herself

just in time. "I'm sorry, but I *am* busy today. Can I call you back later?"

"No. Later I'll be at your place, providing, of course, that it's okay with you."

"Well, it's not okay!"

"Wait a minute, wait a minute. Let's start all over again. I don't know why you have this effect on me," said the voice irritably. "I'm generally considered very suave. Mrs. Bennett, my mother is having one of those impromptu dinner parties for which I gather she is famous in Washington. I wouldn't know; she is the main reason why I took up anthropology as a profession. But this time I'm stuck. She asked me to bring a dinner partner, and last night, in the fascination of your company, I forgot to ask you. I know it's damned short notice, but that's my mother's fault, not mine. She does this sort of thing."

"I'm sorry," Ruth began, and then the meaning of what he had said finally penetrated. "Your mother. . . . She isn't Mrs. Jackson MacDougal?"

"Yes, she is." The voice was defensive.

"Well! I don't know. . . ."

"Damn it, Ruth, you've got to help me out. I can't hurt the old lady's feelings, but those characters she collects drive me nuts. Please?"

"Characters? You mean the most famous conductor in Europe, that Russian ballet dancer who defected, the man who wrote that terrible book, the woman who predicted—"

"Yeah, people like that. I don't know who she's got on tonight. Look, you seem to have heard of her, so you know it's not my fault, this last minute business. She does it all the time—and gets away with it, which is even more fantastic. Please?"

"All right. Thank you."

"Thank *you*." There was a gusty sigh of relief from the other end. "Seven thirty?"

"Come around at six thirty for a drink," Ruth said. "I suspect I'll need it."

"We both will, but not for the reason you're thinking. Hell's bells, darling, it's just a dull party. Bless you."

"Uh—Pat. What shall I—"

The hollow silence on the other end of the wire told her it was too late. She hung up and turned to find her mascaraed miniskirted secretary regarding her with open-mouthed admiration.

"Gee," said her secretary. "Mrs. Jackson MacDougal!"

III

"Who's she?" Sara asked.

"Only the most famous hostess in Washington. Invitations to her parties are more highly regarded than invitations to the White House."

"Is that why you came home early?" Sara demanded incredulously.

"Yes, and that's why we are out right now, to get me something decent to wear. Darn, it still is cold. Unusual for this time of year."

"You Washingtonians always say that." Sara clutched her black leather jacket around her as a strong gust threatened to pull it off. Her black hair lifted, lashed by the wind like something out of a witches' sabbath. "Well, really, Ruth, I'm surprised at you. All this effort for some snobbish old society biddy."

"Darling, she isn't like that. Her husband—good heavens, Pat's father—was Ambassador to England; the family is not only terribly rich, but intellectual, cultivated. She doesn't invite the 'in' crowd, only people she thinks will be interesting. That's why her invitations are so hard to come by."

"Hmmm," said Sara, unconvinced. "Well, my dear aunt, whatever your motives, it is obvious that you must do us credit. So where are we going first?"

"First and last," said Ruth, rounding the corner onto Wisconsin rather more briskly than she had intended. "Heavens, the wind simply roars down this street! We're going to Lili's."

"But you always buy your clothes there." Sara clutched a handful of hair in a vain attempt to keep it out of her eyes. "Let's prowl, we've plenty of time. I do love the Georgetown shops."

Ruth liked them too, so their progress was slow, despite the lashing wind that blew down Wisconsin's curving slope as through a tunnel. The tartans in the Scottish import shop held them for ten minutes; it was hard to believe that those wild blends of color—purple, yellow and black, olive and pale green with a scarlet thread, turquoise and orange-red and indigo—were genuine clan patterns and not the improvisations of a mad Italian designer. The mad designers, Italian and otherwise, were represented in other shops which had names like "Whimsique," and "the place," with no capital letters. Ruth found this distressing and said so, but Sara laughed, loitering before a window framed in enormous orange and purple linoleum flowers and filled with such useful items as an Indian water pipe and a bird cage six feet high, of gilded bamboo trimmed with fake rubies and sapphires.

At the Wine and Cheese shop they stopped to buy cocktail snacks and some of Ruth's favorite hock. Then there was a Mexican shop, where Sara yearned over a bright red, wildly pleated dress embroidered all over the yoke and sleeves with black-and-gold birds; and an Indian shop, where Ruth remarked that, one day, she would like to see

Sara in a sari, preferably that white one trimmed in gold. Then they decided that they really had to start thinking about a dress for Ruth, and passed nobly by the candle shop and the little gallery and the jeweler's that specialized in antique pieces. By this time, strangely enough, they were blocks from Lili's.

Sara stopped in front of a window.

"Look, Ruth. What a darling dress!"

It was a sheath of rainbow iridescence, with long sleeves, a demure high neck, and practically no skirt.

"This doesn't look like my sort of place," Ruth remarked meekly.

"Let's go in anyhow."

The store was small and thickly carpeted, with its stock discreetly tucked away on racks along the walls and only two isolated models in the middle of the floor. The salesladies, elegant young women who looked like college girls, smiled graciously at the new customers and returned to their conversation.

"That's it," said Sara, advancing purposefully on a dress which stood in solitary splendor in the center of the shop. "I saw it the other day, and I thought of it right away when you said you wanted something dressy but not actually formal."

Ruth eyed the creation dubiously. It was one of the new "romantic" styles—a full velvet skirt belted tightly at the waist with a wide, soft belt, and a white organdy top with long sleeves and a cascade of crisp ruffles down the front.

"It would look lovely on you," she began.

"No, no, it's not my style at all," Sara said. "I'm too long-legged for this new length—midi, they call it."

"An ugly name for an unbecoming length," Ruth said, and ran a finger along the fall of ruffles. They sprang briskly back into shape as if they had been starched.

"Try it on, anyhow. You can't tell unless you do."

When they left the shop with a large parcel in hand, Sara

insisted on treating them both to coffee at a local espresso bar. Sipping a liquid which had been referred to as a cappuccino, Ruth did not mention that it bore no resemblance to the drink of the same name which she had enjoyed in Florence four years earlier. She was moved, however, to comment on the price of the coffee and on the decor; the furniture was starkly, uncomfortably modern and the walls were hung with original paintings, in the manner of a gallery. Half the inhabitants of Georgetown painted; the other half bought the paintings.

"I thought these places would be cheaper," Ruth explained. "Like—for students."

"That's right, get with that slang," Sara grinned. "Some students are pretty rich these days. Haven't you ever been in one of these places before?"

"No."

"See what a good influence I am. Two new establishments in one day. I'll have to take you to a discothèque. And you claim to be an old Georgetonian. Or is it Georgetownian?"

"Georgetown is changing," Ruth said dryly. "But I guess people do stay in well-worn tracks. Unfortunately you don't realize you're in a rut until it's too late to climb out of it. You are a good influence, Sara. I'm enjoying having you with me."

"Thanks. I'm enjoying being with you."

They smiled at one another rather self-consciously. Then Ruth glanced at her watch and gave an exclamation.

"We'd better hurry, or I'll be late getting dressed."

"You need shoes," Sara said, slipping into her coat. "No—you have those low-heeled pumps with the big buckles, that's just the thing. Black stockings—"

"Certainly not," Ruth said firmly.

"I've got some I'll lend you."

The total effect—buckled shoes, black stockings, and

ruffles—made Ruth self-conscious until she saw Pat Mac-
Dougal's face. However, he said nothing, beyond a polite
compliment, and Ruth thought she understood why; Sara's
smile was too maternal to be encouraged.

"Cook both those lamb chops," she told her niece. "No
cheating with T.V. dinners. You need something solid."

"Well, actually, I thought," said Sara, trying to look as if
the idea had just occurred to her, "that I might ask Bruce
over to eat your chop. If you don't mind?"

Ruth had laid down the ground rules about guests when
Sara first came to stay with her, and this was perfectly in
order. She heard herself agreeing to the proposal with
unusual warmth. She was in too much of a hurry to try to
analyze why she was glad to have someone with Sara that
evening; a dim discomfort, something connected with the
morning, hovered on the edge of her consciousness and then
was forgotten, as Pat drew her toward the door.

IV

Ruth knew the MacDougal home by sight; it was one of the
famous mansions of Georgetown, and if she had had no
other reason for accepting Pat's invitation, a chance to see
the house would have been excuse enough. Now well
within the borders of the Georgetown area, it had been a
suburban estate when the little town on the Potomac was
first founded. The original George Town, as its present
inhabitants often pointed out, was a cosmopolitan town,
with academies and jewelers and slaves, when the new
capital was still a muddy swamp. Representatives of the
young nation had to be scolded by the President into taking
up residence in the city named for him, and it was with

reluctance that they abandoned the amenities of the town
named after another, less popular George.

The men who had built the house named it, with more
candor than modesty, Barton's Pride. It had long since
passed out of the hands of the Barton family; but it still
stood as it had stood then, on a knoll surrounded by tall
oaks, and it occupied an entire city block, a distinction
which few of the original mansions could still claim. The
driveway was a superb, sweeping circle; Pat's little Jaguar
roared up it with a defiant blast of its exhaust.

After Pat had helped her out of the car Ruth stood for a
moment gazing at the magnificent proportions of the facade,
now blazing with lights which made the bricks glow rose-
pink. The vines which in summer softened the formal
Georgian lines fluttered like tattered curtains, the last
reddening leaves flying in the wind. Shallow stairs led up to
the beautiful doorway with its fanlight and side windows.

The hall was as large as Ruth's drawing room. The
immense chandelier, whose crystal drops chimed delicately
with the breeze of their entrance, had surely been taken
from a Loire château. The rug was an acre of muted cream
and blue and rose; Ruth had seen its like on museum walls,
but never on a floor before. A superb staircase swept up and
divided, framing a circular window. On either side of the
hall were fireplaces; wood crackled and orange-and-gold
flames leaped inside them. Ruth waited until the butler had
turned away with their coats. Then she said out of the corner
of her mouth, "And you had the nerve to admire my
shack."

"Oh, I admire this place," Pat admitted. "The way I
admire the Louvre."

"But you don't live here?"

"People don't live in places like this. They perform, as
on a stage. Wait till you see Mother in action; you'll
understand what I mean."

He took her elbow and turned her toward the wide doors on the left; but before they reached them the panels flew back and Mrs. Jackson MacDougal erupted through them, arms outstretched, face beaming. Ruth gaped.

Washington's most famous hostess was a shimmer of silver: massed diamonds on her high-piled white hair, blazing from her fat little hands and plump throat; and silver, too, in the incredible garment that swathed her from throat to floor and billowed out like a tent as she came flying toward them. A silver lamé caftan, Ruth thought, and stifled a gasp of laughter. Above the ample folds Mrs. MacDougal's much photographed face—superbly, uniquely, magnificently homely—rose like a gargoyle from a cathedral roof.

She threw herself on her tall son, and for one unforgettable moment Ruth saw his rugged face and flaming head swathed in sweeping folds of silver.

"Horrible man, why don't you come more often?" Mrs. MacDougal demanded. "Who's this? Mrs. Bennett? How do you do, very nice, very nice indeed. Much more suitable than the last one. But you only brought her to annoy me. I knew that. Didn't work, did it?"

Pat returned her grin. For a moment the two faces were uncannily alike.

"Not any of my tricks work with you. You were so sweet to that ghastly female that she got the wrong idea. Pursued me for weeks. I had to leave the country to get away from her. Not," he added hastily to Ruth, "because of my brains and good looks, mind you."

"Why should any woman require more?" Ruth asked, since the conversation seemed to be taking that tone. The old lady gave a peal of appreciative laughter and linked arms with Ruth, displacing her flowing silver sleeve and baring another yard or two of diamonds running up her arm.

"That's right, put him in his place. I never trained him

properly. Come in and meet the others. Just a small group; Pat won't come if I have more than a dozen people."

The dozen included the usual lions, a pride of them—so many that their individual distinctions were lost in the general aura of fame. Ruth recognized a much-pursued young senator from a western state and a tall, melancholy man who was the musical half of Broadway's most famous musical comedy team. Ruth's hostess monopolized her, leaving the rest of the guests to fend for themselves; her tactics were so blatant that, in any other woman, Ruth would have recognized them immediately. But she could not believe at first that this descendant of millionaire aristocrats was trying to do her son's courting for him.

"But, Mrs. MacDougal," she protested, after a particularly obvious ploy, "I don't think . . ."

"You think I'm a fantastic old bitch," said her hostess calmly. "I am, it's true, but I'm quite serious about Pat; I'd like him to settle down. It sounds absurd, doesn't it, for a man of his age? He was married before, you know. So were you, I gather."

"He died," Ruth said, stunned into candor by the old lady's sledgehammer tactics. "In the war."

"World War Two? Yes . . . we adults still say '*the* war,' don't we? Pat's wife didn't die; she divorced him. She was a dreadful woman, but I could see her point. He kept dashing off to the jungles of Africa or the deserts of Australia. What fun is that? But it's high time he tried again. He can't go gallivanting around in the wilds much longer; he's getting old. Those places aren't safe."

Ruth's inclination to laugh was quenched by Mrs. MacDougal's expression. It was one she knew well, having seen it so often on her sister's face. Apparently the maternal instinct did not die, even in an eighty-year-old mother for her middle-aged son. Ruth did not find the emotion amusing; rather, it was frightening in its single-minded intensity.

During dinner Ruth watched Pat's expression become increasingly grimmer as the meal went on, through course after superb course. The food certainly could not be the cause of his discontent; Ruth wondered if it might be his dinner partner, who seemed never to stop talking. She was a tall, thin woman, so fair as to be almost anemic looking, with ash blond hair arranged in a peculiarly old-fashioned mass of braids, coils, and ringlets. If Mrs. MacDougal had not been present to dim all lesser lights, the woman's costume might have seemed eccentric: smoke-gray draperies of chiffon which floated dangerously near candle flames and wine glasses whenever she lifted her hands, which she did often, in studiedly flowing gestures.

As soon as the meal was over and the company was being led into the "small drawing room" for coffee, Pat sought Ruth out.

"Let's get out of here," he muttered. "That shameless old—"

The epithet, which presumably applied to his mother, was cut off just in time by the appearance of that matron, who advanced upon him with a purposeful stride.

"Oh, no, you don't, Patrick James," she said severely.

"Mother, you know I hate that nonsense!"

"I know, and I can't imagine why, you dabble in much nastier and less likely subjects all the time. You've never seen Nada, she's the latest rage, and I *insist* you stay. You can't be so rude to Mrs. Bennett, if you won't consider me."

"Oh, all right."

"What on earth is this all about?" Ruth whispered, as they followed Mrs. MacDougal's triumphantly billowing skirts into the drawing room.

"Didn't you recognize that bloodless bean pole I was

stuck with at dinner? Another of the old harridan's tricks, she knows I hate people like that. . . . She's the latest thing in the rich spiritualist circles. A medium."

"I've never attended a séance," Ruth said sedately. "It should be interesting."

"It won't be. These babes don't know any of the good tricks. Someday I'll show you a Hottentot shaman at work. They are masters at crowd psychology."

Despite his jeers, Pat behaved himself very well. Ruth suspected that he was professionally interested after all; just before the lights went out she caught a change of expression that reminded her of her boss's face when a particularly complicated problem arose.

The spirits, Mrs. MacDougal explained, were sensitive to light. That was why most séances were held in semidarkness. It was not—this, with an intent stare at her son, who responded with a bland smile—it was not intended to conceal fraud. No such question could arise with Madame Nada in any case, for that lady was a mental medium and did not indulge in the vulgar demonstrations with tambourines, trumpets, and ectoplasmic hands which were so popular with so-called physical mediums.

Throughout the lecture Madame Nada sat with folded hands, smiling faintly. Only her eyes moved. But they contradicted her studied air of repose as well as her pastel blandness; they were small, dark brown, and piercing, and they darted ceaselessly around the circle of spectators, taking in every detail.

When the lights went out there was a general murmur compounded of nervous giggles, sighs, and one loud yawn, whose source Ruth immediately identified. They were holding hands, since this increased the sympathetic vibrations. On Ruth's right was Mrs. MacDougal. Her fat hand was surprisingly cool and dry, and felt pleasantly like that of a chubby little girl—a little girl wearing lots of dime-store jewelry, which scratched the palm. Ruth thought, "All diamonds are paste in the dark," and realized, with a grin which she hastily suppressed for fear of damaging the vibrations, that she was a little bit drunk. The wine at dinner had flowed freely and it had all been too good to pass over.

The boy on Ruth's left was perspiring, and she wondered whether it was a natural weakness or a bad case of nerves. According to Mrs. MacDougal he had just opened a new psychedelic shop on Wisconsin Avenue, which sold posters of the Beatles in various incredible costumes, luminous pinups of Indian mystics, and atrociously made handcrafted leather sandals.

As her eyes adjusted Ruth realized that the room was not entirely dark; the glow from the fireplace made it possible to see shapes, and glinted redly off objects such as Mrs. MacDougal's diamonds and the silver fillet the medium wore in her hair. After a long silence, broken once by a giggle, and a concerted shusssshing sound directed against the giggler, Ruth felt herself getting drowsy. Warmth and firelight and a little bit too much wine. . . . What a disgrace it would be, she thought comfortably, if she fell off the chair.

The medium's voice made them all jump. It was slow and soft, drawling the words. Accent and tone had changed, but the voice was still recognizably Madame Nada's. The words were strikingly commonplace.

"Good evenin', ladies and gentlemen."

"Good evening, Maybelle," Mrs. MacDougal said in a bright, social tone. "How are you this evening?"

"Very well, thank you kindly. But we're always well here, you know."

"Yes, dear, I know. Maybelle is Madame Nada's control," Mrs. MacDougal explained, in a piercing whisper. "A gently bred young Southern girl. Poor child, she was raped by a Yankee soldier during the War Between the States. But she has no hatred now."

"Love," said the mellifluous voice of Maybelle. The shaggy young man on Ruth's left stirred uneasily. "Only love and sunshine and peace, here."

"Do you have any messages tonight, dear?" Mrs. MacDougal asked.

"Jes' a few. Strange. . . ." The girl's voice sounded puzzled. "There's somethin' holdin' back. . . . A hostile thought. . . ."

Someone across the circle—Ruth was sure it was Pat—coughed suggestively, and Madame Nada's voice hardened momentarily.

"But I'll try. Some of them want so badly to come through, to help. . . . There's someone here who wants to speak to—a lady?—yes, a lady in the room. I can't get the name. . . . The first letter seems to be a G."

There was an audible gasp from someone in the listening circle. The voice went droning on.

"G-R-A— That's the name of the lady. Is there a lady named Grace?"

"Yes, yes," squealed an excited voice.

"Grace, darling, it's Daddy." The medium's voice changed; it was a man's now, deep but shaky, as if with age. "Remember the party? The birthday party, and the pink dress?"

"Oh, my goodness," gasped the invisible Grace.

There was further conversation about the party—Grace's sixth birthday party, said Daddy, and Grace enthusiastically agreed. However, this was fairly dull for the rest of the group, who shared neither Grace's memories nor her susceptibility to suggestion, and before long Daddy was supplanted by a new voice, which described itself as that of an Indian chief named Wamasook, who had lived on the site now occupied by the house, "in the days before the white men came to rob us of our land." Wamasook spoke excellent English. He described his beautiful Indian sweetheart, who had leaped from the Rock of Dumbarton after he was killed in battle, and added that one of the settlers had buried a hoard of gold coins in the well before his tribe was attacked. Since there was now no trace of a well anywhere on the grounds, and since Wamasook's knowledge of the modern geography of the site was somewhat vague, this hint did not arouse much interest among the auditors.

The next visitor from beyond announced himself in a thick Scottish accent as "George," and was promptly identified by Mrs. MacDougal as George Barton, the builder of the house. He remarked that the regions where he was presently living were filled with sunlight and flowers and love. Shortly thereafter Maybelle announced abruptly that Madame Nada was tired.

The lights went on. Ruth almost burst out laughing when she saw Pat; he looked so smug, not only at the confirmation of his predictions, but at his own admirable self-control. Mrs. MacDougal also saw and interpreted his expression. Her voice, as she addressed the medium, had something of the tone of a lady complaining to her dressmaker about the fit of a gown.

"Well, Nada, I'm afraid this was not one of our better demonstrations."

The medium, who was rubbing her eyes and yawning, like someone just awakened from sleep, looked surprised.

"Indeed? I am sorry to hear that. Did not Maybelle come through?"

"Yes, but the messages weren't very—significant."

"But I got a marvelous message from Daddy," said Grace, a well-upholstered elderly lady with a black velvet ribbon around her sagging throat. "All about flowers, and love—"

"And sunshine," said Pat, unable to control himself any

longer. "Not very characteristic conversation from your daddy, Grace, if the tales I hear about the old shark are true."

"Pat, you bad boy, you know people change when they pass on. What use would it all be otherwise?"

"What, indeed?" said Pat charmingly.

His mother gave him a furious look.

"I am so sorry it was not successful," said the medium smoothly. Ruth was reminded of something. . . . Cream? No, olive oil.

"Antagonistic influences, I suppose," Mrs. MacDougal said coldly. The medium gave her a quick, wary look.

"Possibly. Possibly it is simply the house. You know, Mrs. MacDougal, that some places lack the proper atmosphere."

Later, looking back on it, Ruth was never able to understand how it had happened. Surely she hadn't been that drunk! And certainly she was not particularly intrigued by the séance, which had seemed to her both dull and embarrassing. Not even in the light of those events which were now close upon her was she willing to admit another explanation. . . . No, there was no reason, except her loose tongue, which frequently got her into trouble, and some vague idea of being gracious to her hostess, who was visibly vexed with the medium's performance.

When they left the house, with Mrs. MacDougal's enthusiastic thanks ringing in their ears, Ruth was meekly silent. She expected an explosion from Pat; his grim forbearance, which lasted all the way home, was in its way even more uncomfortable.

"Won't you come in?" she asked, when the car had stopped. He nodded.

"I'll give you moral support while you break the news to Sara."

"She'll probably be delighted."

"I expect you're right. What made you do such a thing?"

"I thought it might be fun," said Ruth.

"You're a liar." His long arm swept out and caught her by the shoulders, pulling her to him in a quick, casual embrace. She was relieved to hear him chuckling. "You sure there wasn't a touch of 'screw Pat' in your mind? Excuse the language; I'm trying to clean it up for you, but it's damned hard."

"If you mean what I think you mean, the answer is No. I'm too old for such adolescent jokes. And," she added, moving, "far too old for necking in the front seat of a car."

"It's these damned bucket seats." He released her, and began the complicated operation of extracting his bulk from the little car. "These kids must be contortionists. I've always wondered how they manage to—"

The rest of the sentence was lost as he came around to open her door.

When they entered the hall Ruth heard the voices in the living room, and a jolt of unreasonable irritation struck her. She had forgotten Sara's guest, or had assumed that he would have left. She had smoothed her face into a smile by the time she walked into the living room, there was really no reason why she should let the boy irritate her so.

He rose at once. He had beautiful manners, almost too courteous, as if he were mocking the standards of the society he despised, or considered them so contemptible that they were not worth fighting. His clothes were almost, but never quite, too, too much; an occasional ruffle on a shirt, or a flowery waistcoat, or a pair of trousers that fitted his lean hips and long legs almost, but not quite, too tightly. At least his clothes were well tailored and beautifully kept. His hair was long enough to curl under at the neck; the beard was a neat sort of beard, dark and short and trimmed, with tongues of hair outlining the jaw and the lines between nose and lips—the sort of beard worn by Mephistopheles, or a sixteenth-century Spanish nobleman. As he stood beside Sara, his dark face and Sara's olive beauty and sleek black hair made them look like two young members of the old Spanish royal house—except that none of the Hapsburgs had ever been so handsome.

Sara's flushed cheeks might have been the result of the fire's warmth, but a curve still lingered in the shape of her mouth that made Ruth fairly sure of what she and Bruce had been doing. Then Ruth remembered, joltingly, those few moments in the car out in front, and she decided to forget the whole thing.

Pat greeted the younger man with the ease of old acquaintance.

"Haven't seen you on campus lately. Still protesting?"

"Always, inevitably."

Even his voice, Ruth thought irritably, sounded affected. It was a mellow baritone, but the pronunciation was overprecise and emphatic.

"What's the latest?" Pat asked interestedly. "Segregation, the draft, Vietnam—"

"You didn't get my latest petition?"

Bruce bared his teeth in a gesture that was not even intended to resemble a smile. As he probably knew, the dental effect was heightened by the frame of beard around his mouth.

"I get so many of them," Pat said apologetically.

It was an outrageous remark, and Ruth expected, not an explosion—Bruce was abnormally well controlled for such a passionate defender of causes—but a snarl. Instead, the boy's grin turned into a genuine laugh.

"You know what terrifies me?" he demanded. "The thought that I may end up just like you."

"You almost certainly will."

"I know. That's why it terrifies me."

"Okay, pax. Come into my office next week, and we'll fight some more."

"Yes, let's not argue here," Ruth said firmly. "What are you two drinking? Thanks, no; I don't think I could face vodka in any form at this hour. Pat, would you like brandy?"

"What I really would like," said Pat, "is a cup of tea."

"You constantly amaze me. So would I."

"I'll get it," Sara said. She went out, with Bruce following.

"Now," Pat said, when the tea finally made its appearance; it had taken quite some time. "Tell Sara what you've done."

"Good heavens, you make me sound like a murderer. I've invited a few people to dinner next week, that's all. Mrs. MacDougal and a friend of hers."

"The friend's name," said Pat, "being Madame Nada."

Bruce leaned forward, elbows on his knees, black eyes mocking.

"I didn't know you were interested in spiritualism, Mrs. Bennett."

"I'm not. It was just one of those things."

"A séance!" Sara's eyes danced with amusement. "Aunt Ruth, are we going to have a séance?"

"Yes," Ruth said, sighing. "She thinks this house probably reeks with the right atmosphere."

"But it's tremendous fun," Sara exclaimed. "More fun than Spin the Bottle."

"A parlor game? Is that how you think of it?"

"Sure. Although . . . I've used the Ouija board, and I must admit . . ."

"Involuntary movements," Pat said shortly.

"But I wasn't pushing the board, and I'm sure nobody else was."

"That's what they all say."

Bruce's eyes darted from Sara, flushed and erect on the edge of the couch, to Pat's sour face. Ruth sensed that he was inclined to agree with Pat, but he hated to pass up the chance of an argument.

"I agree that the Ouija board is probably explicable in terms of natural laws," he said pontifically. "But many of the problems of the paranormal have not been properly explored. Take Rhine—"

"You take him. Unscientific and inadequately controlled."

"What are you talking about?" Ruth demanded.

"Dr. Rhine's experiments in telepathy, E. S. P., he calls it. He uses decks of special cards and tries to get a person sitting in one room to send mental images of the cards to a person in another room, who writes down the impressions he gets. It doesn't work. Despite all the juggling with the results."

"The statistical methods," Bruce began hotly; he was now involved in the argument for its own sake.

"Neither you nor I would be capable of judging that aspect. But I know that the controls are inadequate. There are too many ways of faking, deliberate or unconscious. Ask any stage magician."

His eyes glowing, Bruce expertly shifted ground.

"All new scientific discoveries are mocked when they first appear. Take hypnotism—"

"The favorite example of the apologists for spiritualism. Take alchemy, astrology, and the secret of the Great Pyramid. Still pure superstition, all of 'em."

"Boys, boys," Ruth interrupted. "I think either one of you would argue about whether or not the sun is going to rise tomorrow—on either side of the question. Help me decide how I'm going to arrange this ludicrous affair. I haven't even thought about the guest list. How many people does one need for a good séance?"

"The four of us and two guests," Sara counted aloud. "That's six. Do we need more?"

Bruce shot Ruth a quizzical glance. It was so well done that she had no choice but to say, as graciously as she could, "Of course we'll expect you, Bruce. A week from tonight, Friday the tenth."

"Thank you, Mrs. Bennett, I'm looking forward to it," Bruce recited. And then spoiled the effect by adding, with a malicious movement of his lips, "I think you're going to need a skeptic."

"Skeptics I've got," Ruth said wryly.

"Pat's no skeptic, he's the Grand Inquisitor. Burn 'em at the stake, that's his motto. And you—"

"Yes?" This was one of the things she most disliked about the younger generation in general and Bruce in particular—their habit of cheap, pseudopsychological analysis.

"You are fastidious. You dislike the whole idea, not because it's irrational but because it's distasteful."

"Well," Ruth said, surprised, "I guess you're right."

"Sara still hasn't quite given up believing in Santa Claus," Bruce went on. The look he gave Sara was meant to be casually amused, but Ruth caught a glimpse of his eyes, and their expression made her catch her breath. "She's still receptive to wonderment. Trailing clouds of glory. . . ."

"Oh, come on!" Sara was definitely not flattered. Either she had not seen that betraying look or she was too inexperienced to know what it meant.

"So," Bruce concluded, with a sweeping gesture that mocked all of them as well as himself, "I'm your only genuine open mind, completely without prejudice and able to evaluate the evidence."

"There won't be much evidence, I'm afraid. Tonight's performance was pretty sad."

"You caught that, at any rate," Pat said grumpily.

"Oh, yes, it was all very obvious. I was disappointed. I thought she would do better."

"She can, given time for preparation. I told you about Mother's impromptu parties. But I'll wager that in a week Madame Nada will have done a discreet but ample amount of research on you and this house. She will be filled up to here with history—everything she can dig out of the Georgetown guidebooks."

"She'll run into trouble there," Ruth said. "There isn't much about this place in the guidebooks."

"Not even the builder's name, building history, that sort of thing?"

"Oh, well, his name was Campbell, like Cousin Hattie's. Daniel, or was it Abediah? But he wasn't much of a public figure, not like the Bealls and the Stodderts and the really famous Georgetown families."

"Really? Well, that's good."

"Why?"

"Don't you see, Mrs. Bennett?" Bruce was so interested he forgot his affected accent. "The less she can find out from public records, the easier it is to check her sources. If she should come up with something that really isn't in print—"

"Oh, I'll bet she'll come up with something," Pat said.

"Well, I'll spend some time reading up on the house," Bruce said eagerly. "If she slips, I'll catch it."

"Where does the performance take place?" Pat asked, swallowing a yawn.

"We'll need a table, I suppose," Ruth said. "A biggish one. Ten or twelve people. . . ."

"How about the dining-room table?" Sara suggested.

"Over the crumbs and coffee cups? No, dear; you and I will be doing the catering, and I've no intention of scuttling to and fro with trays and sponges in front of guests."

"Then it will have to be in here."

"Yes. We could move these couches farther apart, and sit in front of the fire."

"I think you'll find," Pat said dryly, "that Madame will prefer to be a little farther away from the firelight."

"It's a problem, isn't it?" Bruce began pacing the room, examining it as if he had never seen it before. "I can see why you put the couches in front of the fire, it makes a nice grouping. And the bookshelves at the far end of the room suggest a kind of library corner, looking out over the garden. But the room has an awkward shape. You're losing about a third of your space at this end, next to the street."

"I know, it is awkward. I tried rearranging the furniture, but it wouldn't let itself be moved." The statement, which she had meant as a light comment, sounded unexpectedly alarming. "I mean," she added hastily, "this was the best arrangement; it had been this way for years."

Pat was becoming interested. He walked down the length of the room to the front windows.

"One thing you've got," he said, "if nothing else—an ideal setup for our ghost-raising session. This table in front of the window is round; move it back a couple of feet so we can get chairs all around it, and—"

He was standing with his back to the others, facing the window and the table, on which his hands rested lightly. With the last word his voice broke, and he suddenly bent forward over the table, head bowed and shoulders hunched.

Ruth leaped to her feet.

"Pat!"

"What?" He turned, smiling, and Ruth's nightmare vision of a heart attack faded. "Frog in my throat. A monster. Guess I talk too much."

"Was that all? I thought you were having a fit."

"No, no, I'm fine. Yes, this would do admirably. But you

ought to have these windows caulked. The draft is enough to freeze your bones."

"I did have them caulked. It's just a cold spot, that's all. Too cold for your mother, perhaps."

"No," he said slowly. "This is ideal."

"He's right," Sara agreed. "Ruth, maybe an electric heater. . . ."

"We'll worry about that later." Pat produced another yawn. "Come on, Bruce, I'll give you a lift home."

He lingered in the hall for a moment after Bruce had, reluctantly, gone on out to the car.

"I wish you'd call this off, Ruth," he said, in a voice pitched low enough so that Sara, clearing away cups in the next room, did not hear.

"My dear—why?"

"It's too much for you, too much fuss."

"Don't be silly, I don't mean to try to imitate your mother's style of entertaining. It will be very simple."

"I wish you wouldn't," he repeated, in an oddly flat voice.

"Pat, you look so— Are you sure you didn't have a pain just now?"

"No, damn it, I told you I feel fine! Sorry. . . . I guess I am tired; I didn't mean to yell at you. Good night."

Ruth helped to clear the living room, bade Sara good night, and sat down for a final cigarette in front of the dying fire.

She was worried about Pat. Her father had had that same gray pallor, after his first heart attack. Pat was no longer a young man.

And she? Half her life was over, more than half. . . . And what had she to show for it? An old house which was too large, really, for a single person; a pretty, casual niece who would be gone in another year or two, after she finished college—who would then send a Christ-

mas card and a birthday card every year, with dutiful
messages. Yes, Sara would send the cards; she was a
thoughtful child.

She loved Sara. Drowsing in the dimming light, she
realized that she loved Sara more than was safe or
comfortable, with something of that fierce parental love
which had always frightened her in others. But Sara didn't
love her. Sara would be embarrassed, probably, at the very
idea. In the old days it had been right and proper to love
one's parents, and God; today the tall candid-eyed young
cynics kept their love for erring mankind and their unfortu-
nate brothers; or, occasionally, for their mates. Well, she
had tried that too. Never happy, even at its most intense
peak of longing, it had turned all too soon into misery so
abject that she still felt the echoes of it in her bones, like an
incurable, recurrent sickness. Misery, and love and sickness. . . .

I know what's wrong with me, she thought hazily. I'm
falling asleep. . . .

V

Ruth dreamed that she was lying on the sofa facing the
fireplace, as she actually was. Sara stood before her, and
that, too, was as it might have been. But only the girl's face
was clear; the rest of her body and clothing was dim as a
landscape seen through fog that shifts and thickens and
disperses, giving tantalizing and misleading hints of what
the mist conceals. She saw Sara's face as clearly as if it were
illumined by spotlights; and here the imitation of reality
ended. Ruth had never seen on anyone's face, let alone that
of her pretty niece, a look like the one that disfigured the
dream girl's features, and she hoped she never would. The

eyes were so distended that the whites showed all around the pupils. The complexion, against Sara's black-brown hair, looked gray as ash, and the pale lips were parted in a gasp of terror.

Ruth was so frightened that, even in her sleep, she tried to move. She could not, and recognized that, too, as a common dream symptom. Almost she welcomed the bodily paralysis as a confirmation of the fact that she was really dreaming.

Then the shadow came. It was formless at first, but she knew it had actual form that was somehow concealed from her. All she could see was its size and its menace, and as it loomed up against the dream shape of her niece, Sara's mouth opened in a scream that was all the more pitiable for being silent. The effect of that soundless shriek was so bad that Ruth woke. And then she entered the worst part of the nightmare.

She lay, as she had seen herself in the dream, on the couch that faced the fireplace. Now she could make out the glow of the fading coals—but vaguely, as if she saw them through air saturated with smoke. The table lamp behind the couch was on, casting a dim but adequate light over the whole scene. She felt the roughness of the brocade covering the couch against her cheek, and the stiffness of her cramped muscles. All these sensory impressions proved that she was indeed awake. Sara's dream image had, of course, disappeared.

The shadow had not.

It hovered between her and the fire—dark, heavy gray, smoke-thick and smoke-dark, it was the medium which dulled the crimson coals into tiny sparks. It had no form, but the form was coming, struggling to shape itself, so that the thick, sluggish coils of twilight-dark twisted and moved. . . .

Then, as she struggled frantically against the paralysis

that still held her, deliverance came, in the form of a sound which, if not personally familiar, was at least recognizable as something from the waking world. A voice, dulled by distance and thick glass panes into a mournful echo, calling. . . .

"Come home, come home . . . Sammie . . . come home. . . ."

With an effort that felt as if it must wrench her bones out of their sockets, Ruth swung her feet to the floor and sat up.

And woke, finally and genuinely.

For, of course, the last sequence had been only an extension of the original dream. It was common enough, to dream of waking. Ruth told herself that, but when she raised her hand to her forehead she found that the roots of her hair were soaked with perspiration.

She pushed the damp hair back from her face, drew a long shaken breath, and reached for a cigarette. Half shyly she glanced out of the corner of her eye at the fire. It was almost dead—only a faint reddish glow remained—but it was fading normally with no greasy pall of dead air to obscure it. Ruth let out the breath she had not known she was holding. When she struck the match, her fingers were hardly shaking. But—good heavens, that had been a nasty one!

She wondered what Pat would say about the origins of the nightmare—or Bruce, with his cocky assurance. The last thought brought a faint smile to her lips. No doubt Bruce's interpretation would be shatteringly Freudian.

She finished her cigarette and stood up, conscious of a cowardly disinclination to turn her back on the fireplace—a sentiment which she conquered at once. But she went up the stairs rather briskly, and she left the light on in the living room.

As she drifted off to sleep she found herself listening for a repetition of the call that had roused her. But she heard nothing more. Her room was in the front of the house, and the call seemed to come from the garden side, where Sara's room faced. Sammie certainly picked unsalubrious weather for prowling, she thought drowsily, and then—her last conscious thought before sleep claimed her—funny name for a cat. . . .

Chapter Three

Washingtonians take a perverse pride in the perversity of their weather, refusing to admit that it is, in this respect, like weather anywhere. Ruth had been a resident long enough to feel a sense of personal achievement when Sunday dawned fair and warm after a week of Alaskan cold. Sara had been out until all hours the night before, with the unavoidable Bruce, but she made her appearance at an early breakfast looking as dewy-eyed and rested as a baby. Ruth thought, "Ah, youth," but did not say it, and waved the girl off to a picnic at Great Falls without mentioning that it was not really quite warm enough for shorts. If she had legs like that, she told herself, she would display them too. And the shorts weren't much shorter, in fact, than the skirts the girls were wearing.

Before indulging in a second cup of coffee she tidied up the kitchen, deriving housewifely satisfaction from the look of shining steel and gleaming porcelain. Then she settled down with *The New York Times*.

The kitchen had been built at the tail end of the house, as kitchens of old houses were in that semitropical climate, so that cooking heat and odors would not permeate the rest of the house. The breakfast bay, where Ruth was sitting, had been added in a later century so that the inhabitants could enjoy the view of the walled garden, with its backdrop of firs and magnolias. They glowed greenly in the morning sunlight, and the birds, enjoying the warmth, were out in full voice.

Ruth struggled nobly with the reports of disaster— national, personal, and international—for half an hour, and then threw the paper aside as a particularly penetrating avian shriek reached her ears. Probably just a jay complaining about some private tribulation or fancied affront. . . . But perhaps a passing cat was bothering the birds. She really ought to go out and see.

It took only minutes to change her robe for slacks and sweater, and to run a comb through her short fair curls. When she got outside she realized that Sara was right; it really was too warm for wool clothing. The sun fell like soft intangible fingers on her hands and face. Standing in the middle of the flagged terrace, she threw out her arms and lifted her face in a sudden transport of sheer well-being. It was a wonderful day on which to be alive.

The garden was large for a city house, but then that was one of the features of Georgetown that its inhabitants prized most highly. The house had been built at the very edge of the long narrow lot, so that there was no front yard at all, only an areaway. All the land was in back, and it was fenced high on three sides. Georgetowners lacked the jovial conviviality of suburbanites; they liked their privacy, and did not take offense at others' enjoying theirs. Ruth scarcely knew her neighbors, and there were no gates or doors connecting the yards.

The boards of the fence needed painting, but their ugliness was masked by shrubs and bushes. All but the box and holly were bare now; the lilac and forsythia had lost most of their leaves in the windstorm of the past week, and the ones remaining were sere and yellowing. But Ruth eyed their straggling contours fondly. She had moved into the house the preceding spring, and one memory that would be imprinted forever on her brain was the sight of the garden when she first saw it, with the great heaps of forsythia like sprawling yellow fountains, sending out sprays so bright as to seem luminous. Cousin Hattie had not been able to afford a full-time gardener in her last years, and her part-time boy had spent his efforts on the grass and the roses and let the gnarled old lilacs and other bushes grow as nature decreed. The results had been beautiful.

After the forsythia faded, then came the dogwood—pale rose and white stars against the olive green of the firs—and the gorgeous flaming masses of the azaleas, rose-pink, fuschia and salmon, and white like a spotless drift of snow. There had been lily of the valley in the moist shadows of the pines, and violets thrust green fingers into every possible corner, penetrating the chinks in the brickwork of the patio, invading the rose beds. The lilac, perfuming the whole outdoors, and spirea, and flowering quince. . . .

Ruth had never been much of a nature lover; she had not consciously wanted a garden while she lived in the apartment on Massachusetts Avenue. She had not known how much she missed one until she walked through the back door of Aunt Hattie's house and saw the forsythia blaze out like little fallen suns.

She stooped to pick up some bits of scrap paper, blown in from the street, and then decided to get her gloves and tools and go at the garden. It was too splendid a day to stay indoors.

Trailing the rake, she went back to see how the roses had withstood the wind. They usually bloomed beautifully well into November, so she had not cut them back; the cold spell had taken her by surprise. On the first blustery night she and Sara had dragged in the wrought-iron table and chairs which stood in warm weather under the big oak in the center of the yard. Its spreading branches had been like sunset during October. Now most of the crimson leaves were on the ground under the tree. That would be the next job, after she had checked the roses.

They were in a sheltered spot, and had not suffered so badly as she feared. Colored confetti flakes of petals spattered the ground—pink and white and crimson so dark it was almost black—but several buds still lifted brave heads, and Ruth decided to leave them just in case the warm weather held. She knew she would never make a gardener; it gave her a physical pang to cut the roses back, as if she were amputating legs off birds, though she knew it had to be done.

Some of the buds could be cut; she would gather them before she went in. She was stooping over the bushes when a squawk of outrage erupted above her head and something went scuttling and scraping along the trunk of the fir tree. A big jay swooped out of the green branches, yelling indignantly, and sat down in the topmost branches of the oak, where it swayed and scolded like an animated blue flower.

Ruth looked up and was rewarded by the sight of a face, triangular and furry, peering calmly down at her from the foliage, like the famous disembodied head of the Cheshire cat. She recognized the cat from earlier visits, and yielded to an impulse born of exuberance and the springlike weather.

"Sammie, aren't you ashamed! Chasing birds is not nice."

Sammie gave her a contemptuous blink and vanished, not in stages like the fictitious cat, but all at once. The scraping noise began again, accompanied by quaking branches, and then a sleek tan-and-brown form leaped the last twenty feet to land on its feet not far from Ruth's. The cat immediately rolled over on its rear end and began to clean its tail with frantic energy.

"You're a pretty thing," Ruth said admiringly, and the cat paused, uncannily, to give her a glimpse of two eyes as blue as the back feathers of the jay before it resumed its washing. Its royal self-possession left Ruth amused and absurdly out of countenance. She was familiar with Mr. Eliot's advice on addressing cats, though she had never had occasion to put it into practice. Now, however, it appeared that she had been presumptuous.

"Oh, cat," she began, following the authority, and then jumped as a voice boomed out.

"Bad girl! So that's where you've gotten to!"

For a wild second Ruth was sure the voice, from a source not immediately apparent, was addressing her. She looked around, and, as she saw the face from which the voice had issued, suspended moonlike upon the top of the back fence, she realized that it had been addressing the animal. The face she raised was pink with amusement, and the face on the fence responded with a beam of obvious admiration.

"Good morning, good morning, my dear Mrs. Bennett! I must apologize for our bad child. Is she annoying you?"

"Not at all. She's a beauty, isn't she?"

"Well, we—yes, we think so. Mrs. DeVoto and I. Please feel quite free, however, to evict her if she becomes churlish. Though members of that breed rarely do so. Patronizing, contemptuous, even downright insulting; but never losing the true aristocratic demeanor."

"I'm sure," Ruth murmured. Mr. DeVoto, she recalled, was a retired official of the Department of State. He had something to do with protocol. He was a nice little man, though; he had swept off his genteel golf cap at the sight of her, and his bald head gleamed pinkly in the sunlight.

"Well, Mrs. Bennett," he went on, "if you are sure that

our feline friend does not disturb you, perhaps I will not venture to climb over your fence in order to retrieve her."

"Oh, I'll enjoy her company. But if you want her back I'll be delighted to hand her to you."

"That would hardly be feasible, I fear, though I do thank you for offering so kindly. Kai Lung does not care to be handled except by intimates. Not that she would—er— scratch." Mr. DeVoto's voice sank, as if he were mentioning something faintly obscene. "Dear me, no. She would simply evade your hand if you tried to touch her."

"Yes," Ruth said absently. The bush on the end might be pruned; there seemed to be dead wood there. . . . Then, belatedly, she realized what the man had said, and she exclaimed, "Kai Lung! Isn't her name Sammie?"

"Sammie? Good heavens—gracious me—why, no. She is a female cat, to begin with."

"No wonder she wouldn't speak to me," Ruth said, smiling. "I've not only been familiar, I've been wrong."

"Why would you think her name was Sammie?" Mr. DeVoto was clearly aghast at the very idea.

"Just that I heard someone calling, at night, and I assumed he was calling a pet. There's no reason why I should have thought it was—er—Kai Lung, except that she's the only cat I've seen about, and I know the dog on the south side has another name."

"I can assure you I have not been calling. Good gracious, Mrs. Bennett, I hope you do not think that I would be so thoughtless as to—"

"Of course not. It must be some other cat, or dog, owner."

"I cannot imagine who." Mr. DeVoto's chin sank out of sight as he prepared to retire. "There are no other pets in this block, except for that unattractive beast next door. Well, Mrs. Bennett, it has been most pleasant chatting with you. Perhaps you might join us one evening for a glass of sherry."

"That would be nice."

"My wife will telephone you, then. In the meantime, I do hope you enjoy your gardening."

He lifted the hat he had been holding and replaced it on his head with such perfect timing that, for a second, it seemed to sit suspended on top of the fence as the face below sank out of sight. Ruth allowed herself a broad grin as soon as the face had disappeared, but it was a friendly sort of grin. He really was a nice little man.

She did enjoy her gardening, and she had quite a heap of leaves to show for her efforts when she finished. She had another cup of coffee sitting on the bench built around the oak, and Kai Lung sat beside her and condescended to sample the cream. Then she wound herself into a ball and went to sleep in the sun, and Ruth went back to clipping dead roses. It was a very pleasant day. There was no reason at all why, as she prepared to go in, Ruth should find herself speculating on the identity of the elusive creature named Sammie, and wondering whether he had, in fact, ever come home.

II

The weather held all that week, providing conversation for hundreds of dinner parties. On Friday afternoon Ruth left work early and took a cab home; she was perspiring slightly as she came in the front door, and was not really looking forward to cleaning house and cooking a meal. The first thing she heard was the sound of the vacuum cleaner. In the living room she found Sara, wearing an apron which completely covered her brief skirt, putting the finishing touches on a room which shone with wax and elbow grease.

"Well, that's the pleasantest sight I've seen all day," Ruth exclaimed, as her niece, seeing her enter, switched off the vacuum. "My dear girl, how nice of you!"

"You didn't think I was going to let you do all this by yourself, did you? I don't have any Friday afternoon classes."

"But it's finished; I couldn't have done better myself. All we need now are the flowers. I brought some home with me, they're in the hall."

"What kind?"

"Some carnations and the inevitable chrysanthemums, I'm afraid, but I found some beauties. That lovely bronze. This is a hybrid, with gold and copper streaks."

"I like mums." Sara wound the cord around the cleaner and shoved it towards the door. "What shall I put them in, the blue Delft pots?"

"That would be good. The white ones can go in the copper vases, and the carnations in the silver. There ought to be a few roses left; I'd planned those for the dining room."

"They've been gotten. Take a look."

Ruth pushed open the sliding doors across the hall from the drawing room, and exclaimed with pleasure. The dining room was a dark room, abutting on the neighboring house so closely that that side had been left without windows. Instead of running the full length of the house like the drawing room, it was backed by a high old-fashioned butler's pantry and the kitchen; hence its only outside light came from the street windows, which were kept curtained because they were so close to the sidewalk. The wall sconces and the chandelier had been electrified, and they gave a warm, rich light. The furniture was heavy and dark. Sara had polished it till it reflected objects, and Ruth had mended the worn spots in the exquisite petit point covering the chairs. The table was already set, with Ruth's best damask and silver and crystal; the beautiful old Delft in the corner cupboard, with its scalloped border, had been washed, and the tall silver candlesticks held bayberry candles whose faded green matched the muted shade of the walls.

"Everything is perfect," Ruth said gratefully. "There's nothing for me to do."

"Except the cooking!"

"Yes, I'd better start the rolls. They'll have to rise twice."

"It's such a job. Why didn't you get frozen rolls?"

"The secret of good cooking," Ruth said didactically, "is to stick to what you can do well, but use no substitutes. I can't handle elaborate meals; they require too many hands at the last minute, and I really don't enjoy cooking all that much anyhow. A roast is easy to prepare, but this one I've got is a roast of roasts; I bullied it out of that French butcher on Wisconsin, and paid a week's grocery money for it. The salad is my own invention, but it's very simple—every fresh vegetable I can find goes into it, plus eggs. You'd be surprised how impressive it looks. So the rolls have to be handmade, those frozen ones taste like cardboard and would spoil the total effect."

"I see your point. You know what I'd cook, don't you?"

"Spaghetti," Ruth said.

"How did you ever guess?"

"Well, I used to serve it myself when I started house-keeping. It has the advantage of being honestly peasanty, but I can't serve Mrs. Jackson MacDougal spaghetti. Not that she wouldn't eat it with perfect aplomb."

"What's she like?"

"She's a darling. You'll like her."

They stood for a moment in silence, their arms lightly

touching as they surveyed the room to make sure no touch had been omitted. It was a good moment. Ruth was to remember it later, with a sharp pang of loss.

III

The guests were due at seven thirty. At six Ruth went downstairs to do the last-minute kitchen work which could not be put off any later if she wanted time to dress. The hors d'oeuvres needed to be made, the drink tray set up, the rolls kneaded and shaped—a dozen little odds and ends, time-consuming and annoying, which every hostess knows.

She had done her hair, but her person was attired in mules and a garment unattractively known as a duster. She had just plunged both hands up to the wrists in dough when the doorbell rang. She said "damn," and wondered who on earth it could be. Sara was dressing and was probably unfit for society at the moment. She would have to answer the door herself.

Snatching up a paper towel she stamped into the hall and flung the door open, prepared to give a short shrift to any luckless newspaper boy or lost tourist. One glance and she started to slam it shut.

"Go away! Go away and come back in an hour. Of all the outrageous—"

Pat had thoughtfully inserted one large foot in the door. Now he shoved.

"I'm not a guest, I'm a waiter. Open up."

She had very little choice. He kicked the door shut behind him and headed for the kitchen, without further comment. Ruth trailed along, too curious now to be angry. But if the parcel he carried contained food or wine, she was prepared to rage.

Pat deposited his bundle on the counter and unfolded it.

"My favorite bottle opener, my best carving knife, and," he held up the white material which had contained the other items, "my apron. What needs doing?"

"But you—you. . . . Words," said Ruth honestly, "fail me."

"This last minute stuff is the worst part of the party. I'm trying to demonstrate," he said, with a sidelong glance, "that men are useful things to have around the house. What have we here? Bread or something? Well, I'll leave that to you. What are we drinking? Where do you keep the gin?"

Twenty minutes later Ruth was shaping the last of the rolls while Pat put a shaker of martinis in the refrigerator and swept the kitchen with a comprehensive glance.

"All set, I think. I'll light the fire now, while you change."

"Just a second, till I finish these."

He came up behind her and stood watching, and gradually Ruth's movement slowed. She had expected this sooner or later and had not been sure how she would handle it—or how she wanted to handle it. What she had not anticipated was the mindless lassitude that gripped her at the first touch of his hands.

"Relax," he said, into her ear. "I don't want flour all over my brand new jacket."

Leaning back against him, she heard his quick breathing, felt his hands move from her waist to her breasts. His lips slid down her cheek, seeking her mouth; without conscious volition she turned her face to meet his. So. . . . Those particular nerve endings were not atrophied after all. Through the years she had sought—perhaps unconsciously, perhaps not—partners who did not arouse the deadened emotions, and had told herself that they were gone for good. Now, wherever his hands and lips had touched she felt stripped, not only of clothing but of skin, as if the skillful fingers manipulated the nerves themselves.

For several long unmeasured seconds her consciousness hung suspended on a single pivot of pleasure; then the automatic defenses, never so long defied, snapped into place. She stiffened and moved; and he released her at once, stepping back, hands touching her waist only to balance her.

Staring dizzily at her own hands, Ruth saw a pathetic squeezed lump clenched between taut fingers. Automatically she began to pat it into shape.

"What happened?" he asked quietly. His breathing was slower but still uneven.

"Nothing. I . . . squashed my roll, didn't I?"

"Do you find me that repulsive?"

"Oh, Pat—no." She turned to face him, hands eloquent; with the beginning of a smile he fended off her floury fingers.

"I thought the first reaction was too good. Well, I guess this isn't the time or place to go into the matter. Remove your tempting person from my presence and I'll try to behave myself the rest of the evening. We'll pretend nothing happened."

It was no use pretending; every time her eyes met his she remembered, with her entire body. As Sara deftly removed the plates and served cherries jubilee, Ruth's eyes went back to the magnet that had drawn them all evening, and found his eyes waiting and alight.

When they moved into the drawing room Ruth shook herself mentally. It was high time she paid more attention to her guests, especially now that the main event of the evening was coming up. She had invited a couple from the office, amiable nonentities whose personalities would not be obtrusive, and Sara had added two school friends whose faces, then and forever after, remained pink blurs in Ruth's memory.

Madame Nada, decked in swirling black chiffon for the occasion, led the way into the room. She had already seen and approved the arrangements, but their previous occupation of the drawing room had been confined to the couches near the fire. Now, as the medium approached the table, she suddenly stopped short, her hand outstretched in the act of seeking a chair. Ruth heard her gasp sharply.

"Is something wrong?" she asked, moving to Madame Nada's side. The other guests, chatting and relaxed after a good meal, were not paying much attention. Ruth was the only one who saw the medium's face, and she felt as if she were seeing its true shape for the first time. Genuine surprise and a shadow of some other, less innocuous emotion, had stripped away the mask temporarily.

"It is so cold," said Madame Nada.

"I know, there always seems to be a draft at this end of the room. If it's too bad—"

"Draft?" The close-set brown eyes, still wide with shock, met hers.

"Are we ready?" Mrs. MacDougal asked crisply, at Ruth's elbow. She had changed her personality with her costume, and was wearing a soft dressmaker suit that looked like a thousand dollars, which was probably its approximate price.

"I don't know." Ruth turned impulsively. "It is so chilly at this end of the room. Will it be uncomfortable for you? We could move the table. . . ."

"Heavens, no. Pat told me about the draft—that's why I wore a suit. It seems quite comfortable to me. Where shall we sit?"

Ruth glanced inquiringly at the medium, who replied with a slight shrug and a smile. The mask was back in place.

When they were all seated, Ruth glanced around the table. The scene had an odd distinctness. Colors seemed more vivid, faces sharply cut and memorable. She was struck with a feeling that she ought to remember every detail.

The medium sat with her back to the windows, whose drapes were pulled shut. Ruth's co-worker, Jack Simmons, sat on Madame Nada's right, and Ruth had been directed to the place on the medium's other side. Next to her sat Sara, looking especially vivid and alert; her eyes sparkled with anticipation, rich color stained her cheeks, and her olive complexion was set off by the clear yellow wool of her dress. Bruce sat almost directly opposite her. He had been on his best behavior all evening, except for indicating by his very silence that he found the conversation incredibly dull. As his eyes met Ruth's passing glance, he inclined his head slightly, and his beard twitched. Ruth's glance moved on. Mary Simmons, solemn and self-conscious, her reddened housewife's hands clasped on the table; Pat. That was enough, just. . . . Pat.

"We begin," said Madame Nada suddenly.

IV

Afterward Ruth wondered whether she would have been conscious of that atmosphere if her more delicate senses, those beyond the normal five, had not been preoccupied. A quiver of uneasiness penetrated even that most consuming of all self-interests; for when the lights went out, and the groping hands fumbled and linked, something touched her in the darkness, something impalpable that brushed and passed on; and a long shiver shook her bare arm.

At first the session was not notably different from the other meeting a week earlier. Ruth was conscious of the usual distractions, the annoying little itches which could not be scratched, the intensification of sounds with the loss of sight. The room was quite dark; the heavy drapes cut off all light from the street and the back of the couch shielded the glow of the fire, which had been allowed to die down to a bed of coals.

The medium's breathing deepened and slowed and steadied—the preliminary, as Ruth had been told, to what is called the trance state. Her fingers were linked around the medium's wrist, so she was immediately aware of the moment at which the Madame Nada went into her trance, body relaxed and hands limp.

"A name," the medium droned. "Ann. Something . . . Ann. Mary?"

There was a stir around the table.

"Can she hear us?" It was Bruce's voice.

"No," Mrs. MacDougal answered softly. "Not unless we addressed her directly. She's in light trance now, speaking with her own voice, of impressions she is getting. Later she'll go into deep trance and other personalities will speak through her."

"Mary," the medium interrupted. "Wants to sing. Not doing . . . party. . . ."

Ruth felt Sara's hand contract, and knew she was about to giggle. She squeezed, warningly. However much she shared Sara's feelings, she could not mock her guests.

"Who is Mary?" Mrs. MacDougal asked.

"Pretty! Mary, Mary, quite contrary. That's what Papa calls her."

"Can you describe her?"

"Oh, pretty. . . . Yellow hair. Old-fashioned: long curls. That's funny. . . ."

"Describe her clothing."

"Such pretty, flowery stuff . . . little sprigs, pink flowers. Kerchief around her neck, elbow sleeves. . . ."

Mary Simmons, whose hobby was American costume, gave an involuntary squeak of recognition. The medium, seeming not to hear, swept on.

"A man, too, he's with her. She calls him Papa. Wears

long blue coat, brass buttons. Funny whiskers, long, bushy . . . gray. Close the door, close the door, don't let the damned Yankees in!"

The last sentence boomed out, startlingly, in a deep baritone voice, rough with simulated anger. Sara jumped; Ruth, who had done some reading during the past week, squeezed her hand again.

"She's in deep trance now," Mrs. MacDougal whispered. "Who are you?" she asked aloud.

"Henry. Damn' Yankees, let 'em die. Bolt the door!"

"Henry who?"

"Henry" snorted; he did sound just like a choleric old gentleman.

"Campbell, of course. Henry W. Campbell. My house, damn it; damn' bluecoats can't come in."

"Why don't you want them to come in?" Mrs. Mac-Dougal asked.

"Wait." The voice changed. It was no longer a man's voice; but it was so distorted by some strong emotion that Ruth could not identify it as Madame Nada's. The words sounded strained, as if each one had to be forced through a resisting substance. "No, no. . . . No . . . can . . . not. . . ."

The limp hand flexed so roughly that it pulled loose from Ruth's grasp. The medium's breathing quickened.

"Nada. Listen to me, Nada. Wake up. Wake up. . . . Lights, someone."

The circle broke. Lights flared, leaving everyone blinking. Ruth saw Mrs. MacDougal bending over the medium, holding her shoulders and speaking in a soothing voice.

"All right now?" she asked.

"Yes, yes." The medium straightened and brushed back a lock of hair that had fallen over her forehead. "What happened?"

"An intrusive entity," Mrs. MacDougal said solemnly.

"Strong," the medium muttered. "Strong and. . . ."
She shook herself like a dog coming out of the water.
"Did we get anything of interest?" she asked.

"Oh, yes, splendid. Mrs. Bennett, you know something of the history of the house. Can you verify the incident?"

Put fair and squarely on the spot, Ruth stammered, "Of course the house did belong to the Campbells. I don't recall the name of the man who owned it during the Civil War, but—"

"Yes, it was certainly the War Between the States," Mrs. MacDougal agreed. "Was Mr. Campbell a Southern sympathizer?"

From across the table Bruce said smoothly,

"May I, Mrs. Bennett? Not only was Campbell a rebel at heart—not uncommon in Georgetown—but the incident suggested did occur. When the Union Army fled after the battle of—First Bull Run, I think it was—the wounded, exhausted men streamed back into the city over the bridge at Georgetown. Many of them collapsed on the steps of the houses, and Mr. Campbell ordered his door locked and barred against them."

He waited just long enough for the gasps of amazement to be heard. Then he added gently,

"It's all described in *Old Georgetown Stories*."

The medium was too accustomed to skepticism to show anger, if she felt any. She gave Bruce a sweet smile and said indifferently, "I have never read that book."

"Does the book describe the old man?" Mrs. MacDougal demanded.

"No. But a blue coat and brass buttons aren't unusual."

"What about Mary Ann?"

"I haven't the faintest idea whether or not Henry had a daughter of that name," Bruce said cheerfully. "I doubt if it would be possible to find out."

"That's why it is impossible to convince you skeptics," Mrs. MacDougal said in exasperation. "If you do find verification, you claim the medium could have looked up the information; if you don't find it, you claim it can't be verified."

Bruce gave her a look in which amusement and respect were mingled.

"You're quite right," he said courteously. "It's hard luck, isn't it?"

"Hmmmph." Mrs. MacDougal turned away from him. "Let's try again, Nada, it's still early. Perhaps we can get something which will convince this young man."

"I don't know. . . ." the medium said slowly.

"Come, it's too good a chance to miss. You went quite quickly into deep trance; obviously the atmosphere here is very sympathetic."

The medium was silent. Ruth, next to her, thought she looked more bloodlessly anemic than ever.

"Perhaps Madame Nada is tired," she said, with no other motive than sympathy. "I understand the trance state can be tiring."

"Yes, it is tiring," the medium said. "But that is not why I am afraid—I mean to say, why I am reluctant—"

"No, you mean afraid," Bruce interrupted, staring at the woman. "What are you afraid of?"

Ruth turned toward the boy with a disapproving frown—and realized that he was right. Madame Nada was frightened, badly frightened and, at the same time, excited. Somehow her fear was more convincing than any manifestation she could have produced. Ruth began, "If you feel that way—"

But her gentle voice was drowned out by a booming "Nonsense!" from Mrs. MacDougal; and after a searching glance at her patroness, the medium shrugged.

"Very well. But I have warned."

"We must all concentrate on pure thoughts," Mrs. MacDougal urged. "Perhaps if we sang a hymn—"

"Oh, no," Ruth said involuntarily. The medium gave her a bleak smile.

"I think not. Just—let us begin."

V

The medium sank into trance at once, deeply, frighteningly, almost as if she had been dragged under the surface of consciousness by a force she could not resist. The wrist Ruth held went limp, as before; but Ruth shivered as she felt the undisciplined pulse racing wildly under her fingers.

"Names," the droning voice began. "Mary Ann, Henry, a Frank . . . someone named Hilda."

"Go on," breathed Mrs. MacDougal.

"I see two women. One young, one older. Gray hair. Or is it powder? The quarrel, the girl is crying. Poor Mary!"

Ruth relaxed. This was the same sort of vague talk they had heard before, unconvincing because it could be tailored to fit almost any event. Relieved of her anxiety, her mind began to wander, only half-hearing the medium's descriptions and recitations of names which might apply to anyone on earth, or no one. Something about an Indian in a feathered headdress . . . a hanging man . . . a little white dog. That reminded her of the elusive Sammie, and she was speculating idly on his identity when, as if the memory had been a cue, the terror began.

It came slowly and slyly, like a trickle of dirty water through a crack. A voice, the voice of no one in the circle, began to mutter. It sounded, at first, like a recording played at too low a speed—a dull, forced drone of sound, with no words distinguishable. Then it grew louder, and words began to be heard. But still the mechanical impression was there, as if something were being pushed and squeezed through the wrong sort of machine.

The medium had gone rigid. Her thin wrist was no longer lax; it pulled and pounded against Ruth's fingers. Madame Nada had good cause for alarm; for she, of all the people in the room, knew that the muttering horror of a voice did not come from her own throat. She, and one other. Ruth knew that the sound originated, not from her right-hand side, but from her left. From Sara.

The others, of course, assumed that Madame Nada was producing this voice, as she had produced the others. Yet there was a qualitative difference in this sound, and they all felt it. The room became absolutely still. The cold suddenly seemed intense; Ruth had to clench her teeth together to keep them from chattering.

The muttering, mumbling monologue seemed to go on and on; but in actuality the whole business could not have lasted more than thirty seconds, and the voice had forced out no more than six articulate words, before the medium's strained nerves erupted in a hair-raising scream. It broke the horrified paralysis of the others; there were sounds of chairs being pushed back, cries and questions. The lights flashed on. Ruth had a wild, vivid glimpse of Bruce, his hand still on the light switch, his body braced against the wall, his face paper white as he stared at her. . . . No, not at her. At Sara, beside her. *He knew*. Somehow, he knew.

Making the greatest effort of her life, Ruth turned her head to stare at the thing that sat beside her—quietly now, demurely, head bent and hands still. The features were the same—the narrow nose and flowing black hair, the quiet mouth. The physical identity only intensified the terror; for she knew, with a certainty that defied the senses, that when Sara turned her head, something that was no longer Sara would look back at her through Sara's eyes.

Chapter Four

That night, for the first time in forty years, Ruth left a night light burning when she went to bed. But whenever she closed her eyes a face took shape against the darkness—the familiar, unrecognizable face that had been superimposed on Sara's face for one impossible moment.

From a social point of view the evening could not be called a success, ending as it did with the demoralization of most of the guests and the complete collapse of one of them. Madame Nada had fainted dead away, falling so ungracefully and painfully that even the skeptics knew it was a genuine faint. When she recovered she could think of only one thing—getting out of the house as quickly as possible. Mrs. MacDougal's car took her home, and Pat felt he had to escort the excited women. The other guests made their excuses like people fleeing a house of death. Séances were only fun when they were artificial.

It was clear to Ruth that none of them really knew what had happened; they were simply reacting to an atmosphere as intense as it was unpleasant. The medium was a true sensitive, in that she had felt the unpleasantness more keenly, but she was no more equipped to cope with genuine horror than were the others.

Bruce would have lingered; but Ruth sent him packing. His presence was not the one she wanted, and, in fact, she was not sure that she wanted anyone. She preferred to be alone with Sara.

For Sara it was, once again; no doubt about that. When Ruth turned shrinkingly back to her niece, after administering first aid to Madame Nada, the illusion (if it had been an illusion) was gone. Sara's voice, Sara's expression—the indefinable, essential Sara-ness—were back.

Ruth was left in bed with two equally unpleasant theories for company. The room was comfortably warm, the blankets fleecy, the brushed nylon of her nightgown soft against her recumbent body; but from time to time she shivered with an ungovernable chill.

What is it that defines an individual? Not the body, the color of hair and eyes, the shape of the face, for these may alter with accident or illness, and they do, inevitably, alter with the one unavoidable illness, old age. Opinions and beliefs, the products of the thinking brain, also change; the bright young idealist may become a cynical supporter of bigotry in old age.

So what is it, she wondered, that makes a man or woman, distinctly himself, different from all others? Give that quality a name—personality—though the name itself is meaningless; it may be what some call the immortal soul or it may be simply a cluster of traits, inherited and acquired. Character, soul, spirit, individuality . . . the turn of the head, the expression of the eyes, the responses to pain, fear, love.

When she was little, Ruth had thought of herself—the real Ruth—as a little homunculus living inside her head, busily manipulating the muscles that moved the puppet of her body, arranging the thoughts that animated her brain by

day, sorting and selecting her dreams at night. She wondered now whence she had derived this image; surely there
was something like it in one of Louisa May Alcott's
books. . . . Or perhaps it was an idea which would occur
to any sensitive child—the little soul living inside the brain,
looking out through the eyes.

Tonight something had looked out of Sara's brain,
through Sara's eyes, that was not Sara.

Ruth twisted uncomfortably between sheets which were
already wrinkled and hot. The incredibility of her fancies
was even more apparent when she put them into concrete
images.

In a way, the alternative was less difficult. It was simply
that she, Ruth Bennett, was suffering from hallucinations.
That she was able to entertain, even for a moment, the wild
hypothesis of Sara's differentness, indicated that her own
mind had slipped considerably from normal standards.

People who are losing their minds, they say, do not doubt
their sanity. Ruth suspected that this consoling thought
would not be supported by a psychologist. Heaven knew
she had enough doubts. But at the basis of all her queries lay
one damning fact: that it was easier for her to believe in her
mad idea of possession than in her own madness.

Morning is often a revelation in itself. When Ruth woke
from a brief, but deep, sleep, she could hardly believe in the
dark visions of the night. Sunlight poured in through the
window and the mockingbirds who had made a nest in the
chimney discussed their plans for the day. Downstairs she
heard movement, and Sara's voice, an untrained but sweet
contralto, singing "Where Have All the Flowers Gone?"
Smells floated enticingly up the stair—coffee, bacon, toast.

Saturday was cleaning day. Since Sara arrived Ruth had
gladly abandoned the never-ending search for reliable help.
She and Sara could go over the entire house in four hours,

and leave every bit of glass sparkling and every chair leg polished. If there was the slightest shadow on Sara's soul it was invisible. She sang like a bird and worked like a demon and, after lunch, went dashing off to keep a shopping appointment with a girl friend. Ruth's decision had been made without conscious debate; not for anything in the world would she have mentioned her fears to Sara. She decided that she would call her doctor for a checkup, just to be on the safe side. But Monday would be time enough; Saturday morning was always busy for Dr. Peterson. There was no hurry.

II

She met It again that night, walking in the hall. Sara was barefoot, but the old, uneven boards creaked. Ruth came awake as a soldier in a battle zone jerks out of sleep, alert and fully conscious. She knew instantly what was standing outside her door; and knew, as well, the futility of her former attempts at reason.

The hardest thing she had ever had to do was to get out of bed and go to meet it.

III

"She always wears bedroom slippers," Ruth said. "Ever since she got a splinter in her foot last fall."

Suddenly, without meaning to, she began to cry. Pat, whose face had assumed a deepening expression of concern, slid over and put his arms around her. When the first storm of tears subsided he said quietly, "I don't blame you for being upset, Ruth. But you've got to tell me the rest. What happened after you went out into the hall?"

"I'm sorry." Ruth sniffed, and took a deep breath. "I know I'm not. . . . It was bright moonlight last night; the light came flooding in through the circular window on the landing. It—Sara—" She faltered, seeing his lips tighten at the slip, and then went doggedly on. "She was standing there, on the landing, looking like something out of Mrs. Radcliffe; she always wears nightgowns, not pajamas, and her winter ones are long and high-necked because the house gets cold at night. . . . Sorry again. I'm fighting away from it, aren't I?"

All he said was, "You're doing fine, go on."

"What I'm trying to give you is the picture—a girl in a long pale gown, with her black hair falling over her shoulders. Wraithlike, pale-faced in the moonlight. Her eyes were wide open. . . . No, I can see what you're thinking, but that wasn't it; she was not sleepwalking. My roommate used to walk in her sleep and I know the look. This—Sara—was awake. It was awake, Pat, wide awake; and *it was not Sara.*"

"You're giving me your impressions. You are not describing what happened. We'll worry about subjective sensations after you explain how you got those marks on your face."

"I must look awful," Ruth said drearily.

"You have what is popularly known as a shiner. Plus a couple of scratches on your cheek. How did you explain them to Sara?"

"I didn't. I yelled through the door, told her I had a headache and didn't want to be disturbed. Finally she went out. As soon as she left the house I called you."

"She was—Sara—again this morning?"

"Yes. She offered to get breakfast, call the doctor. She was awfully sweet. . . ."

"All right," he said, as her voice began to quaver. "You've told me everything but the main thing. Sara hit you, didn't she?"

"Yes."

Pat pointed a long finger at the glass on the table beside Ruth.

"Finish your medicine. I know this is a hell of an hour for sherry, but you need a stimulant. Why did she hit you?"

Ruth made a face; for a moment she felt sure that the wine would be the last straw for her churning stomach. Then the warmth spread, and her icy hands relaxed a bit.

"Let me try to be coherent. I saw her standing there in the moonlight. After a minute I spoke to her. She didn't answer. I said, 'Sara, are you ill? What's wrong?' She started. She said—"

"Exact words, if you can remember them."

"Good God, I wish I could forget them! She said the same thing she said at the séance. She said it twice. 'Not dead. Not dead.' Then a sort of sigh, and—I think—the word 'please.' She kept repeating that, faster and faster, till the words ran together. . . . She was screaming by then, Pat; in the middle of it, I thought I caught something that sounded like 'the General.' But I wasn't really listening. I felt I had to make her be quiet. It was when I touched her that she—flailed out with both arms. Honestly, I don't think she meant to hurt me; I'm not even sure she knew who I was."

"Probably not."

"Pat, you know Sara. You know she wouldn't ever—"

"Dear heart, is that what worries you?" He smiled, for the first time since he had entered the house; but the lines on forehead and cheek did not disappear. "I don't think our nice Sara has turned into a homicidal maniac, no. Finish your story before I start lecturing. How the hell did you calm her? She's twice your size, and a healthy young animal."

"I didn't. She almost knocked me out with that blow in the face, but she overbalanced herself. Her foot slipped. When she fell, she must have hit her head. I dragged her back to bed. I probably shouldn't have moved her, but . . . well, I did. She passed from unconsciousness into normal sleep without waking, and when I was sure she was asleep, I went to bed myself."

"I'll bet you were ready for it. Okay. I get the picture."

Ruth drew a long breath.

"I just want to know one thing. Who's crazy—me or Sara?"

"Neither of you is crazy," he said violently. "Don't use that stupid goddamn word."

"I'm sorry. . . ."

"So am I. I'm a hell of a therapist, aren't I. Have another drink. Let's both have another drink."

Ruth took the glass he handed her. In the morning sunlight the light liquid shone like tawny gold.

"Don't think I'm not grateful," she said. "But if you would just tell me, without mincing words. . . ."

"I intend to." He drained his glass in one movement of his wrist. "Dismiss, first of all, the notion that you imagined all this. Such things have happened; people with certain types of mental illness have even inflicted injuries on themselves in order to substantiate a fantastic theory. But not you. This thing happened. So we are faced with the only other possibility. Sara is the one who is mentally disturbed. You're probably right in saying that she didn't know you. Now at this point that's absolutely all I can say; I haven't seen the girl. Something is bugging her, some anxiety; I could guess at the obvious possibilities, but I see no future in doing so."

"Oh, God. What am I going to tell her mother?"

"Nothing, yet. Ruth, you're too intelligent to go into a tizzy at the mention of mental illness; this may not turn out to be anything serious. Let's wait and see before we start screaming."

"But what shall I do?"

"First, you will go and get dressed." He lifted his hand as she started to speak, and solemnly ticked off the points on his fingers. "Next we will go out to lunch and get some food in that queasy stomach of yours. Forget about your black eye, the waiter will think I slugged you, that's all, and he'll admire me greatly. Then we will come back here and wait for Sara. When do you expect her home?"

"Five, or thereabouts. But Pat—"

"I want to talk to her," Pat said quietly. "That's all, just talk. Maybe then we can determine whether she needs a neurologist or a psychiatrist or a gynecologist, or just a good swift kick in the pants."

"But—"

"Theorizing without sufficient data is the most futile of all occupations, Ruth. Wasn't it Sherlock Holmes who said that? It applies to practically everything in life. Now go up and get some clothes on."

Ruth went. After her hysterical plea for help, she could hardly refuse to follow his advice. She wondered, as she dressed, what weird combination of motives had prompted her to call him instead of the family doctor. Some of them were reasonably obvious. Others. . . .

She examined the image in her mirror. It looked abnormally normal, all things considered; trim and tailored in a powder-blue suit, silvery hair serene; carefully applied makeup had even diminished the bruise around her eye.

Others. . . . Her uncontrolled thoughts ran on. Other motives might be in doubt. But one was clear. She had instinctively summoned Pat because he was an expert on the subject that haunted her—literally and terribly. Despite what seemed to her a series of betraying admissions, he had not sensed her true fears—because, she thought bitterly, no sane person would ever conceive of such things. He believed that she had called out to him because she needed him, not as a professional, but as a man.

IV

The sunset was splendidly ominous—indigo and purple clouds rimmed with gold against a pale, clear green sky. The leafless branches of the big oak stood out black against the glory; their complex patterns had an austere mathematical beauty.

Ruth had reached the stage of irrational nervousness when the slightest phenomenon seems prophetic. When the wineglass, one of an old, cherished set, slipped from her hand and shattered musically on the coffee table, she bit her lip so hard that it bled.

Pat bent to collect the pieces. Then they heard the front door open.

Sara was—Sara. But she was not alone. Ruth recognized Bruce's affected speech with mingled exasperation and relief. One could hardly speak candidly to the girl in his presence. On the other hand, it was good to know that Bruce had been with her. Especially with night drawing in.

Now why, she wondered, did I think of that?

Pat's greeting to Sara was, on the surface, casual and without innuendoes. Sherry was offered and accepted; the two young people sat down; Bruce suggested a fire, and was graciously permitted to build one. The darkness fell with winter rapidity, and they sat by the light of the leaping flames and talked about nothing.

Ruth was silent; light conversation seemed impossible.

The devil that Pat had exorcised by the simple fact of refusing to see its possibility slid slyly back, hovering in the gathering shadows. Yet whenever she looked at Sara her brain staggered at the incongruity of it all. Miniskirts and long black leather boots do not suit the supernatural.

As the minutes wore on Ruth felt the tension mounting. Her own silence fed it; so did Bruce's uncharacteristically monosyllabic speech. He sat on the edge of his chair and never took his eyes off Sara. The girl was nervous too; she moved too much, twitching at her skirt, stroking the leather of her boots. She had developed a slight stammer, the first time Ruth had ever noticed any such trait.

"It's dark," Ruth said suddenly. "Let's have some light."

Pat's hand caught her arm as she started to rise. He alone seemed unaffected by the strain.

"The firelight is pleasant," he said. "Leave it."

The words, with their bland assumption of authority, would have irritated Ruth at any other time. Now the sudden need that had sent her groping for light closed in upon her. She sank back onto the couch, not because of Pat's grip, but because her knees would no longer hold her erect. Could no one else feel It? It was coming. It was all around. It was cold and darkness; It fed on darkness. If this went on. . . .

"I understand you haven't been sleeping too well lately," Pat said to Sara.

"No, Pat, don't," Ruth said. "This isn't the time—"

"Of course it is; you're letting this worry you far too much. There's no reason to be shy about it. Everybody has problems at one time or another—nervous strain, over-work. . . ."

"What the hell are you talking about?" Bruce demanded.

"I mean just what I say. Sara has been sleepwalking. That's a sign of nerves, a signal we can't ignore."

"Stop it," Ruth said urgently. "Pat, this is all wrong, can't you feel. . . ." Her voice died, only to rise again in a gasp of terror. Sara was sitting on the edge of the couch nearest the fire. The red light gave auburn gleams to her dark hair, and lit the curve of cheek and chin with a diabolical flush. She had not moved nor uttered a word; but her pose had altered, indefinably but unmistakably.

In the silence that followed Ruth's intake of breath they could all hear the girl breathing in short shallow gasps. The firelight caught the glow of her eyes as they moved. Groping wildly Ruth found Pat's hand and clung to it. She was conscious of a bizarre feeling of relief. He saw it too. The rigidity of his muscles, unresponsive for once to her touch, told of his reaction more graphically than speech. But the reaction that cut Ruth to the quick was Bruce's. He made one small movement, quickly controlled; but she knew enough to recognize it, even from its abortive beginning—the instinctive flight of flexed fingers to his forehead.

"Sara," Pat said softly.

No response. Only that shallow, panicky panting of breath.

"Sara, are you in pain? Tell me what hurts. I can help."

No sound, no movement. Pat freed his hand from Ruth's grasp. He leaned forward as if to touch Sara's arm.

"Don't be afraid. Everything is going to be—"

She flinched away from him, shrinking into the corner of the couch. Pat withdrew his hand.

"You hear me, don't you?"

"I—hear."

The voice was normal enough in tone and pitch; the only thing wrong with it was that it was not Sara's voice.

Even in those two words there was a noticeable difference in inflection. The "I" sound was softer, and there was something about the final "r" that struck oddly on the listening ears.

"You do hear me?" Pat repeated. His voice was soft, but insistent.

"Yes. But I don't know—"

"You don't know what?"

"Who you are."

Pat's arm shot out in a savage silent gesture aimed at Bruce, just in time to keep him in his place. His voice did not lose its even, gentle inflection.

"I'm Pat, Sara. Professor MacDougal. You're taking my course, remember? And doing some typing for me."

"What is—typ-ing?"

"It's a kind of—never mind. You know your name, don't you?"

"Know . . . name. Sara." There was a brief pause; the figure huddled on the couch rolled its eyes, and Ruth felt her hands turn cold. "You called . . . her . . . Sara."

It was too much for Bruce. With a muffled curse he dived, not for Sara, but for the light switch. The chandelier blazed into life, blinding the three who sat by the fire. Ruth's hands flew up to shield her eyes; Pat swore; and Sara, after one muffled cry, turned the color of typewriter paper and fell forward. Pat recovered himself just barely in time to catch her.

"Goddamn it all to hell," he said, kneeling with Sara held across his shoulder like an awkward, long-legged doll; the black boots sprawled pathetically across the rug. "Goddamn you, you young bastard, what the hell did you do that for? Get over here and give me a hand."

"Oh, Pat, don't yell at him; I was about ready to do it myself." Ruth's cheeks were wet with tears of nervous strain. She dropped onto the floor and touched Sara's head. "Is she—"

"Just fainted. Bruce!"

"I'll take her." Bruce held out his arms.

"You'll take her feet. Try not to joggle her. I don't want her to wake up."

At the foot of the stairs Pat handed his part of the burden over to Bruce and let the boy carry her to her room. When Ruth tried to follow them, he held her back.

"Stay with her, Bruce," he called softly. "If she starts to wake, let me know instantly. No, Ruth, you can't do a thing. Come back here."

He took her with him, to the telephone on its little table behind the stairs. When he was about halfway through dialing Ruth woke up. She snatched at his hand.

"Whom are you calling?"

"Whom do you think?"

"Put that telephone down! Pat, you've got to tell me—"

They were both speaking in sharp whispers, their faces only inches apart.

"I'm calling a doctor," Pat said. He was pale; the session had shaken him severely. "If I had realized that matters were this serious—"

"But I told you—"

"It's different when you actually see it." Pat was silent for a moment, staring with creased brows at the telephone. "And I hoped my hunch was wrong. Damn it all—it need not have been this, not from your description. It is comparatively rare. . . ."

"What? What is rare?" With an effort that left her shaking Ruth kept her voice from rising. "What doctor are you planning to call, Pat?"

"A friend of mine. He's a fine guy, one of the best."

"It's after five. He won't be in his office."

"I'm calling him at home."

"But he won't see her till morning anyhow. Can't we—"

"He'll see her tonight—now. Face it, Ruth. I know you love the girl—"

"Yes," Ruth said blankly. "Yes. I do."

"Then you've got to keep your wits about you. This isn't incurable, they've had excellent results with other cases."

"What cases? For God's sake, Pat—"

"He'll want her in the hospital at once, I'm sure," Pat said. "You could go up and pack a bag. . . ."

"Hospital," Ruth pressed her hands to her cheeks. "What hospital? St. Elizabeth's. That's what you mean, isn't it? An insane asylum!"

He caught her by the shoulders and shook her.

"Stop that! St. Elizabeth's is not an insane asylum; it is a hospital for the mentally ill. I thought you were an educated modern woman! Next thing you'll be doing is muttering prayers and making signs against the evil eye! Anyhow, I don't mean St. Elizabeth's. I do mean, and let's get it straight, the psychiatric ward of whatever hospital Jim practices at. Sibley, probably. Ruth, darling. . . ." His voice softened. "After this is over we'll come back and get good and drunk—absolutely stoned. Right now you must be calm or we'll all start screaming. And what good do you think that will do Sara?"

"All right. All right. What is wrong with her?"

He studied her face for a moment; then, as if satisfied, he nodded and let her go.

"Ruth, I'm only an amateur. But the symptoms are so obvious. . . . What you described last night might have been somnambulism—sleepwalking, as a result of some severe nervous strain. But tonight. . . . She really didn't know me, Ruth; she was not putting me on. But the most betraying sign was a single word. She referred to herself as 'her.' 'You call her Sara,' she said."

"Amnesia?"

"Well, it's related, if I understand the problem correctly. But this is more than simple amnesia. We talked to someone tonight who thinks she is not Sara. Ruth, did you ever read a book or see a movie called *The Three Faces of Eve?* Or maybe Shirley Jackson's novel, *The Bird's Nest?*"

"Oh, no," Ruth whispered.

"I'm afraid it's oh, yes. I may be wrong. But it looks to me like multiple personality. What they used to call schizophrenia."

Standing in the hall, with electric lights blazing and telephone near her hand, Ruth knew that she was only half a step away from the cave, and that the gadgetry of the modern world was a thin skin covering emotions that had not altered in centuries. The terms were scientific; the thing they described struck her with the same chill that had struck her primitive ancestors when another word was mentioned.

"Good girl," Pat said, mistaking her frozen horror for acceptance. "I'll call Jim now."

"Oh, no," said another voice. "No, you won't."

They looked up to see Bruce's saturnine beard waving at them. He descended the last few steps.

"You stupid fool," Pat exclaimed. "Get back up there. If she wakes. . . ."

"She won't be any worse off, with what you're planning. Cool it, Pat; she's asleep; she won't wake up for a while. And when she does, it will be here, in her own bed—not in some goddamn ward with a lot of nuts and a bunch of headshrinkers probing into her subconscious."

Pat's face turned dark red. He rolled his eyes heavenward and started counting aloud. After "four" his color began to subside.

"Eight, nine, ten. All right, Bruce, I am not going to knock your front teeth out, as was my first impulse. I will listen to you first, before I knock them out. But make it fast. I'm not feeling awfully calm right now."

"Neither am I." Bruce faced him. Feet apart, hands clenched, he looked like a boxer braced for a blow—except for his face, which was pinched and haggard. He stood in silent thought for several seconds; it was clear that he was choosing his words with care.

"Are you sure of your diagnosis?" he asked.

"Of course not. How arrogant do you think I am?"

"I don't mean the diagnosis of multiple personality. On the face of it, it's a reasonable hypothesis. I'm questioning your general assumption, Dr. MacDougal, not your specific diagnosis. How do you know that this is mental illness?"

Pat was too puzzled to be angry. His brows drew together in an introspective frown.

"How could it be physical? It's not delirium, there's no fever, no—"

"I don't mean that."

"What the hell do you mean?"

Bruce hesitated. Ruth noticed that the scant area of skin that showed on his cheeks was darker than usual. The boy was blushing.

"What I'm suggesting may seem unorthodox," he said at last. "But if you'll try to look at this with an open mind you'll see that there is another possibility, which fits the observed facts even better than your theory of multiple personality."

"Better? What?"

Bruce looked as if he were about to choke. And then, all at once, Ruth knew what he was going to say before he said it.

"Possession."

Chapter Five

"Possession?" Pat repeated. His voice was calmly, mildly curious. "Possession. . . . You do mean what I think you mean—evil spirits? That sort of thing?"

"Yes." Bruce's face was bright red from the hair on his chin to the hair on his forehead. But his eyes did not waver.

"All right. Go on."

"You mean you believe—"

"I think," Pat said, with precision, "that you are insane or joking. I'll give you the benefit of the doubt and assume it is the former. You are, of course, a crypto-Christian—"

"I haven't been to mass for five years," Bruce said in outraged tones, as if he had been accused of fraud or burglary.

"Excuse *me*. I meant that your youthful training, though consciously denied, still affects you. Damn it, boy, you're poaching on my preserves! I know all about the superstition of possession; it's an ancient, widespread delusion among primitive peoples."

"There is still a ritual for exorcism in the church," Bruce said.

"A ritual dating from one of the most superstitious eras

of human history. How many pathetic women were burned, tortured, maimed, because their credulous acquaintances believed they were possessed by the Devil? We know now that these symptoms—if they ever existed, except in the imaginations of vicious neighbors of the accused—were those of mental disorders, schizophrenia among them. Superstition is my field, Bruce; do you suppose I've neglected the richest source of all—the history of the Christian church?"

"I won't argue religion with you," Bruce said. His color was still high, but argument was his meat and drink. "I'll even admit, for the sake of the discussion, that the Christian faith is based on centuries of superstition. My contention is that your modern science of psychiatry is just as irrational— just as much a matter of superstitious faith."

The tension in the dimly lit hall was almost audible, like a high keening. When a log dropped in the fireplace in the next room, all of them started. Pat turned back to his opponent with narrowed eyes.

"This is no time to quibble."

"There won't be another time." Bruce's embarrassed flush had gone; his skin was as pale as ivory against the sharp black lines of his beard. "If you do what you plan to do, she'll lose—"

"Her immortal soul?"

"You could call it that. . . ."

"Show me a soul, Bruce."

The color—excitement, not embarrassment now—blazed up in Bruce's cheeks.

"Show me a subconscious mind!"

"That's not the same thing!"

"God, yes, it's the same thing! Just once try to break through your thick crust of adult dullness and see what I'm trying to get at! I'm not insisting on the possession idea. All I'm saying is that it is as reasonable a theory now, for us, as your theory of multiple personality. We're hypnotized, in our age, by the mumbo jumbo of psychiatry just as the men of the Middle Ages were hypnotized by witchcraft. We've less material proof of our faith than they had of theirs! That's what it comes down to in the end, a matter of faith. You ask me to take the word of Freud and Jung. I don't see why their opinions should carry more weight than those of Thomas Aquinas and St. Paul—and Martin Luther, if it comes to that!"

"You reason like a Jesuit," Pat said coldly. "But doesn't it seem in bad taste to you to debate about Sara's sanity?"

"For Christ's sake!" Bruce brought his clenched fists down on the balustrade with a force that drove the blood from them. "I care more about Sara's sanity than I do about some abstract problem in debate! Why doesn't she deserve the same amount of intellectual effort I give to a problem in logic?"

"This isn't a problem in logic! This is—"

"Wait a minute," Ruth said. She had not spoken in so long that her voice sounded cracked and rusty. Both men turned to stare at her. "You're wrong, Pat. So am I. Isn't this what they accuse us of, the young people—of refusing to keep an open mind? You haven't even asked him why he thinks. . . . I can't say it. I don't even understand what it means."

Hands still clenched on the stair rail, Bruce studied her in openmouthed amazement. Then understanding dawned.

"So that's it," he said slowly. "You felt it too."

"Yes," Ruth said. "If you mean—"

"The Other-ness. The occupation of Sara's body by a force—personality, soul, spirit—that is not Sara. That's possession, Mrs. Bennett. That's what I mean."

"Dear God," Pat muttered. "Ruth—"

"No." She moved back, rejecting his outstretched hand and everything it implied. "Are all three of us mad, Pat? Bruce, and I, and Sara?"

"Not mad, just unbearably distressed and distracted. Damn you, Bruce—"

"At least listen to me!" Bruce glanced up the stairs. There was no sound from Sara's room. "Just give me a chance! I'm not insisting that this is it, Pat. I'm only asking you to consider it as you would any other hypothesis."

"Give me your evidence, then." Pat was livid with anger, but he had his face and voice under control.

"First point—the reaction, not only of myself, but of Mrs. Bennett. Hunches are almost always rationally based; they are value judgments made by the subconscious mind— see, I'm giving you your damned subconscious mind—on the basis of evidence the conscious mind doesn't see. Mrs. Bennett—"

"Ruth."

"Ruth and I are more emotionally involved with Sara than you are. We are more sensitive to her, more able to notice discrepancies. And both of us felt the same thing, and at the same time. Right, Ruth?"

"At the séance. You saw it too."

"Not 'saw,' 'felt.'" Bruce's eyes went dark with memory. "I felt it clear on the other side of the table. And I'll frankly admit it made me feel sick."

"The medium knew too," Ruth exclaimed. "She was terrified."

"Your interpretation of the medium's emotions is not evidence," Pat said flatly.

"How about my emotions?"

"Ah, Ruth—now—"

"And the fact that Bruce and I felt the same?"

"You find now that you felt the same. You're infecting one another. Don't you see—I'm not denying the—the Other-ness, if you choose to call it that. Good God, it's the basis of my own theory."

Bruce rubbed his hands together nervously.

"And Sara's reference to herself, in this last seizure, in the third person?"

"The alternate personalities in this type of psychosis regard one another as different entities," Pat said relentlessly. "Reference to the others as 'she,' or by various nicknames, is common."

Ruth felt herself weakening. He seemed to have an answer for everything. And the proposition he supported had, in a sense, greater hope for Sara's eventual cure than any other; she could not have said why she fought it so strongly, or why she had instinctively supported Bruce's incredible idea. Now her eyes turned to him with a silent plea, and the boy straightened.

"It just so happens that I've read about several of these cases of multiple personality," he said disarmingly.

"I might have known." Under other circumstances the expression on Pat's mouth might have turned into a smile.

"In the first place," Bruce said, "these types aren't homicidal, or dangerous."

"Have you happened to notice Ruth's face?"

Bruce's glance flickered over to Ruth; his knowledge was so intuitively complete that it surprised her to recall that he knew nothing of the previous night's events.

"Sara did that?"

"It was an accident."

"Tell me."

Ruth told the grim little story again. Bruce did not seem disturbed by its ending; what really interested him were the words that Sara had uttered, and he made Ruth repeat them several times. Then he nodded.

"I agree. The attack on you was impersonal. She didn't even know who you were, any more than she knew Pat tonight."

"That will be poor comfort," Pat said, "if she pushes Ruth down the stairs next time, and breaks her neck."

"And it will be poor comfort to me," Bruce said softly, "if your psychiatrist friend sends Sara off the deep end into real psychosis. No, wait a minute, Pat. Remember the Beauchamp case, where four separate and distinct personalities were involved, in one woman? One of these, the "Sally" personality, was almost certainly *produced* by the hypnotic suggestion of the doctor who was handling the case. In another case there were *seven* different personalities which emerged—how, I wonder, and with what help from the inexpert probing of the doctor? Oh, sure, some of these cases were cured—if you can call a random fusion of disparate personalities a cure. My God, Pat, don't your doctor friends scare you just a little bit? They're so damned smug, so sure of themselves—just dig around in the patient's childhood till the probe hits the right little trauma—then, spoing! the pieces all snap back together again!"

"Bruce, I'm not claiming this is simple. Or easy." Pat rubbed his hand across his jaw as if trying to relax tight muscles. His eyes were hooded and sad. "I don't like the situation any better than you do."

"Then listen to me!" Bruce flung his hands wide in a gesture that would have looked theatrical if it had not been so passionately sincere. "Just listen and try to think! Pat, I tell you I know these cases, and this is not like the others! The things Sara has said, and the way she has behaved, do not fit the classic patterns of multiple personality. Nor can I blandly ignore, as you do whenever you strike evidence that doesn't suit your theory, the reactions of other people. Look, I'll make you a proposition. Give me forty-eight hours. Two days. Nothing serious can happen in two days, even if you're right."

"Two days for what?"

"For me to convince you that I'm right." Bruce's eyes

blazed. "I have a feeling that we've only seen the beginning of this, Pat. If the situation hasn't changed within two days, I'll give in."

"This is the craziest proposition—!"

"But you have no choice," Ruth said calmly. "Because, when you come right down to it, I'm the one who has to decide. Aren't I?"

Pat's eyes met hers.

"I could telephone her mother," he said.

"You do, and you'll never enter this house again."

"Damn it, Ruth—"

"I mean it."

Bruce remained silent, with the tact of an expert strategist. He did not so much as bat an eye when Pat, breathing heavily through his nose, said, "All right, I'll give in. Not because I like it. Because I have no choice. But I agree only on one condition. I'm moving in. And I'm staying till this is settled. I'll cancel my classes."

"Good idea," Bruce said coolly. "That makes two of us."

And Ruth said, as calmly as if she were welcoming invited guests, "I'm sorry we have only one extra room. But it has twin beds. I'll call work tomorrow and tell them I've got the flu."

II

They sat around the kitchen table eating pizza. Three of them were eating; Ruth regarded the red-and-yellow circle in front of her with faint repulsion.

"I can't believe you've never eaten pizza," Bruce said. "Where've you been all these years?"

Ruth poked the rubbery red circle with a fork.

"Are you sure it's edible?" she asked dubiously.

The burst of laughter was a little too loud. In the bright, modern warmth of the kitchen they were all able to pretend, but not very successfully, or for very long.

"You didn't want to go out," Pat said. "And nobody feels much like cooking."

The silence fell like fog, wet and clammy.

"Pat, you promised—" Bruce began.

"That I'd give you two days. I'll do more; I'll actively cooperate with anything you suggest doing. I just want to know how Sara feels about this."

Two of them, at least, had been trying not to look at Sara, who sat next to Bruce, her eyes still a bit foggy with sleep, her hand openly holding his. But with the other hand she was feeding herself pizza with the healthy appetite of a young woman.

"As I said before," Bruce remarked, with strained patience, "she has the best right of anyone to know what we're doing."

The argument at the foot of the stairs had not ended with Pat's capitulation. He had protested vigorously when Bruce proposed waking Sara, and it had taken further threats from Ruth to overrule him.

"I'll heat some coffee," Ruth said, abandoning her pizza.

She had not felt like cooking dinner; but there was a sort of comfort now in handling the smooth aluminum of the coffeepot, fiddling with the handles on the stove. The familiar charm of the kitchen seemed like a painting on gauze, that wavered oddly in the breeze of unreason, and might at any moment blow away completely, displaying something the senses could not endure.

Ruth poured the coffee, and no one commented on how badly her hands were shaking.

"Let's take it into the living room," she said.

"No." Bruce caught at Sara's sleeve as she started to rise. "I don't—well, let's say I don't like that room."

"Ah." Pat wriggled around so that he was sitting sideways in his chair. He lifted one foot, raising the ankle on the other knee, and slumped, comfortably. "It is your contention, then, that the living room is a focus of the—er—trouble?"

Bruce gave him a sharp glance; but the older man's manner was irreproachable.

"I'm cooperating," he explained, answering Bruce's look.

"Hmmm. Thanks. I don't know what my contention is. That's half the trouble. But the room is abnormally cold. And that was where this—thing—"

"Are you afraid of your own terms? Possession. By what, if I may ask?"

Bruce stiffened.

"Sara ought to have some ideas about that," he said.

"Well, Sara?" Pat said. "I suspect that you were not—"

"No leading the witness," said Bruce; the words were meant to be mildly humorous, but the tone definitely was not. After a moment, Pat nodded.

"Sorry. Sara?"

"You say something happened at the séance?" Sara looked at Bruce. "I don't remember that. Nor the time I walked in my sleep, the night Ruth fell and hurt herself."

Bruce's eyes caught Ruth's, with a command as clear as words. He had not, then, told the girl everything. Ruth nodded slightly. Out of the corner of her eye she saw that Pat was looking smug, and wondered why.

Sara went on, "But tonight was different."

"You were aware of what was going on?" Pat asked. Ruth wondered if other people could read his face as easily as she could. He was now as crestfallen as he had formerly been smug.

"I sure was. Want me to describe it? I'm not sure I can. . . ."

"If it upsets you, darling," Ruth began.

"Tell it anyhow," said Bruce.

"All right." She gave him a look of such blind trust that Ruth's heart contracted painfully. "You know the feeling, when you're waiting for something that you know will be very painful or unhappy? Like an operation; or somebody is going to die. Something you can't get out of, but that you know you are going to hate. You can't breathe. You keep gasping, but the air won't go down into your lungs. You can hear your own heart thudding, so hard it seems to be banging into your ribs. Your hands perspire. You want to run away, but you can't, it won't do any good, the thing you're afraid of will happen anyhow."

The worst part of the description, for Ruth, was that Sara was not trying to be terrifying, but simply to give facts.

"The feeling was like that," Sara said. "But this time—there was no reason for it. Do you understand? I wasn't afraid of any *thing*. I was just afraid. And that's the worst fear of all, the fear of nothing."

Now Bruce's face was troubled, Pat's confident. Apparently the sensation the girl was describing had meaning to them, though it had none for Ruth.

"Then it came," Sara went on. "It—filled me up. Like water pouring into a pitcher. Pat, I could hear you when you were talking to me—but I couldn't answer. I heard somebody, something else, talking. And I couldn't speak or move a muscle."

"That's all?" Bruce said, after a rather painful moment.

"Yes, it went away, and I fainted, I guess. It's so hard to describe. . . . Did you ever wear clothes that were too tight? Shoes that pinched? That was how—it—felt. Something didn't quite—fit.''

Somehow that was the worst description yet. Ruth's mouth went dry; Pat's face was disturbed.

"All right," he said. "Relax, Sara. You were aware of an invasion—right?—but cannot identify the invader. So far— let's be blunt—this proves nothing, one way or the other."

"I haven't begun to fight," Bruce said grimly. "Ruth, your turn."

"I told you my impressions of the séance," Ruth began.

"I don't mean that. I want to know whether you've noticed anything else out of the ordinary."

"Where? When?"

"Any time, but probably recently. Here. In this house."

"The house," Ruth exclaimed. "You think—"

"Let's not jump the gun. Anything, any impression at all."

For a few seconds Ruth could not think. Her glance wandered around the kitchen—polished brass winking, smooth scrubbed counter tops, mellow brown maple. . . . Then, from nowhere, it came back.

"I had a dream," she said slowly. "Probably just—"

"Describe it."

She did; and it lost considerably in the telling, as dreams usually do.

"The shadow loomed up," she ended, lamely. "And I thought I was awake, but I wasn't. It was an awful feeling, trying to get up, and not being able to move."

"What did awaken you?" Bruce asked. He had begun to lose interest. It was obvious he had no great hopes for the dream.

"I don't remember. . . ." Ruth wrinkled her brows. Then memory dawned, with such impact that she knocked her coffee cup over. Sara dived for it, but Ruth caught at her arm.

"Wait, wait. The voice. Sara, you heard it too; it must mean something. That was what woke me—the same voice you heard. Only there isn't any animal named Sammie!"

It took Bruce almost five minutes to extract a coherent story.

"The time," he said, almost as excited as she was. "What time was it when you woke up?"

"Almost two A.M. And Sara heard it just before dawn. That in itself makes our first assumption ridiculous; who would be chasing a lost pet around at that hour?"

"And through a yard which is completely enclosed," Bruce agreed. "Ruth, we may have something here."

In her triumph Ruth turned toward Pat; and his expression punctured her like a pricked balloon. He looked so sorry for her.

"Now," Bruce said, "I'm going to give Pat a chance for a big ha-ha at my expense. Ruth, did you ever hear any stories about the house being haunted?"

"No. . . ."

"But then you don't know much about the place, do you?"

"I guess nobody does, nobody in the family, at any rate. Cousin Hattie was here so long. . . ."

"Still, it seems to me that we ought to start with the house," Bruce argued. "Nothing like this ever happened to Sara until she came here, and. . . ."

He broke off, his mouth hanging open; and Ruth said hopefully, "And what?"

"Nothing, I guess. I thought for a minute I had an idea, but it got away."

"Maybe you'll catch it in the morning," Ruth said. "It's been a hard day. We all could do with a good night's sleep."

But she knew that none of them would sleep well that night.

III

"How about the Civil War?" Bruce asked.

They were sitting around the kitchen table the following afternoon. Rain slid tearily down the windowpanes, blurring the garden into a gray dismal landscape of bare trees and withered vines.

Inside, the coffeepot was perking and the kitchen was warm and bright as usual; the tiles over the stove glowed in the light of the hanging copper lamp. Ruth had worn pink that day, a bright glowing rose, and Sara's crimson sweater and royal Stewart plaid skirt made another patch of brightness. They had turned to vivid colors as a protest—and not only against the dreary weather.

Bruce leaned across the table, one hand wrapped around his coffee cup, the other shuffling through a pile of papers. He wore a checked waistcoat, which Ruth privately considered the height of affectation; yet somehow it suited the period air of his facial adornment and finely cut features.

The front door slammed and heavy footsteps announced the arrival of the missing member of the impromptu committee. Pat's red head gleamed with rain, challenging the copper-bottomed pans on the wall.

He stood across the room from the others, with one hand braced against the wall, and looked down at them.

"How did it go?"

"We just got here ourselves," Bruce said. "We were starting to compare notes."

"And what a day," Sara said gloomily. "Remember our conversation about Georgetown traditions, Pat? If I was rude to you, I've been punished. I spent the whole morning and most of the afternoon plowing through books on Georgetown history."

"Serves you right." Pat's voice was casual and his smile bland, but Ruth fancied that his eyes lingered on Sara's face with an almost clinical curiosity.

"Some of it was sort of interesting, at that," Sara admitted. "Ruth, did you ever run across the story of Baron Bodisco, who, at the age of sixty-three, fell in love with a sixteen-year-old girl?"

"No. Who was Baron Bodisco?"

"Russian ambassador, about 1850. He lived a couple of blocks from here, on O Street." Sara's eyes twinkled with amusement. "He was a sprightly old gent, obviously. The girl came to a Christmas party he gave for his nephews, and he married her six months later."

"Nasty old man," Bruce muttered.

"No," Sara said, surprisingly. "It was sort of pathetic. He said she might find someone younger and better looking, but no one who would love her more. And he absolutely showered her with jewels and money and gorgeous clothes. There was a description of one of her dresses—white watered silk embroidered with pale pink rosebuds and green leaves. With it she wore emeralds and diamonds."

"I'd be inclined to suspect the young lady's motives, myself," Ruth said, amused at Sara's unexpected streak of romanticism. Did the miniskirted young really yearn, deep down inside, for ruffles and pink rosebuds?

"There was a picture of her in one of the books," Sara said. "She was pretty, all right; but her mouth had a sort of self-satisfied smirk. . . ."

"Did you find time," Bruce inquired with commendable restraint, "to spend maybe five minutes on the Civil War?"

"Why the Civil War?" Pat dumped his coat on a chair, found a cup, and poured himself some coffee.

"The General," Bruce said.

"What?" Pat looked blank. "Oh. Sara said that, didn't she?"

"So Ruth believes. She didn't say it the first time. The words she spoke at the séance were significant, though. I forgot to mention them last night; but they are part of my evidence."

"Ghosts?" Pat asked amiably, sitting down at the table and stretching out a long arm for the sugar bowl.

"Pat," Ruth said warningly.

"Never mind, let him have his fun." Bruce shrugged. "Yes, ghosts. The phenomenon of possession is defined—"

"By those who believe in it—"

"By those who believe in it," Bruce accepted the amendment without a visible change of expression, "as being invasion by the spirit of someone who has died. Oh, sometimes you hear talk of elementals, demons and the like, but I think we can dismiss that for now. The theory is borne out by Sara's own words, which have been reiterated several times. 'Not dead.' That's what the Invader says. It sounds to me like an assertion, almost a defiance."

He lit a cigarette and waited for a comment. None came. Pat's eyes were hooded by drooping lids.

"Additional confirmation—the behavior of the medium at the séance. She said she felt an intrusion—one which frightened her so much that she was reluctant to continue. Now, since she maintains that her contacts come from the spirit world—"

"You suggest," Pat interrupted, without looking up from his contemplation of his coffee cup, "that the Invader tried Madame Nada first, found her unsatisfactory, for one reason or another, and then took over Sara."

"Not exactly. But I think the Madame did sense the Invader. Which doesn't mean that she isn't faking ninety-nine percent of the time."

"That was what scared her," Ruth said. "When she did encounter something genuine, she was petrified."

"And yet she does have a certain talent," Bruce insisted. "I'm thinking of the sensation of cold in that particular part of the living room. She felt that acutely. Ruth and Sara are aware of it—correct me if I'm not putting this accurately—but it doesn't affect them so much."

"That's right," Ruth agreed. "The others didn't seem to notice it at all. Mrs. MacDougal said she didn't."

"I don't either," Bruce said. "Not a quiver. Come on, now, Pat, be honest—you sense it quite strongly, don't you? It almost doubled you up the other night; I thought for a minute you were having a heart attack."

"I felt a chill," Pat said; and, catching Ruth's expressive gaze, he widened his eyes innocently. "I'm giving you as precise and unemotional a description as I can."

"Okay, I won't push," Bruce said wearily. "I won't even mention Ruth's dream, or the voice that calls in the night. We haven't proved yet that they are relevant. I think we have enough, without them, to formulate a theory. As Pat says—ghosts. So I spent the day at the Georgetown branch of the library reading ghost stories."

"While I was plodding through big fat history books!" Sara exclaimed. "You have your nerve."

"I used to enjoy them," Bruce said briefly. "Point is, there is usually a key motif for hauntings. Violence—that's the most common cause. A suicide seeking rest, a victim seeking revenge, a murderer doomed by his sin to linger at the scene of the crime."

"Those aren't the only reasons." Sara began foraging in the cupboards. She put a plate of cookies and another of crackers and cheese on the table, and sat down. Leaning forward, with her chin propped on her hands and her hair swinging in black satin waves across her cheek, she looked enchanting. Only Ruth saw, with an inner pang, the faintest smudge of dark shadow under her eyes.

"Buried treasure," Sara said. "That's a reason. Remember *Tom Sawyer?* Or protection—warning the living of danger to come."

"They may be motives for hauntings, but not for physical possession," Bruce said direly. He swallowed a cookie—it was a small one—whole, and looked a bit more cheerful. "There's another point I wanted to make. Last night I said that nothing had happened to Sara till she came to the house. I was too beat to see the converse—nothing seems to have happened in the house until Sara arrived. That suggests that something lingers, in the house, which finds Sara a suitable host."

He reached for another handful of cookies; and Pat took advantage of his enforced silence to say thoughtfully, "That's ingenious. Completely without solid foundations, of course. . . ."

For a few minutes there was silence except for the sound of Bruce munching. Then Ruth murmured, "It's getting dark. So early these days. . . ."

"We're going out," Pat said firmly. "Out among the bright lights. I need a couple of drinks before I listen to any more of Bruce's theories."

IV

It had stopped raining, but the wind howled mournfully through the trees and shook sprays of leftover raindrops down on their heads. After the sedate silence and darkness of the side street, the garish lights and traffic of Wisconsin seemed like another world. The neon signs and the shifting colors of the stoplights reflected in the shiny wet blackness of the pavement made weird psychedelic patterns of crimson and green and yellow.

The picturesque brick sidewalks of Georgetown were slippery and uneven. Ruth clung to her escort's arm, and found its solidity reassuring in more ways than one. In the light and the cold, rushing air her spirits rose; ahead of her, Bruce looked down at Sara and spoke, and the girl's light laughter floated back to her.

As they passed the entrance to one of the new nightclubs they encountered a group of the new youth who frequented them. Long flowing locks and faded jeans adorned boys and girls alike, and the only distinguishing characteristic of the male was the shaggy, drooping mustache. One of the girls was barefoot. Ruth shivered in sympathy, and Pat began to chuckle softly.

"Quite a contrast," he said.

"Georgetown past and present," Ruth agreed.

"Hoopskirts and hippies? True, but that wasn't what I meant. How the hell can conventional spooks exist in a world which produces that?"

The restaurant—soft lights, candles flickering, the murmur of relaxed conversation—made spooks, conventional or otherwise, seem even less likely. Pat got his drink or two; when the second round arrived he lifted his glass and made Bruce a small ironic bow.

"Go on with the lecture. I'm sorry to have interrupted you, but you must agree that these surroundings are more cheerful."

"Too cheerful," Bruce said dryly. "They cast a glare of absolute unreality over the whole business. Okay, okay. So I gave you the reasoning—much abbreviated—which led me to start investigating the history of the house and the family. The conventional theme of violence, and the mention of 'the General' made me think of wartime; that's why I keep harping on the Civil War. It was a time when sympathies in Maryland were bitterly divided, and when family tragedies often arose out of the tragedy of war. But I don't insist on that; I asked the girls to find out anything they could about family history."

"Well, I'm sorry to disappoint you," Ruth said. "But I found very little. Surprisingly little, in view of how much has been written about Georgetown. Wait a minute. Where did I put those notes?"

She disappeared under the table and the others heard her scrabbling and muttering as she went with both hands into the big black purse, which had to sit on the floor because it was too large to stay on her lap. When she emerged, flushed and sheepish, she met Pat's amused eye and blushed more deeply.

"I have to carry a big purse," she explained defensively. "I have all these papers. . . ."

"You can carry a suitcase if you want to," Pat said tenderly. Bruce cleared his throat and looked disapproving.

"Anyhow." Ruth leafed through the spiral notebook she had unearthed. "Here it is. The house was built about 1810 by Jedediah Campbell (good heavens, what a name!). He was a tobacco dealer."

"Everybody was," Sara remarked.

"Since tobacco warehousing and shipping were the main industries of Georgetown, that isn't surprising," Bruce said impatiently. "Go on, Ruth."

"We'd better order," Pat said, indicating a hovering waiter.

Bruce growled under his breath and ordered chicken without bothering to look at the menu. Pat deliberated over the wine list. Bruce politely intimated that perhaps wine struck the wrong note for the occasion, and Pat ordered it anyhow. Then, just in time to prevent an explosion from Bruce, they got back to business.

"All this is just genealogy," Ruth admitted. "Jedediah's oldest son Ebeneezer inherited the house, and so on, down to eternity. There is absolutely nothing interesting about any of them."

"Then I took up the tale from 1850 on," Sara said, through a mouthful of paté. "Remember the story about the Civil War Campbell that Madame Nada used at the séance? It's the only well-known story connected with the house. But he was an old man when the war broke out and nobody bothered him. Even though by then Georgetown was part of the District of Columbia, a lot of Georgetowners had Southern sympathies."

"It doesn't seem to help," Bruce admitted. "And later?"

"Goodness, I couldn't even find any names of people, not in the books. They must have been nobodies."

"I can give you the names, from family records," Ruth said. "After all, Cousin Hattie was born in the 1880's. Her father's family was large and prolific; when the family fortunes declined, the children scattered. Their children are all over the place now—California, Canada, New England. And my bunch, in the Midwest. And none of them, I assure you, has even been inclined toward violence."

"I'm not interested in the diasporic Campbells." Bruce put a hand over his glass to prevent Pat's refilling it. "Had Cousin Hattie any dark secrets?"

Ruth sputtered into her wine.

"Sorry! But that really is ludicrous. She was the most proper old lady who ever lived; she wore long black dresses from the day her father died till she passed on in 1965. And she died of old age, peacefully, in her bed."

"What a letdown," Pat said with a grin. "I hoped she would turn out to be a secret Satanist, indulging in wild sexual orgies in her parlor, and kissing—"

"Never mind," Ruth said.

"Where did you read about that charming little rite?"

Bruce asked. He too was smiling; his mood had lightened considerably.

"I didn't; I don't read that sort of thing!" They all laughed at her indignation, and she added, smiling, "It was obvious from Pat's expression what he was going to say."

Pat sobered.

"Cousin Hattie is a case in point, though. I'm not seriously suggesting that she was a devil-worshiper; but she could have been, with nobody one whit the wiser. Even if you're right about the roots of this trouble lying in the past, you haven't the slightest hope of finding out the truth."

"I knew it wouldn't be easy." Eyes on his plate, Bruce was crumbling a roll into fragments.

"Easy! It's impossible by its very nature. Look here, don't you see that your theory of a violent act can be proved only if the violence was public knowledge at the time? *Which it wasn't.* If there had been any tragedy, such as murder or suicide, connected with that house, we would have known about it. It would be part of the family history and probably one of the classic legends of Georgetown. The fact that we haven't come across any such legends means that one of two alternatives must be true: Either there was no tragedy, or it was so well concealed that there is no record of it—no trial, no funeral, not even any gossip. And in the latter case—how do you propose to find out about it?"

There was a short but poignant silence.

"Oogh," Sara said, groaning. "That's a nasty one, Pat."

"Nasty, but not unexpected." Bruce sounded confident; but he drained his wineglass with more speed than good manners permitted.

"You mean you knew there wouldn't be anything in the books?" Sara demanded. "And you made me read all those dusty—"

"They had to be checked!" Bruce flung his hands out.

"Can't any of you understand? We're all crazy—all but Pat—and our hypothesis is wildly insane; if we are to get anywhere with it, we must handle our research as sanely as possible."

There was no satisfaction in Pat's expression at this half-submission. Instead his face softened sympathetically.

"I see your point and I agree, absolutely. I'm just a tired old pessimist. . . . What do you plan to do next?"

"The obvious thing. Public records failed, as we expected them to. Now we try the unpublished material."

Pat shook his head.

"Damn it, Bruce, I don't like to be the perpetual wet blanket, but I've had personal experience with the family records of old Georgetown families. I did a paper once, in my distant undergraduate days, on the attitudes of Georgetowners toward the Revolution and separation from England. I went calling, with my big toothy grin, on several little old ladies, looking for letters and family papers. Talk about violence! One of the old darlings chased me out of the house with a rolled-up newspaper."

"Oh, Pat, how lovely," Sara chortled. "What did you do to annoy her?"

"I intimated that maybe her revered ancestor had not been, after all, a Patriot. You know these screwy organizations like the Colonial Dames and the Daughters of the American Revolution insist that you have an ancestor who fought in the Revolution. Turns out, oddly enough, that practically everybody in the Revolutionary Army was a lieutenant or better. . . . You can imagine the furor that would arise if some old biddy's great-great-great were found to have fought in the wrong army! I think they would cheerfully commit murder to keep it a secret."

"How ridiculous," Sara said contemptuously.

"You didn't tell me that you'd done research on Georgetown," Bruce said.

"Hardly amounted to that."

"I'd like to see that paper sometime."

"I don't even know where it is."

"Could you look for it?"

"Oh, for— If it would make you any happier."

"Oh, it would," Bruce murmured. "It sure would.
. . . No thanks, no coffee for me. Nor brandy. Haven't you had enough, Pat?"

The sudden animosity in the last question brought into the open the hostility he had been concealing. Pat refused to take offense. Smiling lazily, he said, "Tact, tact, my boy."

"Sorry." Bruce flushed. "But damn it all, we've got to keep our wits about us."

"Oh, I agree." Pat raised hand sent the waiter running for the check. "You want to get back, I gather. So let's go."

As they walked back to the house, Bruce explained his plans.

"Tomorrow I'm going downtown. I'm not sure whether it's the Archives or the Library of Congress I want, but I know a guy who's majoring in American history, and I can ask him about sources. I might even try to call him tonight. What time is it?"

"Only about ten."

"I thought it was later. It feels later."

"It's a miserable night," Ruth said, shivering as a spray of icy water swept her face. "All sensible people are indoors, in front of a fire."

"I'll call Ted tonight, then. And maybe we can start on another project. One that ought to keep you girls busy all day tomorrow."

"What's that?" Sara asked in a muffled voice. The hair blowing around her face got in her mouth; she pawed at it.

"Seems to me Cousin Hattie ought to have left some papers. What about it, Ruth?"

"She left an incredible amount of junk, certainly. I've

never looked through it. There might be something in the attic, I guess."

They turned up the short walk toward the house. Ruth was in the lead, since she had the key; but as her foot touched the bottom step she stopped, so suddenly that Pat bumped into her. He began to expostulate. Then he saw what she had seen, and fell silent.

The balanced Georgian facade had a door in the center, with long windows on either side—those of the dining room, now dark, on the right, the living-room windows on the left. They had left the latter room brightly lit. The light, shining through the blue satin drapes, gave them a heavenly azure glow, like the robes of a lady saint. But the shining folds were moving.

Ruth's gloved hand clutched at Pat's sleeve.

"Look—"

"Don't say anything," Bruce ordered. Instinctively they spoke in low voices, as though something could hear them. With an equally atavistic impulse they all moved close together, in a huddled, shivering group.

"I'm not going in that door," Sara said.

"Me neither," Pat agreed. "You realize, don't you, that this could be anything from a burglar to an open window elsewhere in the room?"

"Then why don't you want to go in?" Bruce made his challenge in a fierce whisper.

"I'm afraid of burglars," Pat said equably. "Is there a back door?"

"Of course, the kitchen. Come on."

This time no one laughed when Ruth groped in her purse for the back-door key. It took her a long time to locate it. Her fingers were icy cold. The shivering, quivering movement of the curtains continued.

The house was so close to its neighbor that the passageway between them looked like a black tunnel.

"Why the hell didn't I bring a flashlight?" Pat shouldered Ruth out of the way. A tiny flame sprang up and promptly went out. The wind blowing down the passageway was too strong for his lighter. He swore and plunged into the blackness. The others followed, with Bruce bringing up the rear.

The passageway was not only dark, it was cold and windy and damp. Puddles squished under Ruth's feet and splashed her ankles. She was glad to get out of the tunnel. But the backyard was not much better. They huddled again on the paved stones of the patio, now dangerously slippery with rain. Behind them the gloom of the night-dark garden, shaded by pines and unlit even by moonlight, was filled with constant uneasy movement.

The kitchen windows were dark. Ruth silently cursed her inherited Scottish thrift. From now on she would leave every light in the blasted house on, day and night! Very dimly she could make out the white painted steps that led to a little wooden annex at the back, where she kept mops and garbage cans. Through this annex entry to the kitchen was gained.

"Give me the key," Pat muttered, and Ruth gladly allowed him to precede her up the stairs. After a few seconds of muttering and scratching he said grumpily, "I can't see a damn thing. Bruce, come up and hold the lighter, will you?"

Then, for the second time that night, they were gripped simultaneously by the unexpected. Ruth had been hearing the noise for some time. She told herself it was the wind in the trees, but she didn't believe it. But not until Bruce started up the stairs did the moaning sigh form audible words. They were the words she had heard before; but now, with no walls between her and the source (what source???) they were much more distinct. The great sighing voice came at her from all sides and from no sides; from inside her head, from every point of the compass, from the cloudy turmoil of the sky . . . and died away in a long, sobbing cry.

". . . come . . . hooooome. . . ."

Pat said something; it was rather a wordless snarl of anger than articulate profanity. There was a sharp snap, and the door, caught by the wind, crashed back against the wall. The three who stood below fled up the stairs and into the entryway. By that time Pat had the inner door open, and they plunged pell-mell into the warmth of the kitchen, and into a sudden glare of light as Pat found the switch by the door.

Bruce slammed the door shut, and they all stood blinking and gasping—all except Pat, who had not even paused. Huddled in his overcoat with his head retracted like a turtle's, he was plodding toward the room at the front of the house—the uninhabited room where something had shaken the drapes.

They stopped at the door of the dining room; no one cared to go any farther than that. Looking across the hallway and the foot of the stairs, they saw the living room, as calm and bright as any room could be. It was perhaps only Ruth's imagination that made her detect the faintest wisp of gray, no thicker than the smoke from a cigarette, lifting in a lazy coil. . . . The draperies hung in sculptured folds, unmoving.

"Nothing there," Bruce said. His hand touched the light switch in the dining room, and the chandelier blazed on. They stared at one another; and Pat put one big hand on Sara's shoulder where she stood clinging to the wall like a limp strand of ivy.

"Are you all right?"

"Of course she's all right," Bruce snapped.

"Let her talk for once!"

"Stop it, both of you," Ruth ordered. "We're all wound

up like clocks, and no wonder. Bruce, what about that brandy now?"

"Best idea I've heard all evening."

Ruth got the decanter from the side cabinet, and Bruce collected the glasses. Holding them by the stems, two in each hand, like big blown crystal flowers, he looked warily at Pat.

"We're going to have to go into that room sometime."

"Brandy," Ruth said hastily, and swallowed hers in one breath-snatching gulp.

Sara made a face as hers went down; brandy had never been one of her favorite drinks. But it restored some of the color to her cheeks, and Bruce promptly poured another inch of liquid all around.

"I needed that," he admitted. "The place is really turned on tonight. I wonder how much of this activity is in response to what we're doing?"

"Who knows?" Pat muttered. "Who knows anything?"

They stared at one another in bemused silence for a time. Pat's eyes were glazed, and Ruth was conscious of an insidious, what-the-hell warmth that was the product of alcohol on an overstrained nervous system.

"Look here," she said, a bit thickly, "we don't have to do this."

"Do what?" Bruce asked.

"Stand around shaking in our shoes. If the trouble is in the house—then get rid of the house."

"Ruth." Sara held out her hand; her eyes were shining suspiciously. "You can't do that. You love this place."

"My dear child, I'm not proposing a dramatic houseburning by midnight. For one thing, the neighbors might object. I can sell the place. It's worth a lot of money. You and I could go live in a nice apartment on Connecticut, or in Chevy Chase."

"One objection," Bruce said carefully. "You're ash—

ashum—damn it!—assuming that my hypothesis is the right one. If Sara is schizoid she'll be schizoid wherever she is."

"I don't believe in collective hallucinations," Ruth said. "Sara didn't make that sound we heard tonight."

"Not Sammie," Pat said suddenly. "The name was not Sammie."

It was the first sentence he had spoken since Ruth made her proposition, and its very irrelevance had an oddly calming effect. Sara dropped into a chair and rested her head on her folded arms. She looked sideways at Pat with round solemn eyes, like a pensive owl's; and Bruce's breath went out in a theatrical sigh.

"I hate to admit it," he said, "but I was too shook to notice details. What was the name, then?"

"Now who's being unscientific?" Pat said irritably. He rubbed his head, making his hair stand up like a crest, and scowled thoughtfully. "I don't know that it was a name. I do know that there was no 's' sound, that strong sibilant would have been unmistakable. Sara heard the words as 'Sammie' because that is a familiar combination of sounds. Ruth heard the same thing because Sara had prepared her to hear it. To tell the truth, it sounded to me more like 'mammy.'"

After a moment Ruth burst out laughing.

"I'm . . . sorry! Oh, dear! But, Pat—mammy? Shades of Al Jolson! Some poor old nursemaid, like the one in *Gone with the Wind?* And if you knew how funny you all look, standing around this table with your coats on, like visiting burglars. . . ."

They waited respectfully until she had composed herself and dried her eyes. Then Pat remarked, "I'm glad I can supply some comic relief. As for your idea of selling the house—it has some merit, but we don't have to decide anything yet."

"We?" Bruce repeated. He leaned on the table, arms

stiff, and looked at the older man. "How do you feel about your theory now, Pat?"

Pat shrugged.

"Unlike Ruth, I do believe in collective hallucinations. Wait a minute—I'm not saying that was what happened tonight. Though both you and I, Bruce, heard that voice described. . . . You said forty-eight hours. You've still got twenty-four to go."

Chapter Six

Lying flat on her back, staring up at the ceiling, Ruth heard the clock strike four. The clock stood on the landing, probably in the same position it had occupied since it was bought from Josiah Harper, Clockmaker, in 1836. Josiah had built well. The chimes echoed in silver clarity, precise as notes struck on a harpsichord.

As she had done a dozen times since they retired, Ruth raised herself cautiously on her elbow and looked over at Sara. It hadn't taken much persuasion to convince Sara to share her room that night. The room was lit by two rose-shaded lamps on the dressing table; Ruth wondered whether she would ever be able to sleep in a darkened room again.

Sara slept on her back, with her hair cascading over the pillow like spilled ink, and the small movement of her lips, her furled brows, showed that she was dreaming. As Ruth watched, a shade of that alien look spread like a film of water over her features, and faded.

Breathless, Ruth sank back onto her pillow, turning on her side so that she could watch the girl. So this was what it was like, the emotion she had seen in other women's faces. None of the other basic instincts had come down to man from the animals quite so uncontrolled and so primitive. Even the sexual urge had been twisted and condemned and veiled until it was barely recognizable as the simple, amoral need it once had been. Humanity had tried to turn the maternal instinct into a pretty lace-trimmed valentine too, but it had not succeeded; women who would turn sick at the sight of a dead bird could commit any kind of violence to preserve their young.

It was raining again. The soft rustle of raindrops against the window should have been soothing, but Ruth found it too suggestive of other sounds—dry fingers scratching on the glass, for instance, or small bony feet crawling along the sill. The house itself was quiet, except for one oddly soothing sound—that of Pat's resounding masculine snores from across the hall.

Ruth's mouth relaxed as she listened. She was no expert on snoring, but she was willing to bet that Pat's efforts ranked high on any scale. She was getting almost the full effect, since all the bedroom doors were wide open. There was nothing like a haunted house to dispel artificial notions of propriety.

No sound came from Sara's room, which Bruce was now occupying, but the comforting yellow light from his door filled the hall. Ruth had found a box of old family papers in a drawer in the escritoire and Bruce had declared his intention of sitting up with them.

Ruth could remember having seen other papers in the attic. Most of them were obviously junk, the pack-rat hoarding of a fussy old lady; but she had not wanted to discard them as trash until she had time to sort through them. That time, like other hours for matters not urgently desired or needed, had never materialized. Tomorrow—no, today—she would look for them. Though their collective courage, bolstered by brandy, had taken them into the chilly living room, Ruth had flatly refused to enter the dark, gusty attic at night, and no one seemed to blame her.

Tomorrow—today, now—there would be so much to do. Yet they were groping in the dark, clutching a few tattered scraps of isolated fact, with no sign of a pattern and no promise, even, that a pattern existed. Shivering in the warm bed, Ruth faced the dismal fact that no one had yet admitted—that if Bruce's incredible notion was correct, the chances for Sara's cure were even feebler than those promised by psychiatry. The thought brought her drooping lids open and focused her eyes on her niece, searching, and fearing to find. . . .

Sara slept peacefully now. She was young enough to look delectable when she slept, her skin flushed and damp, her lashes long and black on her smooth cheeks. Ruth lay stiff as a piece of wood. Bruce had the right idea; he wasn't even trying to sleep. Sleep was impossible, when the sense of urgency was so great. If there were only something she could do. . . .

The sound almost lifted her bodily out of bed. The muffled crash was followed, after a second, by a faint rustling—innocent enough sounds, both of them, except for the fact that there was no one to make them. They had come from downstairs.

Bruce, in stocking feet and shirt sleeves, materialized in the doorway. He stared at her, and Ruth shook her head mutely.

"I'm going down," he whispered.

"Not alone. Wait, Bruce—"

The sounds of imminent strangulation across the hall stopped; and a few seconds later Pat made his appearance. He was blinking and groggy; the hair stood up on his head like fire on a boulder. He too was fully dressed except for his shoes.

"Where'd it come from?" he mumbled.

"Downstairs."

"Ummm." Pat scratched his head. It was obvious that he was not one of those hearty people who leap, fully aware and ready for burglars, out of their warm beds. He blinked, rubbed his hands over his eyes, and came one stage nearer to consciousness. "Go down," he said vaguely.

By that time Sara was stirring, and when she found out what had roused the others she decided to join the expedition. Bruce had long since left; he had scant patience with the weaknesses of the elderly.

The lights were still on in the living room. Leading the way down the stairs, Ruth could see Bruce bending over some object on the floor near the built-in bookcases. He straightened as she reached the foot of the stairs and came toward her, carrying the object; it seemed to be a book, bound in red leather.

Ruth stopped on the threshold of the living room. It was cold, much colder than it had been upstairs; she was shivering, even in her wool robe. Halfway across the room, Bruce stopped short. She saw the color drain from his face, saw him recoil as if he had run into some solid but invisible barrier; then her eyes turned in the direction of his wide-eyed stare, and she let out a cry of alarm.

"Something's on fire—Bruce—"

Bruce jerked as though he had been stung; the sound of her voice, or her incipient movement, into the room, roused him from his paralysis, and he came bounding toward her, his head averted and one arm up before his face. He cannoned into her, sending her staggering back; and then he turned to face the thing that had sent him into flight—the rising coil of oily black smoke which was forming in the part of the room near the window.

The cold was not the normal cold of a winter night. It rolled out of the room in unseen waves that pulled like quicksand. When Bruce pushed her back she had fancied she felt a sucking, reluctant release. The tentacles still fingered her body; she retreated farther, breathing in harsh gasps that hurt her lungs, back into the space under the stairs. She stopped only when her back touched the wall, and gave another cry as a new wave of cold touched her shrinking side. This was a more natural cold; it came from the cellar door, which was, unaccountably, wide open. Another foot to the left and she would have backed straight down the stairs in her mindless flight.

Bruce had retreated too, step by slow step, as though he were fighting a pull stronger than gravity. He came to a halt at the bottom of the stairs. Pat had seen the thing by now; Ruth heard his wordless bellow of consternation, and Sara's stifled shriek. But most of her awareness was focused on the impossible—the moving blackness that swayed to no breeze, that twisted in upon itself as if in a struggle for form. Smoke where there was no fire; greasy, oily black smoke, that emitted waves of *cold* instead of heat.

Bruce stopped at the bottom of the stairs, one hand on the newel post. By accident or design his body barred the stairs, his arms extended across the narrow space from wall to bannister. He called out something, and Ruth heard the feet above stumble back, up, a few steps. The cold was sickening; it sucked at the warmth of the body like a leech. Ruth knew she was only on the fringe of its malice; the full effect was directed at Bruce.

She saw the book, still clutched in the whitened fingers of the boy's left hand, and in her bemused state she wondered, insanely, where he had found a Bible, and what good he thought it would do. Then she remembered where the thick red volume had come from; she also caught the accidentally blasphemous resemblance, in Bruce's taut body and out-stretched arms, which had brought the first idea into her head. She tried to think of a prayer and finally, as her frozen brain caught up with her instinct, she realized that she had been praying, snatches of incoherent invocation from half-forgotten rituals; and she also knew that the symbols, verbal or physical, were meaningless in the face of the abyss. For the Thing moved, swaying toward them, and put out pseudopods—shapeless, wavering extensions of darkness that pawed the air like half-formed arms.

Then, through the ringing in her ears she heard a sound, as wildly incongruous as shepherd's pipes on a battlefield. It was a small sound, precise and crystalline: the sleepy twitter of a bird on a tree outside the house.

The hovering blackness began to fade.

Once the process of dissolution had begun, it proceeded rapidly; in seconds the pale blue satin drapes showed clear, unfogged, on the wall of the living room.

Through the dead silence she heard again the querulous sleepy chirp; and from Bruce came a shocking, ragged gasp of laughter.

" 'It faded on the crowing of the cock . . .' Or was that a sparrow? 'The bird of dawning . . .' " And, flinging out his arm toward the door, where a streak of sickly gray sky showed through the fanlight, he sat down with a thud on the bottom step and hid his face in his folded arms.

Ruth put out one hand, as delicately as though she feared it might break off, and pushed at the open cellar door. The slam brought another alarmed bellow from Pat.

"I just closed the basement door," she called. "It was wide open."

She detached herself from the wall, feeling as though she must have left the imprint of her body on the plaster, and moved out to where she could see the two faces staring down over the bannister. Sara's was green.

"I'm going to be sick," she said.

Bruce lifted his head. He was still clutching the book; one finger was jammed between the pages like a marker, and the grip of his other fingers was convulsively tight. He was shaking violently, and his face was ashen under a glistening sheen of perspiration; but his mouth was stretched in a wide, exultant grin, and his eyes went straight to Pat's face.

"By God," he said, "how did you like *that*, you damned skeptic?"

II

"I'm selling the house. I won't let Sara spend another night in this chamber of horrors."

Ruth meant every word; but she was forced to admit that Sara looked in splendid condition for a girl who had spent the night in a chamber of horrors. Slim and supple in her emerald green velvet robe, she was scrambling eggs with hungry efficiency.

"Get your hair out of the way," Ruth added irritably. "We've had trouble enough tonight without having you catch on fire."

"Sorry," said Sara amiably. "Ruth, why don't you relax? I'm fine. Bruce is the one I'm worried about."

Wrapped in a blanket and ensconced in a chair by the oven door, Bruce had almost stopped shivering. His symptoms had resembled those of shock; Pat and Ruth had had to drag him out to the warmth of the kitchen. He gave Sara a reassuring grin, but did not speak; there was a glitter in his eyes, though, that suggested he would have plenty to say when the time came.

"He needs food," Pat said, flipping toast onto a plate. "We all do. I'm starved."

Ruth lifted bacon out of the pan onto a paper towel, judged the coffee with an experienced eye, and began laying out silver with more speed than elegance.

"I am too. It must be the nervous strain. I remember once

before when—when I was worried and upset, I ate constantly."

"Is that what you were tonight—nervous? Personally," said Pat, "I was terrified. Come on, Bruce, get some of these eggs into you. That cold is incredibly enervating, and you got the worst of the blast. Hero type," he added amiably.

"Hero, hell; I just had the farthest to run." Bruce took a mouthful of eggs and meditated. "I wonder how many of the great heroes of history would turn out to be slow runners, if you ever investigated the circumstances."

"Let's not be cynical," Ruth said.

They ate in silence for a while, ravenously and with concentration. Ruth finished first; as she reached for her cigarettes she looked around the table at the other three with sudden intense affection. Pat happened to glance up as her eyes reached his face; he grinned, and echoed her thoughts with unnerving accuracy.

"'*Ich hatte eine Kameraden,*'" he quoted.

"How did you know what I was thinking? Yes; I know now why soldiers under fire get so devoted to their buddies."

"There's nobody nicer than the guy who has just saved your life," Pat agreed. "Unless it's the guy who might save it tomorrow."

"Now you're being cynical. It's more than that."

"It must have something to do with trust," Sara offered shyly. "Knowing you can depend on someone, literally to the death."

"Well, you can't depend on me." Ruth pushed her chair back and stared at them defiantly. "I meant it. Sara is not spending another night here."

"Surrender, hmm?"

"Pat, we're not accomplishing anything! It's getting

stronger, and we're helpless. It's dangerous—horribly dangerous—"

"How do you know?" Bruce asked.

Blank silence followed. Finally Ruth said, "You're a fine one to ask that! You looked like a dead man when we pulled you out of there."

"Another cup of coffee and he'll be his old argumentative self," Pat said. "What happened to him was damned unpleasant, but surely it's the worst that abominable Thing can do. It's nonmaterial, after all; how much damage can It inflict?"

"Exactly." Bruce's cheeks were flushed with excitement. "Ruth, I know how you feel. But we are making progress. Don't you realize how much we learned tonight?"

"We learned one of its limitations," Ruth admitted. "Apparently it can't function in daylight."

"Which lends some credence to one of the aspects of spiritualism that has always roused my loudest jeers—the statement that spirits are disturbed by too much light."

"Right. When you stop to think about it, you may recall that the other manifestations—Sara's seizures, and the voice—have also occurred at night."

"Swell," Ruth said gloomily. "A house isn't much good, though, if you can't sleep in it."

"That's not all we learned. Remember this?"

Bruce held up the red book. He had been cradling it in his lap like a baby.

"I'd almost forgotten that. You think we were supposed to find it?"

"I don't think it just happened to fall. You aren't in the habit of leaving heavy books balanced on the edge of the shelf, are you?"

"I don't remember ever touching that one," Ruth admitted. "What is it? Myers' *History of Maryland*. No, it's one of Cousin Hattie's books. It's been there forever."

"Not only was it moved, it lay open," Bruce went on. "That might be accident; but I'm inclined to think that— whatever—could push a book off a shelf could also turn pages."

"The proof of the pudding," Pat said sententiously. "What does your prize say?"

Bruce opened the book.

"This section concerns a minor skirmish known as the Loyalist Plot." He scanned the page, muttering. "Free the prisoners of war . . . hmmph. Yes. It happened in 1780, after the Revolution had begun. Contrary to what the high school history books tell us, not everybody in the Colonies was all that keen on independence. Some fanatical Tory citizens of Maryland decided to strike a blow for the King. They were planning to free the British prisoners at Frederick, and take the armory *at Georgetown*. The Patriots got wind of the plan, caught the leaders, and finally hanged them."

The ensuing silence rang with speculation.

"I don't see it," Ruth said finally.

"Hell's bells, it's just what we've been looking for." Bruce closed the book and put it tenderly on the table. "We're looking for a General and a violent deed. Here's a war situation, divided loyalties—and a specific mention of Georgetown, for God's sake. Somebody—something—has kindly narrowed down our search through history, not only to a given period, but to a particular year!"

"But, Bruce," Ruth protested, "there wasn't even a house here at that time."

Bruce's face went blank—eyes round, mouth ajar. He looked so vacuous that Ruth, in a spasm of alarm, reached out and jogged his arm.

"Huh? No, I'm all right. I just remembered. . . . I'll be damned! I had just found that deed when the big bang came. . . . Sorry, I don't mean to be incoherent. Look here; I was poking around in that box of papers you gave me, and I found the photostat of a deed. It was a sale of land by Ninian Beall, the original proprietor of all this territory—he called it the Rock of Dumbarton—to one Douglass Campbell. And it was dated in the 1760's.''

Ruth poured coffee into her cup so briskly that it splashed. She felt as if her brains needed lubricating.

"Campbell," she muttered. "One of the ancestors, obviously. . . . This house wasn't built till 1810. But there could have been an earlier house. . . ."

"If there was, what happened to it?" Pat demanded. He reached for the coffeepot and Ruth pushed it toward him.

"Torn down, maybe," she offered. "As the family prospered and needed bigger quarters. But Bruce—I thought ghosts were laid when the places they haunt are destroyed."

"Expert authorities differ on that," Bruce said oratorically, and then spoiled the effect by grinning. "You know, when I actually listen to the things we're saying, I can't believe it myself. No, but according to some of the tales I've read, the haunting is connected with a specific building; in others the very soil seems to be permeated with—whatever it is."

"Whatever it is," Sara repeated. "You all sit talking and talking, and all the time I keep remembering . . . that horrible Thing. . . ."

Bruce caught Ruth's anxious eye and nodded.

"Yes. Well, we'd better talk about It. We weren't any of us too coherent the first time we tried."

"It was so *cold*," Ruth said, with a strong shudder. "Was It—that Thing—always there, invisible, when we felt the cold?"

"What a happy thought," Bruce murmured. "Damned if I know. Pat?"

"I don't know either."

The answer was brief, the tone flat. Bruce, after one

penetrating look, picked up the coffeepot and tilted it. A feeble trickle of extremely black liquid dripped into his cup.

"Somebody forgot to fill it," he said mildly, and rose to do so. Over his shoulder and over the rush of running water he said, "Still hedging, Pat, after this morning?"

"I'm trying desperately to keep an open mind," Pat said stubbornly. "Ruth, don't get mad, but—I've seen too much of this sort of thing, all over the world."

"But we all saw it!"

"What did we see? I could have kicked myself later," he added bitterly. "But I was too damned shook up at first to think straight. You know what we did. We sat here shaking and gabbling and compared notes, one after the other. You especially must know, Bruce, how witnesses unconsciously influence one another. What we should have done was write out our separate impressions, without speaking to each other, and then compare them."

"He's right," Bruce said, over Ruth's indignant sniff. He came back to the table carrying the coffeepot, and plugged it in. "Absolutely right. I should have thought of it myself, but I'm damned if I apologize. If that was just a harmless little old hallucination, God save me from the real thing!"

"Even at that," Pat went on doggedly, "we didn't actually see the same thing. Ruth saw smoke—dark, oily smoke. Bruce was babbling about the pillar of darkness by day—not a very apt analogy, if I remember my Bible—whereas, to Sara the thing had shape. It was man-high and roughly anthropomorphic."

"It had arms," said Sara, from behind a veil of hair. "Stubs, that were trying to turn into arms."

"Thanks," Pat said. "I'll dream about that one. Bruce, you can see my point, can't you?"

"Sure," Bruce said agreeably. "We've got to be as critical and logical about the evidence as we can. Hell, I said that myself. But I do think you're leaning over backwards so far you're about to fall on your can. Excuse me, Ruth."

"Don't be so darned polite," Ruth said irritably. "You make me feel like a little gray-haired old lady. I know, I am, but still. . . . Pat, I don't care what Bruce thinks, I'm sick and tired of your attitude. Are you with us or not?"

"Oh, I'm with you," Pat said unexpectedly; and smiled at their stupefied expressions. "At least I'm willing to extend the deadline you proposed. In fact, I'll prove my loyalty by pointing out something you seem to have overlooked. Ruth, did you leave the cellar door open before we went to bed?"

"Why, no; I haven't been in the cellar for ages. Pat! Do you think—"

"I think we may have a very busy ghost. Could the wind have blown the door open?"

"No, no, it catches quite firmly."

Bruce licked his finger and drew an invisible stroke on the air.

"One to you, Pat. Ruth, I want to see your cellar."

He streaked out the door without waiting for an answer. They caught up with him at the top of the cellar stairs.

"Where's the light switch?"

"At the bottom of the stairs."

"Stupid place for it."

"I know." Ruth proffered a box of kitchen matches which she had picked up on the way out. "That's one of the reasons why I detest the basement. I haven't been down here since I moved in."

"You must have," Sara said, picking up her long skirts.

"Wait till he gets the light on; the stairs are steep. No, really, I haven't. The furnace runs like the proverbial charm. People come—" Ruth gestured vaguely— "you know, for meters and things. They go down, I stay up."

The light went on down below, and Bruce called them to descend.

One bare bulb, hanging limply, shed a dismal light over a small cement-lined chamber, occupied only by the big bulk of the furnace and by two ancient iron sinks. There were three windows, all at the front of the house; they were small, even for basement windows, barred and high up.

"It's smaller than I expected," Pat said, after a brief inspection. "Doesn't go under the whole house, does it?"

"No, just the dining room and kitchen half."

"I can't see anything significant down here." Bruce tugged at his beard. "No moldering, brass-bound chests filled with stolen pirate loot, no ancient portraits. . . ."

"The place is far too damp for storage," Ruth said practically. "That's why Hattie kept all her junk in the attic."

"The attic." Bruce gave his beard another tug, harder than he had intended. He let out a yelp. "Damn. There's so much to do—"

"I want to get out of this place," Sara said distinctly.

"What's wrong?" Ruth asked anxiously. "Do you feel—"

"I wish you'd stop jumping at me every time I open my mouth," Sara said. "I just don't like this place."

"I don't either," Pat said. His tone was so peculiar that Ruth transferred her anxious stare to him. He shook himself, like a dog coming out of the water, and smiled at her. "I didn't get my eight hours last night," he said.

"You do look tired, all of a sudden." Ruth took his arm. "Why don't you try to take a nap? Come on, everybody; I hate this place myself and we aren't getting anywhere just standing around."

Bruce waited until they had gone up, and then turned out the light. When he emerged he was still worrying his beard, and Pat had to address him twice before he responded.

"I said, I'm sorry the basement was a bust. Maybe the open door was an accident after all."

"Oh, I dunno," Bruce said vaguely. "Pat, are you going to the university this morning?"

"Hadn't planned to. Why?"

"I want to shower and change, I'm short on sleep myself." Bruce yawned so widely Ruth feared his jaws would split. "And I want to see Ted. His field is Colonial America."

"Georgetown?"

"No. No, he won't know anything I need to know," Bruce said stupidly. He yawned again. "Brrr. He will know what the sources are. And where they're kept—Archives, Library of Congress, the local historical association. Then I'll go there. Wherever there is."

"Take the car, I won't need it. And Bruce—"

"Mmmm?"

"Don't take too many of those damned pep pills—or whatever kind of pills Ted is peddling these days along with advice on Colonial history."

"Ted doesn't—"

"The hell he doesn't. Oh, he's generally harmless; that's why I've left him alone. And I know you don't generally indulge. Just don't start now—especially now. There's no need to push yourself; we've got time."

"I hope you're right," Bruce said.

"We'll start on the attic," Ruth said, still slightly bewildered by the exchange. "And the closets. What are we supposed to be looking for, exactly?"

"Deeds, letters, old newspapers. I've been thinking," Bruce said. "I did get the full blast from our not so friendly ghost, and I'm beginning to think it was no accident. If I had dropped that book, I'd have lost the page and we'd still be groping. So I suggest we look particularly for anything that mentions the name of Master Douglass Campbell."

III

Bruce went upstairs to get his sweater and Ruth headed for the kitchen to clear, accompanied by Pat, who was making hopeful suggestions about more coffee. Ruth plugged the pot in and started to collect eggy plates. She was thinking that nothing is nastier than the remains of cold scrambled eggs when she realized that Sara had not followed her out. It was—she told herself—only concern that made her return, quietly, through the dining room, while Pat was looking for clean cups.

They stood in the hallway, and Ruth's approach would not have been heard if she had worn boots instead of soft slippers. Though Sara was a tall girl, she had to tilt her head back to look up into Bruce's face. Her hands lay on his breast, and his held her shoulders; the curve of her body, in the clinging softness of green velvet, was as eloquent as it was beautiful.

"I hate like hell to leave you alone," Bruce said softly.

"I won't be alone. Ruth and Pat—"

"You know what I mean."

"I know."

"Say it, then."

"I'm alone in a crowd of people, if you aren't there," she said.

His mouth closed over hers, and her head fell back so that the hair streamed in a shining cascade over the arm that had pulled her against him.

Ruth had no conscious intention of moving or speaking; but she must have made some sound, for they broke apart as suddenly as they had come together. Bruce looked at Ruth and started to speak. Then he shrugged slightly, put Sara gently away from him, and left.

Sara stood with hands clasped. She looked, as even the plainest girl can look under some circumstances, utterly beautiful. Ruth said sharply, "Go upstairs and get dressed."

Sara's eyes cleared and focused. She gave Ruth an incredulous look; but her aunt's expression told her that she had not heard wrong. She swung on her heel and fled up the stairs.

"What hit you?" Pat asked, from behind Ruth.

"Nothing," she said shortly. Pat caught her by the elbow as she tried to pass him.

"Nothing my eye. Why so nasty about a couple of kids kissing?"

"I didn't say anything."

"It wasn't what you said, it was the way you said it."

"They're too young to be thinking of—"

"Of what? If they're thinking about what I think they're thinking about, more power to them."

"Oh, Pat! This is no time for—for—"

He waited, giving her plenty of time to find the word. When she did not he said softly, "You've got a problem yourself, haven't you? What—"

Sara came clattering down the stairs. She was wearing stretch slacks and a shirt, and, Ruth suspected, very little else. Her feeling that the slacks were too tight was confirmed by Pat's appreciative stare. The rich raspberry of the slacks and the pink and lemon striped shirt set off Sara's vivid coloring, but her expression was as bleak as the colors were warm. She brushed past Ruth without meeting her eye.

"I'll do the dishes," she said, and vanished into the kitchen.

"She's angry with me," Ruth said wretchedly.

"I don't blame her. Your voice was like ice water; and

coming when it did, after a transcendental minute and a half—"

"I'm going to get dressed," Ruth said. "Then I'm going to look at the closet shelves."

But she knew, as she ascended the stairs, that he was staring speculatively at her; and she knew also that the confrontation she had been expecting had only become more imminent.

IV

By five o'clock Bruce had not returned, and Sara was vibrating nervously between the kitchen window and the tray of cocktails she had prepared.

"Come on in and sit down," Ruth said, taking the tray. "He'll be along any minute."

"You go ahead." Sara was courteous but remote; it was clear that she had not forgotten the morning's episode. "I'm going to start dinner."

Ruth found Pat in the living room lighting the fire. He looked up as she came sidling around the door; they had all started to adopt a circuitous route through the room, avoiding its street end as much as possible.

"Maybe we ought to sit in the kitchen," Ruth said.

Pat took the tray of drinks and set it firmly on the coffee table.

"I don't think anything is likely to happen much before midnight, to judge by past events. Sit down. I'll sit on this side, just in case, and keep an eye on—things."

"No, I'd rather keep my eye on them too." Ruth sat down beside him, on the couch that faced the pertinent end of the room. "Pat, I think we ought to get out of here. At least for the night."

"It's okay by me. But I doubt if Bruce will agree. He'll want to sit and observe manifestations."

"And Sara probably won't go without him. Damn the boy; why doesn't he come home?"

"Tsk, tsk, such language," Pat said comfortably. "What have you got against the kid?"

"Nothing, really. It's just—"

"The beard and the clothes and the supercilious air? I know; they gripe me too. But these things are only a superficial facade; underneath, the little devils are a lot more like the rest of the human race than they care to admit. Bruce is a very sound specimen; Sara could do a lot worse."

"They aren't that serious about each other."

"I don't know about her feelings, but there's no question about his. He's fighting for her, Ruth—tooth and nail."

"Yes, I know . . . and I'm grateful . . . but, Pat, in a way he's enjoying this. It's a game to him—outsmarting you, and me, and the rational universe!"

"I still think you aren't giving him credit. We'll talk to him when he comes in and see if we can't convince him to leave. You and Sara can spend the night at my place, I've got plenty of room."

"That's very nice of you, but. . . ."

He met her quizzical look with one of amusement, but there was a subtle change in his expression.

"Don't worry, you'll be perfectly safe. If I had in mind what you think I have in mind, I wouldn't include Sara."

Ruth leaned back, staring into the leaping flames, and feeling Pat's arm move along the back of the couch behind her. Middle age had its disadvantages, certainly, and one of the losses was the wild singing in the blood; but if one extreme had flattened out, so had the other. The anxieties were gone; the terrors had become only mild anxieties.

"Don't be coy," Pat said softly. His fingers touched her chin. She turned her face toward him, smiling.

"I'm not coy, dear. Only tired."

"That sounds like a challenge."

He was no longer smiling; his eyes moved from her eyes to her lips, and Ruth was aware of the mixed emotions which no woman with any feminine instincts can help feeling under such circumstances—triumph, mingled with a small, exciting touch of alarm.

"Men are so conceited," she murmured. "They—"

His lips cut off the rest of the sentence. It was a cautious embrace, restrained on her side and exploratory on his; when he raised his head, neither had spilled a drop from the glasses they still held, and his hand had not moved from her shoulder.

Ruth let her smile widen just a trifle. He could control his features, but not his breathing; holding the glass was pure affectation, a little boy pretending to show off. Pat's eyes narrowed. He put his glass on the table and took hers from her hand. Without speaking, but with the same look of concentration with which, she imagined, he began a lecture, he took her into his arms.

At first she felt like laughing, there was such deliberation in his movements. She felt pleasantly relaxed, like a cat being stroked; and then, with a jarring realization, she felt her head turning, seeking the mouth which had avoided hers but was moving effectively elsewhere. Pat felt the movement too; his warm breath, then approximately under her left ear, came out in a gust of amusement. Annoyed, she tried to free herself, and found her hands ineffective.

For the first few seconds of the second kiss she was unaware of any emotion except gratification; this, then, was what men starving on a desert island experienced when confronted with their first full meal in months. Only for her it had been years. . . . The new sensation came gradually, insidiously. It was some time before she realized that pleasure had been replaced by terror, and that her body was stiff with revulsion. She tried to move and found she could not; the weight of his body forced her back onto the couch, the pressure of his hands was so painful she wanted to cry out, but could not, because his mouth was a gag, stifling sound and breath. . . . It was a nightmare, all the worse because it had happened before, and because she had not expected, from him, such ruthless contempt for her pain, physical and mental.

Then all the lights in the room went on, in a blinding flash that penetrated even her squeezed eyelids; and from some infinite distance a voice spoke loudly.

Pat was still a dead weight—almost as if he had collapsed—but his hands and body were passive now, no longer actively hurting. After a moment he sat up; and Ruth, blinking through tears of fright and pain, saw Bruce standing in the doorway, his hand on the light switch. He was wearing his coat, but no hat, as was his habit; and the expression on his face made Ruth want to shriek with hysterical amusement.

He's shocked, she thought wildly; poor child, they really are so conventional. . . . Then she realized that she was sprawled awkwardly and embarrassingly across the couch. She sat up and tried to rearrange her skirt.

Bruce gave Pat one quick, appraising look, and then vanished, without comment or apology—an omission which made Ruth think highly of his tact. She had not dared to look at Pat, but she was intensely aware of him. He was hunched over, his face hidden in his hands; but he must have been looking through his fingers, because as soon as Bruce left he turned to Ruth.

"Is there any point in asking you to forgive me?"

"My dear, there's no need—" Ruth's voice was a croak; she had to stop and clear her throat. "You didn't—"

"I hurt you; and that was unforgivable. Good God, I

don't know what came over me!" His clenched hands went to his forehead, and Ruth reached over to pat his shoulder.

"Stop beating yourself. It's happened before——"

She had not meant to say that, nor had she anticipated what the impact of the words would be. They literally caught in her throat and left her staring dumbly at her glass of wine.

"I know it has," Pat said quietly. "I knew something was wrong; it was unmistakable. That's what makes my behavior so viciously stupid."

"How—how did you know?"

"I can't explain; I just—well, felt it. The first time I kissed you I felt it—a mixed-up combination of desire and fear. I knew that; I was so careful—and now I had the unforgivable effrontery to try to force you. Ruth, I'm not apologizing for my instincts, I'm proud of 'em; but I can't forgive myself for my stupidity and clumsiness."

"It's all right."

"No, it's not. But the situation is so fouled up now I might as well plunge on. It's your husband, isn't it? I know about that; he was killed in the Second World War, when you'd only been married a few months."

"Harry. . . ." She let the word linger on her tongue, wondering why, after twenty years, the taste of it should be so bitter.

"It was a tragedy, darling, I know. A terrible thing. But it's been twenty years, and more. You can't bury your emotions for the rest of your life out of some sickly romanticism, no one demands or deserves such distorted loyalty. . . ."

"Loyalty?" She turned, staring at him; and the glass she had picked up began to shake, spilling white liquid, and her whole body shook with silent, painful laughter. "The day I got the telegram from the War Department I got down on my knees and thanked God."

"Was it as bad as that?" he asked, after a moment of silence, in which the truth burst on him like a blinding light.

"It was—there are no words. I was only twenty—Sara's age—and I was so naïve, you wouldn't believe—none of these sophisticated modern children would believe—how dumb I was. At first I thought it was my fault. He called me a prig, and talked about middle-class morality. And I believed him; I was sunk in guilt at my own abhorrence. Oh, Pat, there wasn't a thing he missed!" She gave a choked laugh. The tears were pouring down her cheeks and she swiped at them with the back of her hand. "I read the books later, you know the ones I mean; there was hardly a page I hadn't known, firsthand."

"Why didn't you divorce him?" Pat asked in a deadly quiet voice.

"I told you, at first I thought it was my fault, I thought I would learn. . . . Then, later, he was going away. They were talking about the big invasion, and we knew he would be in it. I couldn't—"

"Yes, I see." Pat's fist beat a soft tattoo against his knee. "It's frustrating," he said casually, "to want to kill a man who's been dead for twenty years. I hope he's rotting."

"I can see now that he was sick," Ruth said, fumbling in her pocket. "I can be sorry for him—now. I didn't realize myself how it had affected me, I just—never thought about it."

"No wonder. All the same, it would have been better if you had proceeded to have a big noisy nervous breakdown and gotten this out of your system. You never had psychiatric help? No, you wouldn't. Excuse me just a minute while I go out on the front steps and shoot myself."

"But—don't. How could you possibly know?"

"I should have known. What the hell are you looking for? Oh, take my handkerchief. Blow your nose. Have another drink. Ruth, I should have known because I love you. Love is supposed to give people insight, isn't it?"

"I think that's one of the sadder delusions of youth." Ruth blew, loudly and satisfyingly. "Unfortunately, it seems to cloud one's vision instead."

"You may be right," Pat said, eying her nervously. "Is that any way to respond to my announcement?"

"I am sorry! I just—"

"I'm not expecting any enthusiasm, under the circumstances. Just think about it." His hands clenched till the knuckles whitened and she knew it was with the effort of not reaching out to touch her. "You feel better now, I know. It was a beautiful catharsis. But it was only temporary; Ruth, you're not through this yet. Just let me try. I'll be careful. This won't happen again. I'll be damned if I know what came over me."

Chapter Seven

The pork chops were sizzling in the pan; Sara cooked them as Ruth had taught her, in bacon fat with plenty of garlic salt and pepper. She looked up at her aunt as the latter came in. Ruth had been upstairs to repair the ravages of the past half hour, but she knew her eyes were red, and she had never appreciated Sara more than now, when the girl greeted her with a smile which held no recollection of the morning's unpleasantness. It was Bruce, vigorously mashing potatoes, who avoided Ruth's eye.

"Do you mind making the gravy, Ruth?" Sara asked prosaically. "I still can't do it without lumps."

"Of course. It was nice of you two to get dinner. But, Bruce—I wondered. . . . I mean, it's after dark. . . ."

"I agree," Bruce said. "We'll leave as soon as we finish eating."

He turned to the table and began ladling potatoes out onto plates.

"Bruce, for goodness sake!" Sara exclaimed. "Put them in a bowl."

"Why get more dishes dirty?" Bruce said.

"Quite right." Pat took the frying pan from Sara and

forked chops out onto plates. "Let's eat and run. You girls are spending the night at my place."

He handed the frying pan back to Ruth.

"Now you can make the gravy," he explained.

"Men," Sara said.

"Impossible," Ruth agreed. They nodded solemnly at each other.

They ate hastily, and in silence. Ruth was occupied with her own thoughts; she was aware that Bruce seemed preoccupied and unusually quiet, but in the confusion of new personal ideas that had overwhelmed her she paid less attention than she might otherwise have done. Bruce finished before the others; he scraped his plate energetically into the sink and began clearing the table with such vigor that Pat had to snatch his plate, with his third pork chop, back.

"Wait a minute. What's the hurry?"

"Ruth is right." Bruce reached for a glass. "We'd better get out of here. I was late getting back. I'd have suggested going then, only Sara had dinner ready. . . . Hurry up, will you? We can leave the dishes till morning; I'll help out then. . . ."

The stammering voice was so unlike Bruce's that Ruth could only stare.

"You must have found out something today," Pat said, studying the younger man curiously.

"Well, sort of. I mean, it doesn't. . . . Look, let's go! I'll talk about it at your place."

Sara rose obediently; and in a quick, convulsive movement Bruce dived across the table and caught her arm.

"Not you—not that way!"

"What on earth—" Ruth began.

"Ruth, will you pack some things for her and get her coat? Then we can go out the kitchen door."

"Why—of course."

As she packed Sara's robe and nightgown and toothbrush, along with her own things, Ruth wondered what Bruce had discovered that frightened him so badly. For he was afraid, and not on his own account. What could be worse than the things they had already experienced?

II

During the drive Bruce continued to ramble, suggesting that the two women go to a hotel, offering to sleep on Pat's living-room floor, and being generally irrelevant. His conversation sounded like the noises people make to conceal the fact that they are not listening to themselves talk—that they are thinking about something else altogether.

Pat lived near Spring Valley, in a tiny house set in what seemed—and proved, by daylight—to be a neatly kept little garden.

"I like gardens," he explained. "Otherwise I'd have taken an apartment. The house is a little large for one person, but I have a lot of books."

That, Ruth decided, was an understatement. Her first impression of Pat's house was that it was built of books. Every wall in the downstairs rooms that was not otherwise occupied was lined with bookcases. There were books on tables, on chairs, on Pat's desk in his study. There were more books on beds and on night tables, and books on every flat surface in the bathroom, including the floor.

Ruth's second impression was that it was the grubbiest house she had ever seen.

Pat surveyed his living room with mild astonishment.

"It's sort of messy, isn't it? I guess what's-her-name didn't come this week."

He leaned over and blew the dust off the coffee table.

"What's-her-name being the cleaning woman, I gather." Ruth said. She picked up a sock from the back of a chair. "It wouldn't be so bad if you wouldn't leave your clothes lying around—and would pick up the newspaper instead of leaving it spread out on the floor—and take out your used coffee cups—and empty an ashtray occasionally. . . ."

She suited the action to the words, and finished by handing Pat the overflowing wastebasket into which she had forced the contents of the ashtrays.

"Amazing," Pat said. Clutching the wastebasket to his chest he looked around the room. "Looks better already."

"Where's the vacuum cleaner? Do you have a vacuum cleaner?"

"Certainly I do. But it's none of your business." Pat put the wastebasket down in the middle of the floor. "You can be housewifely tomorrow, if you insist, but tonight we're going to talk. Don't you want to hear what Bruce has to say?"

"Yes, of course," Ruth said absently.

Even in its present clutter and dust, which had been barely touched by her efforts, the room was a pleasant place, with that air of comfort which comes when a basically well-decorated room is inhabited by someone who cares more for comfort than for elegance. She suspected that Pat's mother had donated the furniture; the chintz on the chairs and couch, with its delicate pattern of lilac and delphinium, in soft blues and lavenders, had certainly not been Pat's choice, but it suited the room, with its low-beamed ceiling and brick fireplace. The rug was a soft textured blue that repeated one color of the flowered print. Coffee table and lamps looked like Pat's contributions; they were of heavy cut glass and their simple, modern lines went surprisingly well with the traditional furniture.

Pursuing her investigations Ruth rounded the corner of

the couch and stopped with a nervous squeal. Lying on the floor behind the couch, unmoved by their entrance, was what appeared to be a dead dog.

Pat rushed to join her, to see what had prompted her yell. Then he relaxed, eyeing the recumbent form—which was that of a very big, brown German shepherd—with disgust.

"That's Lady," he said.

Lady opened one eye and regarded him with remote interest. She let out a short unemphatic bark and closed the eye again.

"Laziest damn' dog I've ever seen," Pat said gloomily.

Sara dropped to the floor and began to rub the dog's head.

"Pretty girl," she crooned. "Nice Lady. Poor thing; how old is she, Pat?"

"Two years old," Pat said. "It's not her age, it's her disposition. She spends half her time lying in front of her food dish where I fall over her every time I go in the kitchen and the rest of her time lying in front of the fireplace waiting for me to make a fire. I've made more fires for that stupid dog."

He was building another one as he spoke, crumpling newspapers and jamming them under the waiting logs. Lady roused, and rolled over from her front to her side. She gave Pat a look of weary approval and he paused long enough to scratch her stomach. "Stupid dog," he muttered. Lady's mouth opened in a grin of affectionate contempt.

"You understand each other," Ruth said, laughing.

"Too true. All right, you stupid dog, there's your fire. Now perhaps I may be allowed to tend to my guests. Coffee? Brandy?"

"Both, please," Ruth said, and went along to help. When they finally settled down, she gave a sigh of contentment. The atmosphere was so restful that she felt completely at home. All of them might have been old inhabitants. Sara was squatting, with black boots crossed, on the hearthrug, and Lady had condescended to shift her big head into the girl's lap, where she lay snuffling and sighing in the throes of an exciting dream. Bruce had propped himself in a somewhat self-conscious pose against the mantel and was staring off into space and displaying his handsome profile to good effect. His close-fitting dark trousers and gaudy waistcoat might have been the doublet and hose of a medieval squire; they suited Bruce's lean height and long legs.

Pat was sprawled out in what was evidently his favorite chair; its cracking leather folds had molded themselves to the shape of his body. He smiled lazily at Ruth and lifted his glass in salute.

"I hate to dispel the mood," Bruce said waspishly.

"Then don't," Pat said.

"Time's running out. In fact, it's run. Forty-eight hours, remember?"

"Oh, that." Pat shrugged.

"You're awfully goddamn' casual about it!"

"I'm sorry," Pat said patiently. "I merely meant to remind you that you don't need to worry about deadlines."

"Deadlines! I'm worried about what we're going to do. Or do you expect Ruth to live with that chunk of fog indefinitely?"

"Don't loose your cool," said Pat, and looked idiotically pleased with himself for remembering this gem of modern idiom. "Naturally we'll have to do something. Let's talk about it. Have a Socratic dialogue."

He smiled at Ruth with the same lazy charm which seemed, at the moment, to be slightly tinged with alcohol. She shared his mood, however, and knew that he was not drunk, except with reaction. One simply did not realize how unnatural the atmosphere of the Georgetown house had become until one got out of it.

Bruce flushed with anger or frustration. Then he took a grip of his beard with both hands, and nodded.

"Okay. Geez, you make me mad," he added plaintively.

"I really am sorry, Bruce. Suppose you do the talking."

"I never refuse that invitation." Bruce's cheerful grin reappeared. "Okay, we'll have that dialogue. Answer Yes or No. We all agree that Sara is not psychotic, and that the manifestations we have seen are, in fact, from the realm which is called supernatural or paranormal."

"Right," Pat said.

"Then let's summarize what we've got. Sara, there's some blank paper in that hodgepodge on the table, you'd better jot this down. If anyone disagrees, or has a point to add, feel free to interrupt."

"Okay," Pat said meekly. If there was a gleam of amusement in his eye Ruth did not see it, but Bruce gave him a sharp glance before going on.

"Point one, a personality has on three occasions taken over Sara's body. Technical term: possession, or, as the English sometimes call it, overshadowing. This entity—whom we will call, for purposes of identification, A—has been pretty damned vague. Its only contribution has been the reference to the general, and a reiteration to the effect that It is not dead."

"Added comment," Pat said. "The accent was not Sara's normal one, but I could not identify it."

"Okay, that's a good point." Bruce sounded mollified. "I couldn't identify it either, except that it sounded softer and broader."

"What we need is a speech expert," Ruth said.

"We can't bring an outsider into this," Bruce said. Then he smote himself heavily on the brow. "Damn it; that's the trouble with us, we just aren't organized. We ought to have had a tape recorder going. We could let someone listen to a tape without giving away the circumstances."

"Thinking about what we should have done is futile," Pat said. "Go on, Bruce. Apparition A is not very helpful."

"Apparition B isn't either. That's what I propose to call that—unspeakable darkness. Yet we respond a lot more strongly to it than we do to the other. I do, anyhow. The entity that overshadows Sara bugs me, I'll admit, but I think mostly because it's not Sara. At the same time it is diluted, so to speak, by being contained in Sara. Whereas the darkness—appalls. The cold which accompanies it is a traditional manifestation of the supernatural, just about the only classic ghostly feature we've encountered. The cold is unnaturally violent and enervating. But the apparition is worse. It is evil."

The dog chose that moment to groan heartrendingly, and Ruth shivered.

"We all agree on that, don't we?" Pat said. "The impression of active, condensed evil—which is interesting. How do we know it's evil? That's a word and a concept which is out of fashion. Is there really such a thing as spiritual evil, and is there a human faculty, a seventh or eighth sense, that can smell it out?"

"You're getting into theology," Sara murmured. "Pretty soon you'll be asking, 'What is the good, Alcibiades?' and then I'll go to sleep."

"Yes, we're getting too philosophical," Bruce agreed. "Though I'd love to go into the problem if we didn't have more pressing matters on hand. All right. Apparition B is evil but otherwise without distinguishing characteristics. Now we come to Apparition C, if you can call a voice an apparition. The Voice. Capital V."

"You're too young to find that amusing," Ruth said, with a chuckle. "Remember, Pat?"

Bruce gave her a glance of dignified disdain.

"Apparition C, if you prefer that, seems to me the most potentially hopeful clue. It has been heard by all of us and it says definite words. 'Come home—Sammie.'"

"Query," Pat's drawl interrupted. "Name uncertain, if it is a name."

"Okay, query Sammie. The voice is indeterminate in terms of sex—"

"Or anything else," Pat muttered. "Direction, location, sense—"

"Or accent. It sounds," said Bruce, with unconscious poetry, "the way the wind would sound if it could speak. Rushing, hollow, immense."

"Good or bad?" Sara asked.

"Neutral, I'd say; wouldn't you?"

"I guess so. It's scary, but just because it is unnormal."

"Right. If Saint Peter himself appeared to me I'd scream and run, just from the unexpectedness of him. Anything else?"

"The book," suggested Ruth. "You believe something moved it."

"Apparition D?" Bruce scowled; he looked beautifully satanic with his brows coming together in a V. "Well, that plunges us into the next question. Which is—do these apparitions overlap?"

"Now you're talking," Pat said. He was so interested that he made the effort of sitting erect. "A and B might be the same entity."

"That occurred to me. The Thing—damn it, we need a name for It; It sounds like something out of a horror movie—"

"I think of It," Sara said, "as the Adversary."

"Hmm. Okay, the Adversary might try to work through Sara first. If it finds her unacceptable, or too fragile physically, it might try materializing."

"It's not a well-read ghost," Pat said. "The ones I've heard about are all tall white things. This dirty, dark mess—"

"Is the only genuine specter I've ever met," Ruth said, with a faint smile. "I've really no basis for comparison."

"Now is there anything to substantiate the impression that A and B are the same?" Bruce continued doggedly.

"No," Pat said.

"No," Bruce agreed. "Possible but not proved. Apparitions C and D—if we call the one who moved the book D—may also be identical. But, whether they are one or two, I think they are distinct from A-B and, what is more, hostile to it."

"Let's have that again," Sara said.

"I think I follow," Pat said. "The entity that moved the book is trying to tell us something. Its action is followed almost at once by the appearance of B, malignant and threatening. And the threat seems to be directed at the person who has the book."

"It's weak," Bruce muttered. "But it's the best we can do. The Voice seems to all of us neutral, if not benevolent. D is presumably benevolent, since it wants to give us some help. A and B definitely are not benevolent. So maybe C and D are the same, as are A and B. Criminey. As logic that isn't very impressive."

"No, but there's a feeling about it. . . . Hell, I can believe in one ghost, or maybe two; but four or five is surely stretching belief pretty thin." Pat tapped his fingers on the arm of the chair. "Suppose we reduce our apparitions to two. You have produced some evidence to indicate that one is helpful and the other hostile."

Sara gave a sigh and stretched out full length on the rug, hands clasped under her head.

"I warned you I'd get sleepy if the conversation got dull," she murmured.

Pat eyed her approvingly.

"You look like a parody of a tombstone," he said. "With the dog's head on your stomach instead of at your feet."

"All bosom and leg," Ruth commented unkindly. "Pull your skirt down."

"I don't think it will go down any farther," Pat said agreeably. "Anyhow, the dog's lying on it."

"You're a hell of a lot of help," Bruce said, addressing his lady love in bitter tones. "You haven't got a thing to contribute, and now you sprawl all over the room, taking people's minds off serious matters. Get up, wench."

"Let's get on to the historical research," Pat said, stifling a yawn. "Then we can get to bed."

"We didn't find much," Ruth admitted. "There's a lot of material around, but it takes ages to go through it."

"Don't I know," Bruce agreed feelingly. "I had a hell of a frustrating day myself. The records for that period are practically nonexistent."

"As the skeptic of this crowd I'd like to raise an objection," Pat said. "You seem to be basing your research on one item—the book. Are you sure you ought to limit yourself to that?"

"Oh, I'm all in favor of cross-checks. If the 1780 Campbell was named Samuel instead of Douglass, I'd be 100 percent sure we were on the right track. Matter of fact, I looked for Sammie today. And I found one. Samuel Campbell, son of George. Died in infancy around—I regret to say—1847."

"Oh, Bruce," Sara whispered. Her mouth had a pitiful droop. "That must be it. Think of it, calling your baby all those years. . . ."

"Samuel was one of twelve children," Bruce said calmly. "Both his parents seem to have been sanctimonious prigs who died in the overpowering odor of sanctity years later. And, if this means anything, there was nothing to indicate that the baby wasn't properly baptized, and all the rest. With all due deference to your sentimentality, luv, I think we can scratch Sammie."

"Your day was a bust, then." Pat yawned. "Sorry. I think maybe—"

"Okay." Bruce extended a hand to Sara and with one seemingly effortless movement pulled her to her feet. There was more muscle in his languid-looking frame than there appeared to be.

"What do we do tomorrow?" Sara asked, leaning against him.

"I go to the Columbia Historical Association. You keep on looking through the house."

"That worries me," Ruth admitted. "Are you sure it's safe for Sara?"

"I'm making two assumptions," Bruce said. "And I hope to God I'm right. One is that the manifestations occur only at night. The other—the other is that they occur only in the house."

Ruth was sodden with fatigue; it took her several seconds to comprehend the last sentence, which Pat had apparently anticipated; he was studying Sara with thoughtful eyes.

"You mean—here? Something might happen here?"

"Not if Bruce is right," Pat said. "You know, Bruce, there is a test we could make."

"What do you mean?" Ruth demanded.

"Hypnosis. Now, Ruth, don't look at me that way. It's a perfectly valid medical technique, not black magic; and I have done it before. I could do it now."

"No," Bruce said. "It's too dangerous."

"But I've had occasion—"

"It's dangerous because it's inconclusive. You guys talk about your friend the subconscious as if you had lunch with it every Tuesday, but the fact is you don't know much about the mind and the way it works. You could unwittingly suggest all kinds of things to Sara, and her subconscious might obligingly produce an imitation of Apparition A just because she thinks we want one. No. I won't allow it."

"Nor I," Ruth said flatly. "Pat, I suspect I'm going to have to make my own bed. Let's get at it, shall we?"

Pat looked stubborn; every hair on his head bristled.

"Very well," he said stiffly. "Bruce, do you want to call a cab?"

Bruce was gnawing his knuckles. He looked up.

"Would you mind if I just flopped down on the couch?"

"Afraid I'm going to pull a Svengali on Sara when your back is turned?" Pat asked nastily.

"It's late, that's all," the boy said mildly. "I won't be in the way."

As it turned out, there were three bedrooms upstairs, and Sara offered to share the big fourposter in one of them with Ruth. So it all worked out, and Pat was suddenly bland and amiable about the whole thing. Ruth was left to wonder precisely what he had had in mind when he made the original sleeping arrangements.

Not until she was almost asleep did it occur to her that there had been nothing in Bruce's discoveries to account for his strange, panicky behavior that evening.

III

Next day was one of the days Washingtonians brag about—brilliant, mild and balmy, with only a hint of cold under the soft breeze, like the bones under a cat's fur. Pat had the car windows rolled down when he drove them to the house, and he said regretfully, "It's too nice a day for that damned museum. If I hadn't had this appointment for a month—"

"You've got to keep it. We'll be all right."

"Hey, I've got an idea. Why don't I bring some stuff—Chinese food, maybe—and we'll have lunch in the garden."

"I thought you were having lunch with the curator."

"I'll get out of that." Pat stopped the car in front of the house.

"But Pat—"

"Look, today I feel like eating lunch with you. Both of you," he added.

Sara giggled, and Pat reached over to give her a fatherly smack as she got out of the car. Or maybe, Ruth thought, it wasn't so fatherly.

"Bruce may be back for lunch," she reported, putting her head back in the car window.

"The more the merrier," Pat said resignedly. He put the car into gear. "What do you like? Sweet-and-sour pork? Egg foo yung?"

"Anything but chop suey," Ruth said, and followed the car with her eyes as it swooped down the street, avoided a woman with a perambulator, and darted around the corner into the stream of traffic on Wisconsin.

Sunlight twinkled off the windshields and chrome of passing cars and warmed the rosy red brick of the houses opposite, bringing out the precise, geometric patterns of the whitened mortar. Most of the shades were still drawn and the dignified facades looked like sleepy old ladies snatching a catnap with hands folded primly in their laps, dreaming of their long honorable lives. One of the trees was alive with starlings holding one of their mysterious conferences; the squawking, which sounded like the United Nations in the lively old Khrushchev era, was unmusical but vigorously alive, and the sidewalk under the tree was already white with droppings. Washingtonians cursed the starlings, but Ruth had a sneaking sympathy for their vulgar, uproarious bustle. They were ugly rusty-looking birds, but when the sunlight glanced off their feathers they glowed with iridescence as brilliant as that of a sequined dress. It was with conscious reluctance that Ruth turned away from the sun and life of the street into the quiet house.

The living room was shadowy and still with all the drapes pulled; when Ruth opened them the sunlight streamed in, filled with dancing dust motes.

"Goodness, the place is dirty," she muttered.

"Ruth—"

"What's wrong? Do you feel—"

"No, nothing. That's what amazes me. How can the place look so normal?"

"Yes, I know. . . ." Ruth's eyes traveled from the window, where the drapes hung placidly in azure blue folds, across the patterns of the carpet. There ought to be a great charred spot, the mark of burning. . . .

"Well," she said, giving herself a brisk shake to dispel phantoms, "I think perhaps we ought to stay out of this room, for all it feels so innocent. I remember that there were some papers that looked like letters in a box in the hall closet. Let's take them into the kitchen and look them over while we have another cup of coffee. Then we can try the attic."

The letters turned out to be fascinating; they were still reading them several hours later when Pat's emphatic pounding was heard at the front door. He was using his foot, not his fist, as Ruth discovered when she opened the door; his arms were loaded with parcels which he dumped on the kitchen table, demanding, "Where's Bruce?"

"Not back yet."

"Let's eat this while it's hot. We can warm his up for him."

Bruce appeared while Pat was still sorting little packages of soy sauce and mustard, and they all sat down together.

"You look particularly smug," Ruth remarked, as Bruce dug into a beautiful concoction with an unpronounceable name which contained, among other commodities, shrimp and snow peas. "You must have made a discovery."

"Something," Bruce swallowed, and the rest of his

speech became considerably more intelligible. "But I don't want to discuss it while we're eating."

"We got bogged down," Sara said. "I've been reading some ancestress's love letters, and they are a panic. Do you know she called her husband 'Mr. Campbell' after they had been married thirty years?"

"That's what's wrong with our modern society." Pat shook his head and spread mustard with a lavish hand. "No respect. Old values breaking down."

Ruth laughed.

"Gosh, it's a beautiful day," she exclaimed, in a sudden burst of well-being. "Let's not talk about anything important till after lunch. I feel too good to start worrying."

"It's partly the weather and partly this damned picnic atmosphere," Bruce said. He stabbed a shrimp and looked at it fondly. "We seem to spend half our time eating and/or drinking, under the most peculiar conditions."

"'And, my dear husband, do not forget to take food regularly and in good quantity,'" Sara quoted. "She wrote him that when he was off on a business trip. I think it's great advice."

Looking at Bruce, Ruth was inclined to agree. He was beginning to develop visible shadows under his eyes, and there was a look in them, particularly when he watched Sara, that Ruth found disturbing.

The light mood lasted through the meal, which Pat cleared by dumping everything into a paper bag and depositing it in the garbage can. When he came back in, he said,

"Are we having coffee or more tea? Whichever, let's take it outside."

The sunlight was seductively warm. Ruth produced a blanket for Sara, knowing her habit of sprawling on the lowest surface available, and Bruce sat down beside her on a pile of leaves.

"I feel like Luther," Pat announced, and they all stared at him. "I don't believe in anything," he explained.

"No ghosts," Bruce said, with a faint smile.

"No ghosts."

"I wish you were right." Bruce leaned back on his elbows and contemplated the sky.

"What did you find out today?" Sara asked. The question broke the relaxed, sunny mood; Bruce sat erect, and Ruth felt herself stiffening.

"There was a house here in 1780," he said. "Douglass Campbell's house. I ran into a piece of luck, a collection of family letters. The Page letters, they're called. The Pages lived up the street a way, but the family died out in the late nineteenth century and the last Page left the papers to the Columbia Historical Society. That's where I've been all morning."

"Okay, okay," Pat said. "You don't have to explain every goddamned source. What did the Pages have to say about the Campbells?"

"Not much, most of them were business letters about land and tobacco. But in 1805 Alexander Page's eldest daughter got married and moved to Annapolis. Mrs. Page wrote the girl several letters telling her the hometown gossip. The Campbell fire was a good juicy tidbit."

"Fire?" Sara repeated.

"The house burned down . . . and Douglass Campbell with it."

In the silence the squawk of a blue jay sounded like a scream. Ruth was remembering the impression she had felt that morning—that there should be marks of scorching where the apparition had been. As she looked at Sara she knew her niece was thinking along the same lines; her face was pale with horror.

"That black, coiling smoke," she said in a whisper. "Bruce, could it be—*him?*"

"Cut that out!" Bruce exclaimed.

Simultaneously Pat said sharply, "Don't be morbid, Sara. The suggestion of smoke is purely subjective. Bruce, what happened, that the old boy was caught in the house? He must have been old, if he had already built his house by 1780."

"The fire was thirty years later," Bruce said. "He could have been as young as fifty-five or as old as eighty. It's possible that the smoke knocked him out before anyone realized that the house was on fire. It was stone; the letter mentioned that. The walls weren't burned, of course, but the whole inside was gutted and the roof collapsed. When the heir, who was Campbell's sister's son, moved to Georgetown from Frederick, he leveled the walls and built a new house."

Ruth was silent. The sunshine and birdsongs seemed far away, and the orange beads of the bittersweet against the fence had faded. The ancient tragedy had affected her spirits unaccountably.

"I don't see any connection between this story and our apparitions," Pat said. "The smoky impression is meaningless. If the old man's name had been Samuel, now. . . ."

"It wasn't. But there was something funny. . . ."

"In the letter?"

"Yeah. The trouble with letters is that the writers have all sorts of background knowledge they don't bother to explain. Why should they? Their readers know it. But it leaves a modern researcher groping. Old Lady Page described the fire and clucked over the sad tragedy. Then she said—wait a minute. I wrote it down." Bruce pulled a notebook out of his pocket. "Here we go: 'Some have been heard to say that it is a judgment for his having withdrawn, not only from the offices of his neighbors but from the loving kindness of God following his affliction, he not having been seen at the services these thirty years. But I am sensible of his former zeal as a true Samson among the Philistines, not only in support of the Sunday laws, but in despising the heretics who are now so favored by the wretches across Rock Creek.'"

Bruce closed the notebook.

"Then she starts to complain about how dear muslin has become. She's a rip-roaring old Tory. Her handwriting was vile, too."

"Who were the wretches across Rock Creek?"

"The distinguished officials of the United States Government," Bruce said with a grin. "Many Georgetowners resented having the seat of government so close, and some were lukewarm about the whole idea of independence."

"How about the heretics?" Ruth asked. "The old lady had a fine vocabulary, didn't she?"

"She was a mean old bitch," Bruce replied briefly. "The heretics, I'm pretty sure, were the Catholics. They weren't allowed to build churches around here until after the Revolution, you know."

"The letter is funny, all right, but not, I expect, in the sense you meant," Pat said. "What struck you as odd?"

A mockingbird swung from a branch of bittersweet and addressed them mellifluously. Bruce contemplated the bird before answering.

"Let me restate what she says. Douglass Campbell, back in the 1770's, was a good devout Protestant and a man of some substance—you got that reference to supporting the Sunday laws? Then something happened to him—some affliction—and he shut himself up in his house. He didn't even go to church. There is no mention of anyone else's dying in the fire, which suggests that he was a widower or a bachelor."

"If the heir was his nephew, maybe he was a bachelor," Sara said.

"Bachelors were rarer in those days," Pat pointed out.

"He could just as well have been a widower whose children had died young. Infant mortality was high."

"Maybe that was the affliction," Sara said. "The death of a child, an only child."

"Hmm." Pat leaned back against the tree, staring up through the leafless branches at the cloudless blue sky. "Possibly. You know, Bruce, we may be interpreting the clue of the book too literally. Our invisible informant may have wanted to indicate a date, not a connection with a specific event."

"I thought of that. You realize that the Page letter gives us that cross-check we hoped for? The affliction occurred thirty years before the fire, which was in 1810. That takes us back to the crucial year, 1780. But I can't get around the fact that the Loyalist Plot involved Georgetown and Georgetowners. Can that be a coincidence?"

"Was Campbell a Tory?" Ruth asked.

"He wasn't involved in the Plot, that's for sure; the book mentions not only the names of the men who were hanged, but also the ones who were accused and acquitted."

"Maybe," Pat suggested, "he was one of the loyal— damn it, terms are confusing—loyal Patriots who helped foil the Plot. Then, thirty years later—"

"That's rather long to wait for revenge," Bruce said.

"So he died a natural death. But he could have suffered his affliction during the Plot. Some personal tragedy. Maybe he was blinded, or crippled."

"Or he could have lost his child or his wife or his money." Bruce banged his knee with his fist. "Damn it, we're just guessing. It's all so vague!"

"If you could find out whether he was married and all like that, it might help?" Sara asked anxiously, with the air of a mother looking through her purse for a lollipop. "Ruth, what about the genealogy?"

"Good gracious, I am a dolt," Ruth exclaimed. "Of course—the Bible."

"What Bible?"

"It's old; I don't know how old, but the pages are so fragile they crumble when you touch them. Cousin Hattie kept it wrapped in dozens of layers of plastic. It's one of those enormous ancient Bibles with a family tree in the front, and it was kept up for generations. Sara, there's a copy of the genealogy somewhere—in the desk, I think. See if you can find it. I hate to disturb the book, I've been meaning to take it to some museum to see about preserving it, but. . . ."

Sara was off, her hair flying. She came back with a sizable scroll, which Ruth passed on to Bruce without unrolling it.

"This must have been Hattie's copy. She was rotten with family pride."

Bruce unrolled the parchment on the grass; his black head and Sara's bent over it.

"Here's Douglass," Bruce said, his finger tracing the family tree, with its brilliantly colored coats of arms and crabbed writing. "Halfway down the tree. Wow—Cousin Hattie wasn't modest, was she? Here's Robert the Bruce back here, and Alfred, King of England. . . . This later part looks a little more authentic. She must have picked it up from family papers and tacked the royalty on to make it look more impressive."

"Her writing was nothing to brag about either," Sara said, crouched over the scroll.

"Get your hair out of the way." Bruce brushed at it; his hand lingered, but not for long. "Douglass Campbell, 1720–1810. Married Elizabeth Sanger, 1740–1756. . . ."

Sara caught her breath.

"Sixteen years old! That must be wrong."

"Not necessarily," Ruth said. "They did marry young. If

he married her when she was fifteen, and she died, perhaps in childbirth. . . ."

"Yes, look here. There was a child, born the same year, 1756. . . . That's funny," Bruce said. "No name. Just a question mark."

Sara sat up, tossing her hair back over her shoulders.

"What a terrible thing. Sixteen years old, dying when she had her baby. . . . That's four years younger than I am."

"If I were a parent," Ruth remarked, "I couldn't let that one pass."

"You'd be right too, much as I hate to admit it." Sara smiled at her. "So we don't have it so bad these days. And he was . . . let's see. . . ." She crouched over the chart again. "He was thirty-five when he married her, twenty years older. . . ."

"A real aged creep," Pat said morosely. "Thirty-five, my God."

"Oh, Pat! To a girl of fifteen—"

"Maybe he was romantic as hell."

"And maybe not."

"Bruce, what's the matter?" Ruth asked, interrupting the dialogue.

"I'm trying to figure out why Douglass's only child has no name."

"Maybe it died before it was baptized," Sara suggested.

"I don't think they would even mention a stillborn child, and any other would have been baptized. The dates are odd, too—1756, and then a blank. Do you suppose Cousin Hattie got this from the family Bible?"

"I don't think the Bible could be that old," Ruth said. "Do you mind if I look?"

"Well, I do, rather. It's very fragile."

"I'll be careful."

Ruth looked at his protruding lower lip and grimaced. She was coming to know that expression well.

"All right," she said coolly. "Sara, it's in the lower drawer of the bookcase. . . ." She shivered. The sun had gone behind a cloud and the garden suddenly looked bleak and depressing. "Let's all go in," she said. "It's getting cold."

The book was enormous. It was wrapped in two layers of plastic and one of faded silk. As Ruth carefully unswathed it, on the piecrust table in the living room, Pat gave an exclamation.

"What criminal neglect! This should have been under glass years ago. The old lady's cheap plastic bags are no substitute."

"I meant to have it looked at, but you know how it is. . . ."

"You find the place, Ruth," Bruce ordered. "I'm afraid to touch it. Sorry; I didn't realize how delicate it was."

Ruth found the place, at the cost of some destruction. The yellowing pages were almost impossible to touch without crumbling the edges.

"Goodness," she said, forgetting her irritation with Bruce in her interest. "Here's Douglass—the first name. Looks as if he must be the original ancestor."

"He was probably the first one to emigrate," Bruce said. "Starting a new line in a new land, that sort of thing."

"I keep telling you, I don't know a thing about the family history. But he was a Scot; a lot of them left in something of a hurry after the '45."

"This must have been his Bible," Sara exclaimed. "How amazing. Two hundred years old!"

"And a bit," Pat said. "He wrote a fine, bold black hand, didn't he?"

They contemplated the page in awed silence. It is said that Americans are unduly impressed by sheer age, being so relatively young in the world scheme themselves. But there was something breathtaking about the angles and curves of the thick black ink, unfaded by time—the visible remnant of a man whose other remains were long since dust.

"Campbell and wife," Pat muttered. "Here she is— Elizabeth. . . . Yes, Hattie must have cribbed that part of the genealogy out of the Bible. The names and dates are the same."

"And here," said Bruce, in an odd voice, "is why there was a question mark for Douglass's child."

The entry was there: one name among the many blank spaces provided for possible progeny. It had been covered completely by a wide, dark blot.

"Somebody goofed," Sara said.

"Hardly." Bruce bent over the page till his delicately chiseled nose almost touched it. "This was deliberate; it's too neat to be accidental. Looks as if Douglass scratched the kid's name out. Corny, weren't they?"

"The ink used for the scratching out is paler than the original," Ruth said. "I can see marks underneath."

"You're right." Before Ruth realized what he was about, Bruce had begun picking at the page with his fingernail. A flake of blue ink chipped off.

"Bruce," she warned.

"It's okay, I'm not doing anything," Bruce said with palpable untruth, amid a shower of fine flakes. "This is cheap ink—locally made, maybe. It's coming. . . . That's an A, surely A-M—"

"Amaryllis," Sara suggested.

"Well, it obviously isn't Samuel," Pat said. "Damn. Another good theory gone west."

". . . A-N . . ."

"Amanias." Sara giggled.

"Shut up. . . . D . . . A."

"Amanda."

"A daughter," Ruth said.

"A bad daughter," Pat contributed.

Transfixed, Bruce remained in the same position, like Brer Rabbit stuck to the Tar Baby. When he straightened, his eyes had a wild glitter.

"Don't any of you see it? I guess maybe you wouldn't. I happened to run across it, as a nickname, in that book on Georgetown ghosts, and I never thought. . . ."

"What on earth are you talking about?"

"Not Sammie. Pat was right about that. But it is a name. It's not Samuel the voice is calling. It's Amanda. Ammie."

Chapter Eight

The first recognizable sound to come out of the babble was Pat's unmelodious baritone crooning, "I think he's got it," to the well-known tune from "My Fair Lady."

"You're awfully frivolous for an anthropologist," Ruth told him.

"Anthropologists have a reputation for frivolity. It's the wild lives we lead. 'Exotic sex customs among the Andaman Islanders. . . .' Sorry—I'm babbling. But, by God, now I really am convinced. It's too neat to be wrong."

"Almost too neat." Bruce tried to sound calm, but he was grinning from ear to ear. "But it's got to be right, it was so damned unexpected. I felt the same way you did, Pat; I was sure the name would be Samuel, and my heart went down into my boots when it wasn't."

"Then. . . . It is Douglass Campell who calls," Ruth said, and her tone sobered them all. "He's calling his daughter. Ammie. Who died. But she says she isn't dead. . . ."

Pat turned to look at her from the middle of the rug, where he had chasséd, a la Henry Higgins, to the tune of his song. The late afternoon sunlight slanted through the

164

window, setting fire to his coppery hair and exposing the
lines that had appeared around his mouth.

"Wait a minute, let's not jump to any more conclusions
than we have to. It was not death that caused a beloved only
daughter to be erased from the pages of the family Bible."

"Beloved?" Bruce repeated in a peculiar voice.

"Oh, all right, scratch the adjective. It just seemed to
me. . . ."

"Yes, well . . . the point remains." Bruce scowled; his
hand went up to his beard. "If she had died he'd have
recorded the year in the usual way. Let's see. There's no
record of any marriage for Amanda. In 1780 she was
twenty-four—a hopeless old maid, in those days. She must
have been the dutiful daughter who kept house for dear old
dad. What could she have done to make him want to
obliterate her name?"

Sara curled up on the couch, kicking her shoes off and
tucking her feet under her.

"They used to disinherit boys for disobedience," she
offered. "Like taking up a profession the father didn't
approve of."

"There were only two disgraceful professions open to
women in those days." Pat grinned. "The other one was the
stage."

"But Campbell was one of the gentry," Bruce objected.
"His well-bred daughter wouldn't cut loose at the sedate
age of twenty-four and join a bawdy house."

"Oh, men are so obtuse," Ruth said impatiently. "She
ran off, of course. With some worthless rapscallion her
father didn't approve of. Or she got pregnant by same."

"Is that the famous woman's intuition I keep hearing
about?" Pat was amused.

"Well, what else could the girl do?" Ruth demanded.
"This wasn't London, with its organized sin and gaudy
night life; it was a provincial village. And if she reached the

age of twenty-four without marrying, she'd be ripe for seduction by any glib male who passed through town."

"And they say men are cynical!" Pat shook his head.

"Oh, you're being silly. Let's have some sherry. We need to talk about this."

Ruth switched on the lights as she went out. When she came back, with a tray, the other three were still arguing.

"It doesn't matter," Bruce said, nailing down the essential point. "We'll probably never know what she did. The thing that matters is that she left, under a cloud."

"Okay, I'll buy that," Pat said, taking the tray from Ruth. "What does this do to our varied alphabetical apparitions?"

"The Voice is Douglass," Ruth repeated. "And if C and D—the entity that moved the book—are the same, then— then Douglass is trying to help us."

"Poor guy," Pat muttered.

"Why poor?" Bruce took a sip of his sherry, grimaced, and set the glass down. "Seems to me he was a mean old bastard. There's malevolence in that big ink blot."

"Oh, no, Bruce," Ruth exclaimed. "The voice is terribly pathetic; I've felt that all along. Of course he'd be angry at first, especially if she had left him to go to certain misery or disgrace. But afterward. . . . He still misses her and wants her back, can't you feel that?"

"I guess so." Bruce scowled at his glass.

"Is there something wrong with the sherry?" Ruth asked.

"Well, to tell you the truth—" He grinned sheepishly at her. "I can't stand sherry."

"Then for goodness sake don't drink it! You poor suffering martyr, when I think of all the times. . . . Make yourself a drink, the stuff is in the dining room."

"No, never mind. Thanks. Listen, it's getting late. Maybe—"

"Let's talk about our other apparitions," Pat interrupted.

"I want to get this straight while I can. We hypothesized two ghosts, one hostile and one neutral or helpful. I think what we learned today bears this out. Douglass may or may not be the Voice, but he certainly is not the entity who speaks through Sara."

"Of course," Ruth said slowly. "We forgot to make that point because it was so obvious. Apparition B is female. Not just the voice—the gestures, the manner. . . ."

"Oh, yes," Bruce agreed. He had forgotten his preoccupation with the time in contemplating this new idea. "No doubt about it, I'd say. Apparition B is Ammie, all right."

"Yes," Sara said. "I wonder what she wants."

"Ugh," Ruth said, with an involuntary shudder. "Nothing good."

"How do you know?" Bruce asked.

"Why, I—she—maybe I'm prejudiced, but there's something wicked about walking into another person's mind."

"Not very ladylike," Bruce said. "Maybe she was desperate."

"For what?" Ruth repeated. "And why Sara?"

"That's not hard." Bruce began pacing, hands behind his back. "Sara makes a perfect vehicle for Amanda—blood kin, same sex, approximately the same age."

"But what does she *want?*" Ruth slammed her fist down on the table, and the others stared at her. "I'm sorry," she muttered. "But this is. . . . Bruce, I think we've done amazingly well, far better than we ever hoped, and most of the credit goes to you. But don't you see—practically speaking, we haven't made any progress. What, precisely, are we going to do?"

"Ruth, we are doing something." Bruce stopped his pacing and sat down beside her. "If we can find out what the girl does want—"

"And suppose she wants Sara's body?"

It was out at last, the fear that had haunted at least three of the four. Ruth knew by Sara's face that this was not a new idea for her; surely it would be the ultimate in horror to feel one's own body slipping out of control—as annihilating as death, but malignant, personalized. And Bruce's silence showed that he had no immediate answer.

"That's only one possibility," Pat said; but his voice lacked conviction. "Maybe she wants to reach her father. To be forgiven."

"I don't really care what she wants," Ruth said clearly. "I want to get rid of her."

"There is a way," Pat said. "Bruce mentioned it, that first night."

"Exorcism. Well—why not?"

"You know what it signifies," Bruce said. "The ritual casts It—the intruder—out into oblivion."

"Why not?" Ruth repeated stubbornly.

"It does seem awfully final," Sara said, with a feeble smile.

"Worse than that. It probably won't work."

"It's worth a try," Ruth insisted.

Bruce glanced helplessly at Pat, and seemed to find some support in his answering shrug.

"Ruth, how the hell do you propose to go about it? I can see myself telling this yarn to some priest."

"What's the alternative?"

"Continuing to search for the rest of the story. We may find—"

"And we may not. Bruce, don't you see how dangerous it is to wait?"

"I see something else," Bruce said, in a voice that turned her cold. "Look at the window."

The balmy weather had betrayed them. It was not spring; it was late fall, almost winter, and however brilliant the sun it had to obey the laws of nature. In winter the sun sets earlier than in summer. The days are shorter. This day was over.

Ruth got to her feet. There was no sign as yet of the ominous thickening of the air near the window, but in this she preferred to take no chances.

"Come on, Sara," she said.

Then she saw her niece's face.

"No," said the light girl's voice. "No, not . . . help!"

"Good God," Pat whispered. "Do you think she heard what we said—Ammie?"

"I don't know." Ruth took a step forward, toward the stiff body of her niece. "Amanda. You are Amanda?"

"Ammie," the voice agreed, and faded into a sigh. "Help . . . Ammie."

The light outside the window was gone; Ruth was cold with apprehension, not only for what had happened, but for what might yet occur.

"Help you?" she said sharply. Her tone was the one she might have used to a stenographer at work, but she was unaware of the incongruity. "How can we help you? Why don't you go away and leave Sara alone? Go to—to your father."

Bruce moved, his eyes wide and startled; he held up one hand as if in warning. It was too late. The stiff figure on the couch doubled up and then soared erect, hands lifted.

"Father . . . no," It cried. "No, hate, hate, hate. . . ."

Ruth had never heard a word that expressed its own meaning so vividly. Sara's body stumbled clumsily to its feet, still clawing the air. No wonder it's awkward, Ruth thought, no wonder it speaks with such difficulty. It's like trying to drive an unfamiliar type of car, when you haven't driven for—for two hundred years. . . .

She cried out and fell back as the familiar, unrecognizable figure stumbled toward her, mouthing hate. Bruce was the first of the two men to move and he did so with obvious reluctance. Ruth saw the last vestige of color drain from his face when his hand touched the girl's arm, and she remembered, only too well, the reaction of her own body to contact with that abnormally occupied flesh. Bruce's mouth twisted as if in pain, but he kept his hold. Swinging the shambling figure around he brought his fist up in a careful arc. Sara folded like a doll, into his arms; and without a glance for anyone or anything else in the room, Bruce left—down the length of the living room, through the arch, and straight out the front door. If it had not been for Pat, Ruth would never have made it; his hand propelled her through the door. Huddled in his car they sat and watched the windows, where the folds of the satin curtains had begun to move.

II

They stood on the doorstep of the neat new house in its well-tended lawn. Pat's hand was on the knocker, but he was still arguing.

"Ruth, I wish you wouldn't do this."

"I told you you didn't have to come." She reached past him and pushed the bell.

"You'll need my help," he said significantly. "But I keep telling you; this man is not the right man. Let me try downtown—"

"I know this man personally and he knows me. That's important, considering how crazy—" She broke off, smiling formally at the elderly woman who had opened the door. "Is Father Bishko in, please? Mrs. Bennett to see him."

Father Bishko greeted them with the suave charm Ruth had encountered at several Georgetown dinner parties. He was a strikingly handsome man, with dark hair and gentle brown eyes. He blinked once or twice during Ruth's story, but did not interrupt. When she had finished he said mildly, "I—er—must confess, Mrs. Bennett, that you leave me— er—speechless. If anyone but you had told me this story—"

"I hope you consider my corroboration worth something," Pat interrupted.

"Naturally. If it had not been you two—"

"Then may we ask your help, Father?"

"But, my dear Mrs. Bennett!" Father Bishko waved his hands in the air. "This is not a project to be undertaken lightly."

"You can do it, can't you?"

"There is such a procedure," Father Bishko admitted.

"Then—"

"It is necessary to consult other authorities. For permission to act."

"Oh, dear." Ruth felt her smile sagging. "How long will it take?"

"Why, that is difficult to say. Several days, I expect. Assuming that the response is favorable."

"We can't wait. . . ." Ruth broke off, hearing her voice quiver.

"Is it that serious?" The priest's voice had more warmth; her distress had moved him more than her reasoned description.

"Yes, it is," Pat said. "Father, I know I haven't so much as made my confession for a good many years, but—"

"Are you by any chance trying to bribe me, Pat?" the priest asked. He sounded less vague, much younger, and wholly human; there was a faint grin on his face.

"With my immortal soul?" Pat returned the grin, and shook his head. "You know me too well, Dennie. But this lady is in serious trouble and she thinks you might be able to help her."

"You don't think so, do you?"

"Well, I—"

"Never mind. Well." Father Bishko rubbed his chin with a long ivory finger. "I'm not sure I can help either, but I'll certainly be happy to try. Suppose I drop by one day, just to look the situation over."

"Would you really?" Ruth was limp with gratitude and relief. "I don't know how to thank you."

"Don't get your hopes up," the priest warned. "If you weren't a pair of unbelievers I'd admit I have certain reservations about parts of the ritual. And, Pat—I don't believe in ghosts."

"Come on around this afternoon," Pat said, rising. "And we'll see what we can do to convince you."

When they were once more outside, Ruth turned impulsively to her companion.

"I'm sorry, Pat. Why didn't you tell me you and Father Bishko were friends?"

"Or that I, like Bruce, am a renegade?" Pat smiled down at her, not at all discomposed. "It seemed irrelevant."

"Well, he was awfully nice. It's funny; he didn't promise a thing, and yet I can't help feeling encouraged."

"That feeling is Dennie Bishko's stock in trade," Pat said, a bit grimly. "And that's why I said he wasn't the man for the job. Oh, sure, he's a howling success in a fashionable sophisticated parish; maybe he has even given genuine spiritual comfort to some people. But behind that handsome face of his there is not enough strength of faith or belief. We'd do better with a man from a slum parish— someone who has had to wrestle, if not with malignant spirits, at least with the vile things human beings do to one another."

"We'll see," Ruth said.

Pat took her elbow to help her across the street and

looked down ruefully at the shining head that barely reached his shoulder.

"In your own quiet, ladylike way, you're just as bullheaded as I am," he said.

III

It was many months before Ruth could recall that afternoon without an inward shudder. The Terror—and it rated a capital letter in her thoughts—was painful enough, but this episode violated a sense of human decency as well.

Father Bishko was looking slightly wary when she opened the door, but the charm of the house and of the formal tea service she had carefully arranged soon relaxed him.

"This is a selfish pleasure for me, in fact," he said, graciously waving away her expression of thanks. "I've longed to see this house. Now that our acquaintance has developed, I may venture to ask if we may include it on our house tour next spring. It's for a very worthy cause, you know."

"She may not be here next spring," Pat said, before Ruth could compose a suitably vague but pleasant reply. Father Bishko, accepting a cup of tea with lemon, looked up at him with an arch smile.

"Indeed? Well, we shall just have to make sure that if Mrs. Bennett does leave it will not be because her charming house is inhabited by unwelcome guests."

They had agreed, during an impassioned consultation the previous evening, that the clerical visitor should not be informed of the details they had worked out.

"It sounds convincing to us," Bruce had insisted, "because we've seen it develop and we've experienced the disturbances personally. But to an outsider it will seem absolute balderdash. If you inisist on this dam' fool stunt, just tell him it's spooks and let him cope."

"That's all he needs to know," Pat had agreed. "Furthermore, it will provide another check. If he sees anything, it will not be influenced by our descriptions."

Ruth was to recall, later, the strange expression on Bruce's face when Pat said this. Bruce had been, unaccountably, against the whole idea of exorcism. Or perhaps, Ruth thought, offering Father Bishko a plate of cookies, it was not so unaccountable. Bruce was probably as ill at ease as his coreligionist in the presence of a priest.

By now, though, Pat had gotten over his self-consciousness and was behaving charmingly. He and Father Bishko were reminiscing about their mutual school days, and both of them seemed to be enjoying themselves.

The streaks of sunlight on the floor were turning from gold to bronze before Sara came in. With her, of course, was Bruce, looking particularly bland and blank. He shook hands with the priest, bowing slightly as he did so, and joined amiably in a discussion of the avant-garde theater. After another half hour of polite chitchat, Father Bishko began making going-home signs.

"Mrs. Bennett, I assure you I'll try to bring your problem before my superiors at once. You'll forgive you if I was a bit brusque this morning—"

"Oh, you could never be that."

"Incredulous, then. But now that I've gotten to know you better, you and your charming niece. . . . Obviously, if this matter distresses you, it must be looked into. That in itself is cause enough for me to take action."

"You are very kind," Ruth said sincerely. "Especially since you must rely on our word alone for what is admittedly an extraordinary story."

"I could hardly expect you to conjure up an apparition for me," Father Bishko said with a smile.

"I was hoping we could do just that," Pat said. "It's getting on toward that time of day. . . ."

The priest put his cup on the table and looked up alertly.

"Do you mean that it consistently appears at a particular time? And, by the by, what is It? You haven't been very clear in your description."

"To the first question—no, not exactly, but It normally does not appear until after dark. As for a description—" Pat hesitated, and Father Bishko nodded.

"Yes, I quite see your point. Independent corroboration. Dear me; I must confess, this intrigues me."

"If you could stay a little longer. . . ." Sara suggested.

"Unfortunately, I'm dining out. In fact, I'm already late for an appointment." He smiled at Pat with the quick, mischievous look which undoubtedly entranced a number of his parishioners. "If you were alone in this, Pat, I'd suspect you of putting me on. As it is . . . well, my morbid curiosity is nearly at fever pitch. I would dearly love to see something of this sort with my own eyes."

Studying those bright, innocent eyes, Ruth was seized by a horrid qualm of apprehension which twisted her stomach muscles into knots. It was a common enough feeling, the sort of feeling that is hailed as a premonition if later events bear it out, and dismissed as "nerves" if they do not. Pat had been right. This nice, happy, shallow man must not encounter their dark visitant. His combination of rationalism and optimism would be the worst possible equipment for such a meeting; they might even act as a challenge to the malignant darkness.

"I'm sorry we can't oblige," she said with a forced smile, in the tone experienced hostesses adopt to indicate— to experienced guests—that the party is over. Father Bishko rose to his feet.

"Is your apparition confined in space as well as in time?" he asked, peering hopefully about as if he expected a misty white form to be lurking behind the couch.

"It comes—there," Pat said, pointing.

"Where? Here?"

Father Bishko stood motionless, his face lifted and his eyes half closed, as if he were listening to a voice inaudible to the others. Ruth's apprehension lightened momentarily. Perhaps he might sense something after all.

"No," Father Bishko said, in a matter-of-fact voice. "I sense nothing abnormal. But my gift does not lie along those lines, as I ought to have warned you."

"Nothing at all?" Pat asked. He was standing next to the slighter, shorter man and Ruth saw him give a quickly controlled shiver. The priest shook his head. Evidently he did not even feel the cold which was apparent to Pat.

Casually Bruce had wandered down the room into the entrance doorway, drawing Sara with him. From the gathering shadows of the hall his pale face, oddly distorted by the camouflaging beard, peered into the living room like a mask hanging on a wall.

"Before I go," Father Bishko said, "perhaps you would allow me to say a blessing. It can do no harm and—who knows?—it might do some good."

He bowed his head without waiting for the answer which common courtesy would have forced on Ruth. She was unable to speak. The formless apprehension had gripped her even more strongly than before, dulling all her senses but one. "Do no harm?" Or would it? She felt something now, just as, it is said, a few individuals sense an earthquake before the first tremor rips the earth apart. The signs were the same—the constricted, aching head, the breathlessness, the hushed air. And the sensation struck her dumb. She could not speak nor move, not even to call a warning.

Father Bishko, his eyes closed and his other senses

apparently unresponsive, had no warning from within. Pat had fallen back a few paces at the beginning of the prayer—a rather childish attempt at dissociation, Ruth thought at the time—and when the darkening of the air became visible, he recoiled still farther.

Thus it was from Bruce, hitherto demurely silent, that the shout came. He bellowed, "Father!" in a voice that would have roused the dead, and simultaneously the effect seemed to strike the priest. He opened his eyes then, to find himself face to face with a boiling, seething mass of blackness. It had taken shape with frantic speed—gathering strength with practice, Ruth wondered, or stimulated somehow by the presence of the priest? For Father Bishko, the effect was like waking from sleep to find a visage of dreadful, distorted hate pressed against one's own; the sudden shock of such abominable proximity would have been as bad as the horror itself. But this was infinitely worse; for few men can claim to have found themselves rubbing noses with evil incarnate.

Perhaps no human being could have withstood such a shock; and Father Bishko, despite his calling, was only human. He let out a high, shrill cry, and stumbled back; and the thing bubbled and slid after him.

Bruce's face disappeared, and then a flood of gray light poured into the hall as the front door opened. Ruth knew he was getting Sara out of the house.

Then she caught her breath as Father Bishko, in the doorway, turned at bay. She had never—as yet—seen a more magnificent exhibition of sheer courage, for the man was obviously frightened almost out of his wits. Shaking and pale, he nevertheless stood firm, and presented his crucifix to the face of the Adversary.

It stopped, swaying; again Ruth half expected to see a charred, smoking spot where it had been. For a second it seemed to shrink in, and she felt an upsurge of hope. But it was only gathering itself for the next move. With a sudden, jerking shiver it shook itself into a new shape. The column thickened and darkened, the top shrank and grew round; two projections shot out from a spot about three-fourths of the way up. Ruth cried out and threw her hands up before her eyes; in another moment the Thing would have had the form, but not the face, of a human being.

It was too much for flesh and blood to bear. Father Bishko finally broke, broke and ran, his face altering terribly, dropping the crucifix in his wild flight and sending Pat staggering back.

Not until that moment did Ruth realize that the sounds she had been hearing were coming from Pat. They were not cries of anger or fear, but they were, in a way, even more shocking. Pat was laughing.

IV

"I'll never forgive myself," Ruth said. "Never."

They sat in Pat's dusty living room. All the feeble aids of physical comfort had been applied—a bright fire, brandy glasses and cigarettes, draperies pulled against the night. Night lights, as Bruce had said, for the frightened children. Each time the efficacy of the gestures grew less; each time it took more effort to shut out the memory of the inconceivable.

"You've no reason to reproach yourself." Pat's face was lined with chagrin. "I'm the one who should be ashamed. To laugh at a man at a time like that. . . . But, you know—if you had seen his face—"

"I did," Ruth said. "Pat, call him again."

"Honey, he must have gotten home, or to help of some kind. Bruce saw him catch a taxi."

"I was so worried about you, Ruth," Sara said. "I

couldn't see how you were going to get out. But it just—
went away?"

"Yes, as suddenly as it came. It came for him—Father
Bishko—didn't it?"

"I'm afraid so," Bruce said tightly. The physical strain
seemed to be telling on him, even more than on the others;
his lean cheeks looked sunken, and the glitter in his eyes
was almost feverish. Strangely enough it made him look
younger instead of older.

"Why afraid?" Sara asked.

"Because the strength and rage are so violent. I swear, it
looked like a deliberate attack. But that's not all. I didn't
really believe any of the conventional symbols would affect
it, but I guess I was still hoping. . . ."

"It means we've found that one potential weapon does
not work," Pat agreed heavily.

"One? What potential weapons are there?" Ruth demanded.

"Oh, dozens, that's the trouble. The religious symbols
are the most popular—crucifix, holy water, prayer—but
there's garlic, iron, various herbs, beeswax, fire—you name
it. You can get rid of an evil spirit by transferring it into a
stone, or an animal. . . ."

"How?"

Pat glanced at her and laughed mirthlessly.

"I never imagined I'd use this book this way." He went
to the bookcase by the fire and pulled out a worn green
volume, one of a set that filled half the shelf. "Here's the
encyclopedia of magical lore, the recipe book for witches,
Frazer's *The Golden Bough*. I've acquired a few new ones,
but he has most of the tricks right here."

"Are you ruling them all out because the crucifix had no
effect?" Bruce asked. He joined Pat at the bookcase and
took down another volume of the set.

"I'm not ruling anything out. I just don't know where to begin. But can you really bring yourself to believe that we should hang a chicken around Sara's neck and wait for Ammie to move into it?"

"Fire," Bruce muttered. "That doesn't seem very helpful in the present case, does it?" He flipped another page.

"I remember the iron bit," Sara said. "It's in that lovely Kipling book, is it *Puck of Pook's Hill*, or the sequel? 'Iron, cold iron, is the master of them all. . . .'"

"I loved that book too," Ruth said, momentarily diverted. "The fairy people can't stand iron; that's because they aren't cute little sprites in nylon petticoats, but the Old People, the little dark people who used bronze and were driven underground by the iron weapons of the new invaders."

"How cute," Bruce said crushingly, without lifting his eyes from the book.

"Something about running water, too," Sara muttered.

"Or we could acquire some masks and dance around Sara banging pots," Pat said with sudden violence. "How can one decide which of two impossibilities is more possible?"

Bruce looked up.

"I thought we had agreed that this is possible. Damned if I see why you cavil over a little thing like devil dances, if you admit devils. Or," he added gently, "do you?"

"Of course I'm still fighting it," Pat shouted. "Everything I've been taught for fifty years is fighting it. Danm it, Bruce, allow me my moments of sheer incredulity, can't you?"

"I'm not sure I can." Bruce closed the book but kept one finger inside the pages; Ruth was reminded of that other book and the circumstances of its discovery. "Pat, if you weaken. . . . We need all the belief we can get."

"I'm trying."

"Are you? Or do you begin to suspect, again, that we're hallucinating? You can't claim anything so simple as schizophrenia now. Not with that ghastly thing in the parlor every afternoon."

"I don't make any such claim, of course."

"There's another possibility," Bruce went on carefully. "One we've not mentioned, but one which I'm sure has occurred to you."

"Some natural phenomenon? Gas, or subterranean tremors, or something?"

"No, not something. I mean fraud. Deliberate, conscious fakery."

"I'd have been a fool not to have thought of it," Pat said.

Bruce put one hand casually on the back of a chair. Ruth was the only person near enough to see that he was inobtrusively supporting a good deal of his weight on that hand, and to note the tiny beads of sweat on his upper lip.

"We know you aren't a fool. All right, let's drag it out and look at it; I hate things festering in the subconscious. If it were fraud, who would be promoting it—besides Sara?"

Sara smiled; Ruth gave a gasp of protest.

"Naturally Sara would have to be in on it," Pat said calmly. "She's Ammie. The medium as well—the séance was the opening gun in the affair."

"I had the dream," Ruth said.

"That could have been induced—by the same phonograph record or tape that produces the 'Ammie-Come-Home' voice."

"You're crazy," Ruth said indignantly. "And the—the Adversary? I suppose that could be produced by a tape?"

"It could be produced," Bruce said coolly. "I don't know how, just off hand, but I'll bet any good stage magician could reproduce any of the effects we have seen. Including the cold."

"And the story of Douglass Campbell and his daughter, which we so painfully ferreted out?"

"If we found it, someone else could. Someone who used it as the basis of the plot."

"You'd make a good Devil's Advocate," Pat said, smiling reluctantly. "Now you've got me turned around so that I have to defend the case. What about motive?"

"I can think of at least three possibilities, just off hand."

"One," Sara challenged.

"Someone wants to buy Ruth's house cheap," Bruce said promptly. "Buried treasure in the basement, maybe, or just a passion for old houses."

"Two?"

"Hatred. Of Ruth, or you, or even Pat. Get him mixed up in something like this and then expose it in a blaze of publicity. It wouldn't do his scholarly reputation much good. Three, some nut trying to prove spiritualism—and don't ask me to explain the kind of mentality that creates fakes to prove truths; I can't. I just know they exist."

"I see you've given the matter some thought," Pat said.

"I'm no fool either. Only I happen to know Sara wouldn't do such an insane thing. Of course there is that convenient item, hypnosis. Sara could be unwittingly producing her bit of the supernatural through posthypnotic suggestion."

"An outside villain?" Pat considered the suggestion.

"Not necessarily." Bruce cleared his throat. "I thought of you, naturally. In a mystery story you'd be the obvious suspect. You protest too much."

Pat choked; then his sense of humor came to the rescue, and he laughed.

"Okay, Bruce, you win again. We're committed. Let's be consistent in our folly, at least, and not waste time."

Bruce's breath came out in a louder gasp than was compatible with calm nerves. But he said coolly enough,

"Then let's look at Frazer. I balk myself at the Bantu ceremonies, but we could try some of the herbs. Vervain, Saint John's-wort, garlic—"

Sara giggled.

"What are you going to do, make a lei and hang it around my neck?"

"The big problem will be finding the stuff," Ruth said. "Garlic we can get, but vervain is not exactly in stock at the grocer's."

"You can look for it tomorrow," Bruce said. "It'll be a nice job, out in the open air for a change. Find out the scientific name of the stuff, it's in here someplace—" He was again flicking through the pages of Sir James Frazer's classic. "Funny," he muttered. "The standard remedies, in western culture, are the holy relics. We lost a big group there."

"You know," Sara said, "that reminds me of something I read—"

At the same time Pat remarked, "Maybe we need holier relics. A sliver of the True Cross or a bone of a saint."

And Ruth chimed in with, "Pat, do try to call him again!"

Faced with two people talking at once, Pat turned to Ruth.

"Okay, dear. If it will make you feel better."

The telephone was on a table by the couch. They could all hear the muffled ringing at the other end, and they heard the ringing stop when the instrument was lifted.

"Dennie?" Pat's face lightened. He had not voiced his concern, for fear of encouraging Ruth's, but it had been profound. "Are you all right? Where've you been?"

The listeners could hear the tinny rattle of the other voice, but could not distinguish words. For them the conversation was one-sided but perfectly intelligible.

"I'm more relieved than I can say. . . . No, no, Dennie, you mustn't feel that way; quite the contrary. Mrs. Bennett has been beside herself with worry. . . . Yes, she's here. . . . Sure."

Ruth took the telephone with some trepidation. The priest brushed her stumbling apologies aside; he had other, more important things on his mind.

"Mrs. Bennett, I've made an appointment, the first of the necessary steps for the procedure we discussed. It will take a little time; this is a busy archdiocese. In the meantime, I want you to promise me that you won't enter that house again, or allow anyone else to do so."

"But, Father. . . ."

"I am . . . deeply shaken and ashamed. I do not say this in defense of my own behavior, but in fear for you— this visitation is strong, strong and evil. You must not risk yourself."

"I know the sensations are dreadful," Ruth said, very much moved. "But you saw it at its worst—and faced it, may I say, with a courage that few people could have shown. But it is impalpable; I'm sure it can't do any physical harm."

"Physical?" Father Bishko's voice rose. "My dear, my dear—that is not the danger. Promise me. I shan't sleep tonight unless I have your promise."

"I promise," she said; and then, on request, handed the instrument back to Pat. A few more sentences passed, and then Pat hung up.

"Poor guy," he said. "He's all shaken up."

"It might not do him any harm," Bruce said sharply. "A priest, enduring the universe, ought to be shaken up now and then. People ought to be shaken up."

"The trouble with the young," Pat remarked, "is not that they speak in platitudes, but that they are so damned intense about them."

"Don't, Pat."

"Sorry, dear. We are none of us at our best." He ran his fingers through his hair so that it stood up in the familiar cockatoo crest. "What did you promise?"

"That I wouldn't go back to the house. I had to," she said defensively. "He was genuinely distressed. And say what you will, I feel responsible. We should have warned him."

Bruce gave her a disdainful glance. He did not need to tell her that he did not feel himself bound by her promise. All he said was, "He's going to try the exorcism?"

"When he gets permission."

"I have to admit I admire his guts, then," Bruce said grumpily. "If a little bitty prayer produced that outburst today, God knows what a full-scale exorcism will bring out. I wouldn't care to face it myself."

"Maybe it will work. He seems to think so."

"He's going on the theory that if one pill doesn't do the trick, maybe six pills will," Bruce said. "I'm afraid this is a case of if one pill doesn't work, why bother with more? The technique is wrong. Sara, let's start on *The Golden Bough*."

It was like a well-rehearsed play, Ruth thought; take your places for Act One, Scene Two. They had only played these roles for a few days, but they had come to accept them. Sara found pen and paper; she made an unorthodox secretary, squatting cross-legged on the hearth rug, with the falling waves of her hair curtaining her face. Bruce, shoulder against the mantel, slim height lounging, moved his hands as he spoke; Pat slouched in his worn leather chair with the light setting the crest of his hair ablaze and leaving his face shadowed, remote. And Ruth herself was on her way to the kitchen to put the coffeepot on, so that the great minds might be stimulated to think. In the doorway she paused, appreciating the warmth and homely charm of the family scene: the vivid colors of Sara's forest green skirt and sweater, Pat's coppery bright hair, Bruce's black-and-white elegance, the glint of light off the silver bowl on the table. They might have been any comfortable family, chatting casually after dinner.

"Transference into a tree," Bruce said. "Bore a hole in the trunk, insert a lock of the sufferer's hair. Then plug up the hole. . . ."

Ruth didn't know whether to laugh or cry.

Chapter Nine

They all overslept the next morning, and two of them refused breakfast.

"And it's not because I'm hung over, either," Ruth said sullenly. "I had the most ghastly dream last night—witch doctors in feathers and masks chasing Sara around a fire. It ended with somebody getting eaten, I'm not quite sure whom. Me, probably. I'll just have coffee, thanks."

Sara rose and obliged.

"I had a dream, too," she said; and something in her tone made the others stop in mid-swallow and mid-bite to look at her.

"Messages from the beyond?" Pat asked. His attempt at lightness was not a success.

"I don't know."

"Well, what did you dream?" Bruce asked.

Sara settled down with her elbows on the table. Ruth started to point out that her hair was unsanitarily involved with her plate of scrambled eggs, and then decided not to bother. There were obviously more important matters at stake.

"I dreamed I was in the house," Sara began. "Just

walking through the rooms. I started out in the kitchen, and it looked funny; I mean, I couldn't make out any of the details, just the view of the garden. The room was all blurry and unshaped. Then I walked through the dining room and things got a little clearer, but the furniture was still shapeless blobs."

She paused, her eyes dark with memory, trying to choose her words.

"I couldn't see into the living room. There was like a curtain pulled over the doorway. In the hall things were still misty, but I noticed one thing. The cellar door was open."

"The cellar again," Bruce muttered. "Damn it, I just don't see. . . ."

Pat waved him to silence.

"Was that all you dreamed?"

"No, there was one bit more. I tried—I wanted—" Again she paused; she had gone a trifle pale. "This was the only bad part," she said. "I told you what happened in the dream, but I haven't described the atmosphere. The feeling of it. I was anxious all through this, but not really frightened; just—like trying to sneak something out of the house before Mother could catch me. But it kept building up, the anxiety, and when I was in the hallway I knew I was getting near the source of the trouble. I wanted to go into the living room. But I couldn't. Something held me back, something that almost gibbered with terror. Finally the struggle got to be too much. I woke up."

She took a large bite of toast, and Ruth said, in a voice that was tart with relief, "You don't seem particularly upset this morning."

"No, I told you it wasn't that bad," Sara said thickly.

"The cellar," Bruce mumbled. "It must mean something."

"What?" Pat demanded. "We looked once. There wasn't an extra cobweb that shouldn't have been there."

"Something under the cellar?" Sara said. Ruth looked at her, somewhat startled.

"Douglass Campbell's buried treasure?"

"God, I hope not," Bruce said morosely. "The floor is concrete. If we have to drill that out and then excavate the whole bloody floor area—"

"Our spirit guides are going to have to be a little more specific before I tackle that one," Pat agreed. "I suggest that if the dream does have meaning it lies in the latter part. The suggestion that there is something in the living room that we haven't found."

"Books?" Ruth guessed wildly. "There are more of Hattie's in the bookcase at the back, the same one the Maryland history book came from."

"It sounds crazy," Bruce said despondently. "But we might as well look. I keep thinking that, with the old lady's interest in family, there ought to be more in the house that we've missed."

"I promised Father Bishko—"

"Well, I didn't," Bruce said. "I wouldn't consider such a promise binding, Ruth. I'd like you to come, if only to show me likely places to look, but you don't need to."

"Bruce is right," Pat said. "I don't consider myself bound by any such promise."

Bruce studied him thoughtfully; Ruth thought she could see the dark eyes weighing possibilities.

"There's something you could do that would be a helluva lot more useful."

"What's that?"

"Trot over to Annapolis," Bruce said.

"What the hell for?"

"State papers. I've gone through most of the material at the Library of Congress, but there are all kinds of local records at Annapolis. Two such collections—the Red and Blue Book papers—have letters relating to Georgetown people during this period. And somebody ought to look through the newspapers. *The Maryland Journal and Baltimore Advertiser* is the one covering our period, I think. They'll have it on microfilm at Annapolis."

Pat's face took on the stubborn look Ruth was coming to know so well. She could understand his reaction. Bruce was right; but his glibness and inclination to assume authority were extremely irritating.

"Why don't you go?"

"A, I don't have a car. B, I lack your academic prestige. And C," he added quickly, as Pat's mouth opened in protest, "I'm having trouble with my eyes and I'd rather not drive."

"I didn't know you had eye trouble," Sara said. "Bruce, what is it?"

"I have to use drops, and they blur my sight," Bruce said.

"But you never told me—"

"What do you expect me to do, give every girl I date a list of my physical disabilities? Forget it. Well, Pat?"

"I can hardly refuse, can I? Okay. I'd better start right away. It's getting late."

"We'll meet you back here about six," Bruce said. "The Hall of Records probably closes about four or five. We'll have left the other house by that time, so don't go there. Can you give us an extra key, in case we get here before you do?"

"All right," Pat said without enthusiasm.

He got up and promptly tripped over Lady, who was, as predicted, flat on the floor in front of her food dish.

"Stupid dog," Pat said automatically.

Lady moaned.

Bruce stared at the dog.

"Hey, Pat. Can we borrow Lady?"

"What in heaven's name for?"

"As a canary," Bruce explained.

Sara giggled, Ruth stared, and Pat explained, "He's not over the edge yet. They used to use birds in coal mines in the old days to detect the presence of lethal gases. Being so much smaller the birds passed out before the concentration got high enough to damage men. You may certainly borrow Lady, but you ought to consider three factors. First, you will probably have to carry her out to the car, and she weighs almost as much as Sara; second, we have no proof that the supposed sensitivity of animals to supernatural influences is anything more than an old wives' tale; third, even if most animals are sensitive, Lady is such a lump that she probably wouldn't stir if Satan himself came up and leered in her face."

"I'll risk it," Bruce said. "It's worth a try."

As she went in search of her purse and coat, Ruth knew that there was one implication of the dream which none of them cared to explore, or even comment upon. If Sara had been visited in sleep, then her immunity was broken. She was no safer out of the house than in it.

II

Bruce refused Pat's offer to drive them to the house. Ruth felt almost certain that he had been lying about his eye trouble. The conclusion was inescapable: He did not want Pat to come with them. Why?

On the way over, Bruce made the taxi stop before a supermarket. He came out carrying a small bag and wearing a slightly sheepish expression. He refused to let Sara see what was in the bag. She took it as a joke, teasing and pretending to snatch; but Ruth could not enter into the game. Doubt assailed her. Was it possible that, after all, she had been led astray, her weakness expertly played upon by an unscrupulous or deranged young man? When they reached the house it took all her willpower to force her to enter. With every visit the atmosphere got worse; the whole house now seemed to vibrate with sounds just below the range of hearing, the air to quiver with unseen forces. Her newborn doubts made the situation even more unpleasant.

Once inside, however, Bruce seemed to improve. At least his odd behavior about his purchase was explained, to Ruth's satisfaction, when she saw what it was. Bruce opened the bag in the kitchen and produced a handful of objects that looked like little gray-white oranges.

"Garlic!" Sara said, with a whoop of laughter. Then she suddenly sobered. "Oh, no, you're not," she said, backing away. "Oh, no!"

"Oh, yes." Bruce eyed his purchase doubtfully. "Ruth, have you got a drill? I don't know how else—"

"I think a big darning needle," Ruth said, smiling. "I suppose you want to release the juices? Otherwise we could just tape the bits all over her."

Sara exclaimed in outrage, and Bruce began to laugh.

"What a gaudy picture! We'll settle for the conventional necklace."

When it was done, Sara studied herself critically in the mirror and admitted, "It's not bad. I've seen worse-looking things in those psychedelic shops on Wisconsin."

"And you could always give away a free set of nose plugs with each ensemble," Ruth suggested, pinching her nostrils together.

"I don't know what you're complaining about," Sara said. "You're a lot farther away from it than I am. Luckily I like the smell of garlic."

They dragged the banter and laughter out a little too long, reluctant to leave the warm modernity of the kitchen for that other room. But when they entered, they found Lady stretched out in front of the fireplace, and Ruth's spirits rose. Up to this point they had not found the conventional trappings of the supernatural particularly reliable, so Lady's calm was meaningless until it had been tested—an eventuality which Ruth hoped would never occur. But she felt, somehow, that it would be impossible for anything to look so comfortable unless the room really was clear. Bruce obviously felt the same way; he made a detour just to scratch Lady behind the ears. She twitched one of the ears feebly but made no other acknowledgment, and Bruce said, as he straightened, "That dog manages to convey the impression that she's worn out from a hard day's work. I wish I knew how to do it."

"It makes me feel one hundred percent better just to look at her," Ruth said. "Now. Where do we start?"

"Here." Bruce advanced upon the bookcase.

They found several astounding things, including a copy of *Ruth Fielding in the Rockies*, whose cover showed an adventurous damsel in long skirts and a pompadour preparing to mount a horse. Sara appropriated this masterpiece, and sat chortling over it for some time, reading excerpts aloud.

"It's the old-time equivalent of Nancy Drew," she said. "Imagine Cousin Hattie keeping this around."

"Who's Nancy Drew?" Bruce asked, distracted.

"The girl's equivalent of the Hardy Boys," Ruth said. "Bruce, here's something called *Recollections of Old Georgetown*."

"No soap. I looked through it at the library." Bruce got up off the floor in one effortless movement. "Nothing else. Let's try the attic."

Ruth groaned with dismay at the sight of the place; she had forgotten how many articles had been put away "till I have time to sort through them." There were boxes and cartons and old trunks and suitcases; there was a dress form, and a chair with one leg broken, and a sofa that had lost most of its stuffing. There was an untidy stack of old pictures. . . .

"I wonder," Bruce said, heading toward them, "if anybody we know is here?"

Nobody was. The pictures were daguerreotypes of desperately bearded gentlemen and grim-faced ladies, or engravings of classical subjects in funereal black frames.

"You wouldn't find anything that old in the attic," Ruth said, as Bruce tossed the last of the pile aside with a gesture of disgust. "Colonial portraits are chic; they would be downstairs."

"I can't help wondering what she looked like," Bruce murmured. Ruth nodded.

"I know. I've wondered too. But it would be too much luck to discover a portrait of her."

"I guess so. Well . . . I'll take the big trunk, you take the little one."

They worked steadily for three more hours and then stopped for a quick lunch. Lady roused at that—Sara swore she heard the can opener being removed from the drawer—and dragged herself out to the kitchen to indicate that she might consider joining them. Bruce pointed out that she was only supposed to be fed twice a day, but the argument convinced neither Lady nor Sara, who persisted in sneaking tidbits to her under the table.

The hours in the airless, dusty attic had given Ruth a headache, so after lunch they adjourned to the living room, whither Bruce had taken several promising-looking cartons. They spent an unprofitable and increasingly tedious afternoon reading yellowing newspapers and clippings of recipes, fashions and gossip columns—all fascinating under most circumstances, but none dating back to the period they were interested in. Finally Ruth's eyes gave out; she rose, stretching cramped muscles, and went to draw the drapes. The sunlight was too explicit; it showed the dust on tables and bookcases.

"Don't do that," Bruce said, looking up. "I don't want to lose track of the time. You ought to have a clock in this room."

"Don't you trust the garlic?" Sara asked lightly.

"No, and I suspect Pat may be right about Lady. She doesn't look very sensitive."

"She wants me to light the fire," Sara said.

Bruce gave the recumbent rump of Lady a disparaging glance.

"How can you tell?"

"She communicates. Telepathy."

"Go ahead and light it," Ruth said. "It seems chilly in here to me. . . ."

She stopped, with a catch of breath, but Bruce shook his head.

"No, it's not that kind of cold. I turned the thermostat down when we came in."

Sara crawled over to the fire, and soon the flames were leaping up. Lady grunted appreciatively and rolled over.

"Stupid dog," Sara said affectionately.

"Are you giving up?" Bruce asked severely. "There are two more boxes upstairs."

"We'd better have some coffee," Ruth said. "I'm falling asleep over this stuff."

When she came back with the tray she found her assistants in a state of semicollapse, Sara in her favorite prone position before the fire and Bruce stretched out vertically across the couch like an exclamation mark. They stirred when she put the tray down.

"I guess we'd better not start another box," Bruce said, with a wide yawn. "Wait a minute. There was one thing I did want to look at. The cellar."

"But we've been down there," Ruth said. The coffee had revived her a bit, but she was not fond of the gloomy basement.

"One more look." Bruce's beard jutted out in a way which was becoming too familiar.

"Shall we take Lady?" Sara asked.

"Not unless you feel like carrying her down. I don't."

At Bruce's suggestion Ruth found a flashlight and located a hammer and screwdriver in the pantry drawer when he asked for tools. He gave the screwdriver back to her but kept the hammer; and when they had descended the stairs he began banging on the walls.

"My dear boy," Ruth said, amused.

"We've tried everything else." Bruce vanished behind the furnace. The beam of the flashlight wavered like a big firefly, and steadied. "By God! Ruth, come here."

"Not on your life." Ruth advanced to the side of the furnace and peered behind it. "What's back there?"

She could see for herself. No one had made any attempt to hide it, but she had never poked her nose into the dark, spidery corner.

"A door. Where does it go to, I wonder?"

Bruce gave the encrusted wooden panel an exploratory tap with the hammer. The sound that came back was not encouraging; it had a solid thunk that denied any idea of empty space.

"The panels must be six inches thick," he said. "This isn't a door, it's a barricade. And it's going to be a helluva job breaking it down."

"Why should we want to break it down?" Ruth asked in surprise. "This part of the cellar is bad enough."

Bruce sneezed violently and wiped his face with his sleeve. He backed out of the corner. His eyes were bright with excitement and his beard was draped with cobwebs.

"The outer part of the cellar only goes under the dining-kitchen area. This other section must lie beneath the living room. Once upon a time somebody was moved to block it off. That would be reason enough to explore it, even without the other clues."

"Oh, dear," Ruth said blankly. "I don't think I like this."

"I don't either. I'm the one who'll have to swing the ax. But it's got to be done."

"Bruce, I don't even own an ax. There's a little hatchet someplace. . . ."

"No, I'll have to pick up some tools. This is going to be a rough job. And I don't intend to start today, it's getting late. Why don't we—"

At the top of the cellar stairs the door stood open. They heard the sounds at the outer, street door—the turn and click of the knob, the slam of the door closing. Footsteps echoed in the hall.

Ruth's reaction was puzzlement rather than alarm. Those sounds were not connected in her mind with the manifestations. Bruce's response alarmed her more than the sounds. He made a convulsive movement with the flashlight in his right hand. The footsteps were on the stairs now. Before Ruth had time to be frightened Pat's familiar form came into view.

"I thought you'd still be here," he said. "Wait till you hear—"

"I told you not to come to the house," Bruce said shrilly.

"I finished early." Pat raised his eyebrows and sat down unceremoniously on the bottom step. "What are you all doing down here?"

"Bruce found another part of the cellar," Sara explained. "There's a door, all blocked up, behind the furnace."

"Really?" Pat's eyebrows shot up to his hairline. He stood up and wandered over to investigate the discovery, and Ruth felt her neck prickle, for as the older man passed him, Bruce made another of those abortive, violent gestures.

"I can't see much." Pat drew back. "It's not important anyhow."

"How do you know it's not?" Bruce asked.

"Because today I found out the missing parts of the story." Pat beamed, waiting for the effect of his verbal bombshell to be felt. "I know what happened to Amanda Campbell."

"Really? Pat, that's marvelous."

"How did you find out?"

The two women spoke at once. Bruce said nothing.

Pat propped himself up against the wall.

"It was in the newspaper," he said. "Amazing, eh? I found it right away; if I were endowed with psi faculties, I'd think I had been led to it."

He took a deep breath, prepared, it was clear, to launch into a detailed account.

"Let's go to your place and you can tell us all about it," Bruce said.

Pat glared.

"You trying to spoil my effect? What's the matter—mad because the wild goose chase laid a golden egg after all?"

"Pat, of course we're pleased," Ruth said hastily. "I'm dying to know. What did happen to Ammie?"

Pat's scowl relaxed.

"You were right, Ruth, I'll never sneer at your intuition again. She did elope. Wait a minute, let me read this to you. It's classic. I copied it word for word."

He searched the pockets of his overcoat and jacket before he found the paper. Bruce moistened his lips nervously and shifted from one foot to the other. Ruth met his eye and shrugged slightly. Short of picking him up bodily she did not see how they were going to move Pat. He was never very amenable to suggestion, and this afternoon he seemed so delighted by his find that he was more stubborn than ever. Undoubtedly the boy's earlier successes had riled him; he was prepared to rub this one in just a bit.

"Here it is," Pat said, unfolding his paper. "You know, I didn't realize they did this sort of thing back in Colonial times. It's like a 'Whereas' ad in a modern newspaper, only much more detailed." He cleared his throat and began to read:

"With regret and shame the undersigned finds himself under the necessity of advertising his daughter. Painful though it may be to a fond parent, he does by these presents make known that Amanda, his daughter, has eloped from his house with one Anthony Doyle, Captain in the Army of Independence, who has long attempted to seduce her from her faith and her loving duty to her parent, and has finally succeeded; for which her disconsolate father does not hold her to blame, but promises that, should she discover her error and regret her sin, she shall be received into his home without question." Pat glanced up. "The signature," he concluded, "I leave to your imaginations."

"Douglass Campbell," Ruth whispered. "Oh, Pat, you were right too—the poor man."

"You two are prejudiced," Sara said, lifting a firm chin. "You always side with the parents. I think it was frightful of him to make a public announcement of her elopement!"

"The ad was meant for her," Pat said. "Can't you read the real meaning? He wasn't trying to shame her, he wanted her to know that she could always come home."

"That's sweet, I'm sure," Sara said impudently. "But I'll bet she was glad to get away. Who wouldn't prefer a dashing Irishman, and an officer at that, to a dull dad?"

"Perhaps the young man had tried to court her properly," Ruth said, trying to be fair; she was somewhat stung by Sara's remark about prejudice. "And Douglass considered him unsuitable."

"Naturally," Pat said. "He was Catholic."

"How do you—oh, that business about seducing her from her faith. And it's an Irish name, of course. . . ."

"A Catholic and a Patriot," Pat said. "Campbell was a fiercely intolerant Protestant and a Tory. She couldn't have picked a more unpopular combination in a boyfriend."

"You're awfully damn dogmatic about your deductions," Bruce said spitefully.

"They seem quite reasonable to me," Ruth said, trying to make peace; Pat's face had darkened again.

"Okay, okay," Bruce mumbled. "Do you mind if we—"

"I wonder what Doyle was doing in Georgetown?" Sara said. "Were there any battles in these parts?"

"There must have been a detachment guarding the British prisoners," Pat said. "He may have been in command of that."

"We might look him up," Ruth suggested. "Aren't there army records? We don't even know where he came from. Maybe he took Ammie home, wherever home was."

"Camden, New Jersey," Pat said absently. He was staring at the furnace with his forehead slightly furrowed, as if some new, disturbing thought had just entered his mind.

"Was that in the newspaper too?" Bruce asked. He had become very still, the nervous gestures in abeyance; and his eyes seemed to want to follow Pat's gaze toward the blocked and hidden door.

Pat did not reply. Bruce walked toward him, stepping delicately.

"Pat, could we—look, I don't know what time it is, but it must be late. Can't we adjourn now?"

"Sure," Pat said. "It's a nasty night out, though. It started to rain when I turned off Wisconsin, and the wind is rising."

The words were simply descriptive; there was no reason why they should have created such an unpleasant picture in

Ruth's mind. When she reached the top of the stairs she could not repress an exclamation of dismay. The splintered reflection of the streetlight brightened the fanlight over the door. It was not quite night, but it was too near to be comfortable—dusk, twilight, deepening into darkness. She plunged toward the hall closet where they had left their coats, calling Sara.

Bruce was the third person up the stairs, and he was as anxious as Ruth to be gone. Pat, still carrying his coat, followed them obediently along the hall. Ruth thought he seemed subdued, and attributed it to their reception of his news. She promised herself she would make it up to him as soon as they reached a safe place.

Safe. . . . The house was not. She could almost hear the humming, like an electric motor, plugged in and building up a charge. . . .

"Wait a minute," Pat said, as Bruce reached for his raincoat. "Where's that stupid dog?"

"Oh, goodness, I almost forgot her." Ruth, already wearing coat and hat, went back toward the living room. It was in darkness except for a faint glow from the fire, but she could make out Lady's silhouette, like a low lump, against the reddish glare. She switched on the lights.

"Come on, baby," Pat said.

Bruce dropped his coat.

"I'll get her. Pat, why don't you go on out and—uh—get the car started?"

"The car'll start when I want it to," Pat said, giving him a puzzled look. "Get up, Lady, come with Papa."

Ruth stood just inside the doorway, her hand still on the light switch. As she watched Bruce her suspicion and alarm came back in double strength. He was so nervous that she expected momentarily to see him start wringing his hands. He vibrated distractedly just outside the door, looking from Sara, who watched him in growing bewilderment, to Pat, who was nudging the dog's snoring form with his toe. Indecisiveness was not normally one of Bruce's problems.

"I am not going to carry you," Pat told his dog. She was not visibly moved by the statement.

Bruce hunched his shoulder, in a gesture that resembled a shudder, and made up his mind. He plunged into the room like a swimmer entering a lake in December.

"I'll carry her," he said. "Pat, you go on and—"

"Are you crazy?" Pat demanded. "She'll walk, it just takes me a while. . . ."

"She'll come for me," Sara said. She threw her coat down on a chair and entered the living room. "Lady, baby, come to Sara."

They were all there. It came to Ruth with the sharpness of a blow in the face. They were all in the living room and night crouched outside the walls. She could hear the wind moaning like a frightened child around the eaves, and through the trees, lashing the windows with raindrops.

"Sara," she said, her voice strangely hoarse. "Sara."

At the same moment Pat bent over to touch the dog.

Lady roused. She came up stiff-legged and aware, in the instantaneous response to peril which no human being can learn. Her haunches had been under the coffee table; she sent it over, spilling decanter, glasses, and ashtrays. Ruth did not even glance at the havoc. She had eyes only for the dog—for Lady, the somnolent, who stood with every hair on her neck up and bristling, with lips drawn back to display long ivory fangs. Her dark eyes were fixed on her master; and for a moment Ruth thought the hundred pounds of bone and muscle and tearing fangs were about to spring. But what happened was, in its way, infinitely worse. The snarl in Lady's throat changed to a horrible whine. She dropped to her belly and began to crawl, whimpering like a puppy. When she had cleared the couch she sprang up and fled. Ruth heard the crash of the heavy body against the front door, and the howl, the almost human howl of frustration and terror when the door refused to yield. Then there was another muffled crashing sound, and silence.

Ruth had no conscious memory of having moved. Her body had simply recoiled, with the same sort of reflex that jerks a hand back from a licking flame. There was no way out through the door, it was too perilously close to the spot where, once again, the foul blackness seethed and coiled. It was stronger tonight, worse than she had yet seen it, as if it drew strength from each successive appearance. And the cold beat at them in pulsating, paralyzing waves.

"The French doors," a voice said. "Out . . . into garden. . . ."

Ruth's retreat had carried her halfway down the length of the room. She stood pressed up against the wall, next to the round piecrust table. She could not turn her back on the blackness, nor could she bring herself to look at it directly; it contaminated the air by its very existence; it was an affront, a violation of normalcy so acute that it amounted to blasphemy.

And Pat was facing it. Ruth felt a touch of dim pride that penetrated even her terror as she saw him stop after the first automatic withdrawal. His face was hard and expressionless; his feet were planted widely apart, like those of a man thigh-deep in racing water.

By contrast, Bruce made a pitiable showing. Stumbling, making odd inarticulate sounds, dragging Sara by the hand, he retreated toward the tall French doors at the end of the room. When he reached them he dropped Sara's hand and began struggling with the catch that held the windows closed. The clumsiness of fear frustrated his intent; the catch refused to give, and when Bruce brought his fist down on it, his hand slipped, slamming into one of the glass panes. The glass broke, letting in a gust of freezing rain; and Bruce pulled back a hand that was streaming blood from half a dozen cuts. He held it up before his face, staring blindly.

"Bruce—wait—" Ruth found speech incredibly difficult. Her vocal cords, like her other muscles, seemed frozen.

The boy heard her; he whirled around, his movements still erratic and undisciplined. Then his expression changed, altering his features so terribly that if Ruth had met him on the street she would not have recognized him. He plunged forward; his hands clawed at Pat's sleeve.

"Pat . . . don't. For God's sake—"

"It can't hurt," Pat said dully. "Can't hurt me. Let go. Got to do something. . . ."

"Don't . . . no . . . stop. . . . Pat, wait, let me tell you—"

Pat's rigidly controlled expression did not change. He simply lifted his heavy shoulders and heaved. Bruce went reeling back, missing the fireplace by two feet, and hit the wall so hard that one of the pictures fell with a crash.

There had been no sound from Sara; Ruth could see her at the edge of her vision, standing near the window, staring blank-faced. Ruth's time-sense was completely distorted; the scene seemed to have been going on forever, yet she knew everything was happening very quickly. Pat was on the move even before Bruce's body struck the wall. The column of darkness did not move as he came toward it. It waited. It did not menace or threaten, rather it shrank in on itself like—

Like a coiled spring. The analogy completed itself in Ruth's muddled brain, as the spring was released.

Standing off to one side, she had a clear unobstructed view of what happened. But at the final moment something fogged her eyes—mercifully, for such things were not meant to be seen, could not be seen in safety. When her vision cleared, the coiling smoke had disappeared. But it was not gone. It looked at her from Pat's eyes.

Ruth heard the whistling exhalation of Sara's breath, and the sound of her body dropping to the floor. She wished she could faint too. Pat was a big man, tall and heavily built. He looked bigger now. His hunched shoulders seemed hulking and swollen.

The eyes—not his eyes—saw her, and were indifferent, and passed on. But that one fleeting contact with the venom of the Adversary, now concentrated and focused, wiped every emotion out of her except for a sneaking, cowardly relief: She was not in Its direct path; It did not want her. She fell to her knees, huddled like an embryo, making herself small. Anything to avoid meeting, ever again, the blackness of its regard.

From first to last her heart had not measured more than a dozen beats. It took Bruce that long to get his breath back and to move out, from the opposite wall, into Its path.

Movement seemed difficult for It. Its steps dragged. It stopped when Bruce barred Its way, and raised Its heavy head to look at him; and Ruth saw him jerk back and fling a hand up before his face. She knew the impact of that gaze; and she knew the effort it cost Bruce to stay where he was, on his feet, and to lower his shielding hand. The change in his demeanor, from the terrified panic which had driven him, woke an answering spark in Ruth's brain. Now that the thing he most feared had happened—the thing he alone of them all had seemed to foresee—he was ready to face it. Slowly and painfully Ruth began to drag herself erect. That brand of courage demanded all the support she could give it.

Even as she swayed to her feet the final transformation came, the great overshadowing of the present by the shapes of the dead past. The bodies of the two men seemed to waver and grow insubstantial. They were the same, but not quite the same; surely, she knew, these two, or two others indentical in intent, had stood like this, in silent confrontation, once before. The older man, a heavy, hulking shape, head lowered like a bull ready to charge, fists clenched, arms dangling at his sides; the younger, slender and poised in breeches and ruffled shirt, the long blade in his right hand ready but not yet raised, his coat discarded in the warmth of a spring night. . . .

A gust of air from the shattered pane struck Ruth's face, and her mind went reeling; for the air was not the damp cold air of a winter night in Washington. It was balmy and fragrant with the scent of lilac: the smell of an April night which had passed out of time two centuries before.

Chapter Ten

"Call him, Ruth."

The voice came from far away. Ruth shook her head, feeling the soft spring breeze against her closed eyelids. The fragrance of lilac filled the room, heavy and sweet.

"Call him. Call his name. Ruth, please. Help me."

The voice was nearer now, and somehow familiar. It was a man's voice. The wind touched her face. . . .

The wind was cold, carrying rain. Ruth opened her eyes.

She was looking straight at Bruce, who stood swaying on unsteady feet, his face ashen and his eyes fixed unblinkingly on that other face, as if the force of his gaze held it back. Then the looming form took a step forward, and Bruce's right arm lifted. Blood still dripped from the cuts on his hand; his stained fingers were tight around the handle of the poker from the fireplace set.

"Call him, Ruth, see if you can get through to him. . . . I don't want to have to kill him. . . ."

As the Other moved again, Bruce fell back a step, casting a frantic glance over his shoulder. He could not retreat much farther. Behind him was the closed window, and Sara, sprawled like a dead woman against the wall.

"Pat," Ruth said. "Pat, it's me, Ruth. Can you hear me?"

For an instant she thought the heavy shoulders shifted. Only for an instant.

"Pat—darling. Listen to me. Pat. . . ."

"It's no use," Bruce said. "Ruth, get out of the way. It's as strong as an ox. It doesn't know you. . . . God!"

The last word was a gasp, half-drowned by the rush of the heavy body across the carpet. It was quick, for all Its bulk, and Bruce was slowed by a fatal handicap—the body It occupied. Ruth had not even thought of it as Pat; it was so unlike him in all the significant ways. Yet the head at which Bruce aimed the poker was Pat's red head. He brought the weapon up in a whistling arc; but he could not bring it down. And in the instant of hesitation, the thing was upon him.

They went crashing backwards together. The impact of the fall, and of the heavy body on top of him, knocked Bruce out as he hit the floor. He lay still, face upturned and eyes closed, the poker fallen from his hand, while the blunt fingers settled around his bared throat, and squeezed.

Ruth was so close that she could see the separate reddish hairs on the backs of the hands, red-gold lifted threads in the lamplight—the same light which fell brilliantly on Bruce's face; and she watched while his cheeks and forehead turned from white to mottled red, and darkened.

Forever afterward she was to wonder what will guided her hand—blind luck, or unconscious knowledge, or—something else. The object her groping fingers lifted from the table at her side was heavy enough to stun, and necessity guided her aim. But there was this, and she would never forget it: As the Book left her grasp, the thing that crouched on the floor reared up, lifting clawed hands in menace or protest, Its face upraised, Its mouth stretched in a snarl. The massive volume struck It full in the face, obliterating Its features momentarily, and then dropped back onto Bruce's chest. The Thing followed the book down, falling flat across the boy's body; but not before Ruth had caught one glimpse of a face which was, once again, the face she knew, gone lax in unconsciousness.

She ran forward, avoiding the fallen figures. The window latch gave sweetly, and she shrank back, throwing her arms up before her face, as the wind shrieked in, snatching the double leaves of the window and hurling them back against the wall. The lash of the cold rain stung her forehead; the blowing drapes bellied out like live things.

She heard Sara groan and stir as the freezing damp struck her face, but she had no time for lesser casualties. Pat was lying face down on the floor, arms out above his head. She caught him under the arms and tugged. Nothing happened, his dead weight was too much for her. She transferred her grip to one wrist, straightened up, and leaned back on her heels. The heavy body moved a few inches.

Ruth gasped with terror and frustration. She had to get him out of here before he woke, and the rough handling itself might rouse him faster.

She heard a gasp and a whimper from Sara, and turned. The girl was on her feet, one hand twisted in the lashing folds of the drapes. She was staring wide-eyed at Bruce. The dusky color had faded from the boy's face, but the marks of Pat's hands, and nails, were plain on his throat. He wouldn't be of any help for a while, Ruth thought coldly. She reached out and caught Sara by a strand of black hair as the girl stumbled past her.

"He'll be all right, there's no time for that now, I need help," she said, in one breath, as Sara's head jerked back and she gave a squeal of pain. "Take his other arm. Hurry, for God's sake, before he wakes up."

Sara gave one agonized look at Bruce and obeyed.

Between them they got Pat as far as the windows, and there Sara got some of her wits back.

"He'll catch pneumonia," she said, between chattering teeth. "And it's t-t-ten feet down into the rosebushes. Ruth, you can't—"

"Oh, yes, I can." Pat was beginning to mutter and move. Fear gave the final surge of strength to Ruth's muscles. She grabbed his legs and shifted him so that he lay across the ledge; after that one good hard push was all it took.

From the sounds, she could tell that he had landed, and hard. She turned on Sara and caught her by the shoulders.

"Out you go," she said, and shoved.

She did not wait to see what happened, but whirled in the same movement and ran back to where Bruce lay. She dropped to her knees beside him; but her shaking concern was not for the unconscious boy. It was the poker in his hand that she wanted. If Pat tried to climb back through the window she would have to use it.

The sounds from outside, audible even over the sigh of the wind, were reassuring. Pat was plainly awake now, he was thrashing and bellowing in the bushes; but the tone of his fury was obviously, blessedly, Pat and no one else.

The handle of the poker was unpleasantly sticky when Ruth touched it; when she pulled her fingers back, they were smeared with red. Bruce's hand had stopped bleeding, but it was a gory mess. She had not been able to bring herself to look at his face for, despite her reassurance of Sara, she feared he was dead. But she could not leave him without so much as a glance; pity and affection and profound gratitude finally broke the shell of ice that had shielded her, and the tears began to slide down her cheeks as she shifted, still on her knees, to where she could touch his face.

II

The car slid jerkily through a red light and went on.

"It's a good thing there isn't any traffic," Ruth said, with a shaky laugh. "I'm not at my best tonight."

Her efforts at conversation fell flat. In the back seat Sara was too preoccupied with Bruce to hear an explosion. He was awake, but his sole remark so far had been to the effect that his head felt as if it were about to fall off and roll across the floor. Ruth was not too concerned about him; since the moment when her hand had touched his cheek and his eyes had opened and stared quizzically at her, she had simply thanked heaven for the resilience of youth.

It was Pat she was worried about—Pat, who sat hunched and silent beside her, his head bent and his eyes focused on his own limp hands, where they hung between his knees. One of the reasons why she had run the red light was the certainty that a sudden halt would have flung him against the windshield.

It took them some time to get settled down after they reached Pat's house. First aid and dry clothes were the immediate needs, and Ruth had to tend to the dog, whom she had found shivering and pathetically subdued by the front door and had bundled into the car with the other wounded. Lady seemed to feel that a hearty snack would do wonders for her nerves, so Ruth took the hint, and also scrambled eggs and made coffee for the others. Finally she had them all settled down before the fire. Sara, in her green velvet, looked unbelievably normal. Seeing her clear eyes and unmarked skin, Ruth felt another deep surge of gratitude for the boy who occupied the couch.

They had bedded Bruce down though Ruth suspected, from the gleam in his eye, that he had no intention of remaining down. He was the most battered of the lot; there was a lump the size of an egg on the back of his head, and the marks on his throat had begun to darken.

Pat's injuries were superficial. His face and arms were crisscrossed with scratches from the rosebushes. All down the bridge of his nose, extending across his forehead, was a curious reddening and roughening of the skin. Ruth told herself that this must have come from the harsh nap of the carpet when she had dragged him. Oddly enough, however, there was no corresponding patch on his chin, and this area, it seemed to her, would have borne the brunt of the rubbing.

Whatever its origin, the physical manifestation was only a chafing of the skin. What frightened Ruth was the look in Pat's eye, and the frightening formality of his manner. He moved like something that had to be wound up, and was almost run down. It was not the overshadowing that she feared now. She knew what was tormenting him; and she gave Bruce a look of furious reproach when he said in his frog's croak, "You've got a grip like a wrestler, Pat. No more soapboxes for me for a few days. Talk about a fate worse than death!"

"Bruce—" Ruth began.

"It's all right," Pat said. "We might as well discuss the fact. The fact that tonight I tried to kill Bruce and almost succeeded."

"It wasn't you," Sara said.

Pat lifted his hands before his face and looked at them.

"Your hands but not your will," Ruth said intensely. "You're no more responsible than someone under hypnosis."

"A hypnotized subject," Pat quoted, "cannot be made to do anything against his will."

It was as if he had plucked the words out of a box of alphabet letters and arranged them on the table for their inspection.

After a moment Bruce said, "I've heard that theory questioned, as a matter of fact. But it's irrelevant. You weren't hypnotized. You were being used, just as a gun is used by the man who squeezes the trigger." The lecture ended in a squawk as his vocal cords protested, and he added, in a voice which was less formal and far more convincing, "Hell, Pat, don't be morbid. I know you think I'm a pain in the neck, but you wouldn't try to kill me under any circumstances, in your right mind or out of it."

There was a clicking sound from the hall, like steel knitting needles, and they all looked up as the dog padded sedately into the room. She stood next to the fireplace regarding them all in turn, with her red tongue lolling; then she walked over to Pat and collapsed at his feet with a weary sigh, putting her chin on his shoe.

Pat reached down and patted the dog's big head. When he straightened up his expression was almost normal.

"I wonder what she thinks of it all," he said. "Has she already forgotten, or does she shrug mentally and write it all off as human folly, beyond a sensible dog's comprehension?"

"No," Ruth said with conviction. "She's welcoming you back. She knows that wasn't you, back there. Pat, you have no idea—I can't explain—how alien It was."

"Trouble was," Bruce croaked, "it was your body wrapped around the damn thing. I couldn't bring myself to smash your skull."

"I appreciate your consideration, believe me. But if you didn't stop me, who did? I feel like Snoopy, I don't even know what was going on. I could feel the thing come into me, and it was just as Sara said—something pouring in, filling me up, something that didn't quite fit. That was a bad moment, the thing was so ravenously triumphant; and after that I don't remember a thing."

"I stopped you," Ruth said. She held out her hands. "So don't give us any more of your melodrama. How the hell do you think I feel about these hands of mine?"

"Language, language." Pat grinned at her and took her shaking hands into his own scratched palms. "When I came up out of that hellish rosebush you were hovering in the window with the poker. Would you really have used it?"

"Yes."

"Thanks." He lifted her hands to his face and then held them on his knee. Ruth moved closer and the dog, drowsing, made a soft grumbling noise.

"I missed the exciting part myself," Bruce remarked. "What did you do, Ruth? Not that I mind being outsmarted by a mere woman, but still. . . ."

"I threw the Book at him," Ruth said, and then gave an astonished gasp of laughter. "Sorry about that. . . . I did, literally. It was the big family Bible."

"That must have been some pitch," Pat said. "I didn't think the Book was massive enough to knock me out. It's big, and clumsy, but. . . ."

"I don't know!" Ruth exclaimed. "I wonder. . . . But it couldn't be that. The crucifix didn't work. . . ."

"I wonder myself," Bruce said. He was sitting up, despite Sara's objections; wrapped in one of Pat's wilder robes, a silk paisley affair that must have been a Christmas present because it had so obviously never been worn, he looked like an Eastern prince instead of a Spanish grandee.

"You know what really burns me?" Pat asked. "Not my attempted murder so much as my incredible stupidity. Bruce, you knew what was going to happen; you tried to stop me; I remember that much. You expected this."

"Suspect is the word, not expect. But—my God!—I died a thousand deaths trying to get you out of that room before it happened. I was sweating bullets."

"Why the hell didn't you tell me?"

Bruce flung out his hands. His eyes were wide and dark with the memory of that terrible frustration.

"How could I? You wouldn't have believed me, any of you. I didn't have a fact to my name, just a crazy hunch. . . . And you're so bloody bull-headed, Pat, you'd have stuck around just to show me."

"Hmmmph," Pat muttered. He cocked his head, eyebrows lifted, and studied the younger man with unwilling respect. "What made you suspect?"

"Oh, don't be so stinking humble; you couldn't have seen it coming—don't you understand? You were already half-shadowed."

Ruth moved, with a soft questioning sound, and Bruce nodded gravely at her.

"Yes, the night he had you down on the couch was the first time. I gather you were all wound up in certain private emotions, so you didn't see, as I did, how nasty it looked. It was out of character for Pat, very much out of character, especially with you—it was pretty obvious that he was getting—uh—sentimental about you. I mean, there are women you seduce and women you rape, and the women you—"

"You make your point," Pat said, trying to maintain a feeble semblance of dignity, although his face was almost as red as his hair.

"Oh. Well, the second time was when Father Bishko ran. You may not be devout, but you're polite. Your behavior on that occasion, again, was alarmingly atypical. But tonight, in the cellar, you really scared hell out of me. You kept coming up with those odd flashes of intuition, bits of knowledge you couldn't possibly have known—unless you were in some sort of contact with It, getting Its thoughts."

"Yes, I see," Pat said thoughtfully. "Amanda failed with Sara. She had to try someone else."

"No!" Bruce's voice rose. "No, Pat, you still don't get it. You've got it wrong. We all have it wrong. We were on the wrong track from the beginning."

In the silence the crackling and hissing of the flames were the only sounds, except for the dog's comfortable snoring breaths. Ruth never forgot the picture they made, her friends and allies, wearing their battle scars and fatigue like medals. The firelight ran bronze fingers through Sara's tumbled hair and made dark sweet shadows at the corner of her mouth. Bruce, leaning forward in his eagerness, his bandaged hand lifted for emphasis; Pat swathed in a horrible old bathrobe furred with dog hairs, his own hair standing on end like a cockatoo's crest, and his face crisscrossed with scratches. . . . And her own hands, at rest in his.

When Bruce began to speak, he had as intent an audience as any lecturer could hope for.

"We decided, early in the game, that we might have two ghosts. As soon as we learned about Ammie, it was obvious that she was the entity who came to Sara. Where we made our big mistake was in identifying her with A, the thing that materializes in the living room. I'd begun to have my doubts about that even before tonight; because, if there was one thing we agreed on, it was that the smoke, or fog, was evil. It produced an overpowering repulsion and terror. Ammie never affected us that way."

"But, Bruce," Ruth protested. "She wasn't very—well, very nice."

"She was frightened and confused," Bruce said, with a curious gentleness. "The—well, the residue, let's call it—

of Amanda Campbell that lingers in the house is not a conventional ghost, a complete sensate personality. She's more like a phonograph record, stuck at a certain point. That's why she has been so incoherent and so unhelpful when we have contacted her."

He paused, waiting for a comment. None came, not even from Pat; and Bruce continued, "But Ammie, though vital in the arousing of the house, is not the source of danger. That entity, as dark and violent as the smoke and fire it suggests, is still aware, still reacting."

"Smoke and fire," Ruth said thoughtfully.

"No." Bruce answered her thought rather than her words. "I don't think the form of the apparition is necessarily conditioned by physical fire. It conveys the emotions that drive him, even beyond death—violence, darkness, threat. That was what possessed you tonight, Pat. And it was not a woman, however malevolent. I had already come to sense this presence as that of a man, a man like you in many ways, Pat—hot-tempered, passionate, potentially violent. That's why he was able to reach you, and why you didn't sense the change yourself. Ruth didn't realize because—well, because . . ."

"That's all right," Ruth said wryly. "This is no time to spare my feelings. I didn't realize because I was operating on the assumption that all men are beasts."

"You saw the overshadowing tonight," Bruce said, passing over the admission. "Was there any doubt in your mind that what you saw was male, not female?"

"Overpoweringly male," Ruth said promptly. "Bruce, of course! It works out like those little syllogisms of Lewis Carroll's. The thing that overshadowed Pat was a man. The thing that overshadowed Pat was the blackness. Therefore the blackness is male. Ammie is female. . . ."

"Ammie is not the blackness," Bruce finished. "So who is? It can only be one person, I think."

"Samson among the Philistines," Ruth said. "Samson was a husky specimen, wasn't he? The man who died by fire. . . . I know you don't agree with that, Bruce, but I can't help feeling that it must have shaped him, somehow. Of course. It's Douglass Campbell."

Bruce nodded.

"That explains why the Bible stopped It, when the crucifix didn't."

"You're so damned smart I can't stand you," Pat said gloomily.

"Douglass was a rabid Protestant," Bruce said with a grin. "He had no respect for Papist mummeries while he was alive. Why should he pay attention to them after he was dead?"

"Whereas the Bible. . . ." Ruth began. "Good heavens—it was probably Douglass's own Bible! How pertinent can you get?"

"But that's what I tried to say once before!" Sara's voice rose, and they all stopped talking to stare at her.

"What was it you tried to say?" Bruce asked.

"Oh, I didn't think much of the idea myself," Sara said. "And then you all drowned me out the way you do. . . . It was just something I read in a book of ghost stories. The man who wrote it was a psychic investigator and he said, someplace or other, that he always suspected ghosts couldn't be exorcised by rites they didn't accept when they were alive."

Bruce sank back onto the couch. Pat hid his face in his hands.

"Sara. . . ." Ruth began.

"Well, I'm sorry," the girl said defensively.

"What are you sorry about?" Pat's hands dropped from his face; it was red with amused chagrin. "It's so damned typical of us, bellowing our loud-mouthed theories, and ignoring the small voice that had the vital clue."

"I don't suppose we'd have paid any attention if she had been able to get it out," Bruce said glumly. "Sara, I've been lectured on my sins by a lot of people, but nobody ever made me feel quite so small and wormy."

"If it's true," Ruth murmured. "If it should be true—it opens up a number of incredible possibilities. . . ."

"All sorts of possibilities," Pat agreed. "Multiple after-worlds, diverse heavens, created by the belief of the worshipers. . . ."

"And it explains why the methods of exorcising evil spirits vary so much from culture to culture," Bruce said. "Devil masks and loud noises in Africa, crosses and holy water in Europe. And—" he glanced with oblique humor at Pat—"the analyst's couch and hypnotism today."

"What a heaven that would be," said Pat, still fascinated by his idea. "The Great God Freud and his disciples. Sort of a Brave New World, without sex taboos and frustrations. . . ."

Bruce sat up with a grimace of pain.

"There are more immediate applications for us." He leaned forward, and the firelight played on his set features, deepening the shadows under his eyes and cheekbones, giving a satanic flush to the flat planes of cheek and forehead. "We're all a little giddy with relief just now, but we have to face the unpleasant truth. Which is that our situation, bad enough to begin with, is steadily getting worse. Now that this force has been aroused, it is gaining strength." He looked at Ruth. "You said once that It was impalpable, and thus incapable of doing physical harm. Maybe that was true at one time. But now Douglass has found himself a body."

Pat stirred.

"No, he hasn't. Once, maybe, because I didn't know what to expect. . . ."

"We can't count on your powers of resistance," Bruce said ruthlessly. "It took Douglass longer to find a host than it did Ammie; maybe the tie of blood relationship has meaning, I wouldn't know. But now that Douglass has succeeded once, he may find it easier a second time. Your friend Bishko has the wrong idea, Pat. It's not Ruth who's in danger in that house. It's you."

"And Sara," Ruth said. "You think Ammie is harmless, but I'm not convinced."

Sara tossed her head, throwing the hair back from her face, and smiled at her aunt.

"Ammie won't hurt me, Ruth. I guess I've always known that."

"No, not Ammie," Bruce said. He heaved himself up with a grunt of pain, and extracted a sheaf of papers from his hip pocket. "Maybe you've forgotten that dream of yours, Ruth; but I wrote it down, that first morning. The core of it was a threat to Sara, and the thing that threatened her was a shapeless darkness. Why do you think I got in the way of that hellish thing tonight? Because I could see where its eyes were looking and where its steps were heading. It wanted Sara."

"I knew that too," Ruth said dully. "And even then I couldn't—do what you did. If you hadn't. . . . I can't say it. I can't even think about it. Bruce, I've made up my mind. I'm going to sell the house."

There was no immediate reaction. Bruce sat back, lids lowered. Pat, intent on the cigarette he was lighting, said nothing.

"You could," Bruce said finally.

Pat raised his eyes from his match to encounter Ruth's waiting gaze. His mouth twisted in a grimace which was a poor imitation of the smile he intended.

"You aren't beating a dead horse, Ruth; you're beating

the wrong horse. If you mean to give up, the thing to avoid is not the house. It's me."

It was an inappropriate moment for Ruth to become aware, finally and positively, of the fact she had denied so long.

"We'll be living here," she said calmly. "I won't need the house in any case."

Pat swallowed his protest the wrong way and began to cough violently.

"You're both jumping to conclusions," Bruce said; his expression was an odd blend of amusement, embarrassment, and sympathy. "Ruth, you can't sell the house; if someone else had experiences there your finicky conscience would devil you all the rest of your life. And, while I think Douglass is bound to the house, I can't be certain; and you can't spend your declining years toting a twenty-pound Bible around under one arm."

Cherry red with coughing and emotion, Pat tried to speak, but Bruce cut him off with an autocratic wave of his hand. Ruth was brooding about the phrase "declining years," and did not interrupt.

"We've got to get rid of Campbell for good," Bruce went on. "That's the only way out. The situation is not as hopeless as it looks, we've already learned a great deal. So far the only thing that has had the slightest effect on our visitant is the Bible. The logical conclusion, I suppose, would be that we should turn for help to a Protestant minister. But frankly, I'm dubious. I don't think there is such a thing as a ritual for exorcism in any of the Protestant creeds; and even if there were we'd be taking a terrible risk in exposing someone else to Douglass. A certain type of personality might be driven hopelessly insane."

"What a cheery little optimist you are," Pat said bitterly. "You've just eliminated the last possible hope."

"Man, you are obtuse," Bruce said scornfully. "We've

found out a helluva lot in the last couple of days, but we're still missing the one vital clue. What does Douglass want? What is it that is keeping him from his rest?"

"He wants her—Ammie," Ruth said despairingly. "How can we satisfy that desire?"

"How do you know that's what he wants?" Bruce countered. "Even if it were—suppose he's obsessed and haunted by not knowing what became of her. Maybe we could find out. Maybe that would satisfy him. Myself, I can't believe his desires are that innocent. He's seething with rage and malevolence; the whole house is rotten with his hate. Why? I tell you, there's a part of the story we still don't know."

"You may be right, at that." Pat was looking more cheerful. "You know, Bruce, there are several factors that don't fit into your interpretation. The voice, for instance. It's not malevolent; it's kind of pathetic. How do you account for that?"

"I can't, and I'm not sure I need to. Maybe it's Douglass at one moment of time, and the apparition is the old man at a less attractive period. Maybe the voice is Ammie, echoing the cry that calls her back. The thing that interests me is what we called Apparition D. The one that moved the book."

"It wasn't Douglass," Ruth said. "He was the one who tried to prevent us from finding it. So it must be—"

"Ammie," Pat finished. "But she isn't much help, is she? Was the book only meant to give us the year, so that we could identify the right Campbell? Or does the Loyalist Plot have a specific meaning that we haven't yet discovered?"

Sara, pensive and shy in her squatting position, raised her head, swept the hair back from her brow, and broke her long silence.

"Why," she said simply, "don't you ask Ammie?"

III

The clock struck midnight, and they were still arguing. Bruce had worn himself out in outraged argument; he was reclining, his profile very young and sulky.

"I won't do it," Pat said. He folded his arms. "That's final."

"We'll never find out otherwise," Sara said, for the fifth or sixth time. "It's the only way."

"But the risk, Sara," Ruth exclaimed. "We opened the door once before for Ammie, and see what happened! So far this place is safe—uninvaded. We can't—"

"You said that before," Sara pointed out. "And I said you have to take risks to gain anything worth having. Even safety."

"It's more than safety that interests you," said Bruce, staring malevolently at the ceiling.

"I feel so sorry for her!" Sara burst out. "I've felt her; you haven't. Bruce is right, she's confused and lonely. . . ."

"Emotionally involved with a ghost!" Pat groaned. "Well, I won't hypnotize you, and that's flat."

"She would come tonight," Sara pleaded.

"Well, she can't come." Bruce continued to contemplate the ceiling. "Tomorrow Ruth and I are going to finish searching the attic. We haven't exhausted the conventional sources yet."

"Bruce," Ruth said reluctantly, "I hate to bring this up, but—maybe I'd better search the attic alone."

She had never seen Bruce so surprised. He swung his feet to the floor and sat up.

"Why?"

"It just occurred to me tonight, when I saw you and Pat facing one another. . . . There was a third person involved in the story. If Captain Doyle was a young man, desperately in love with Sara—I mean, Amanda—"

"A third overshadowing?" Bruce brooded. "I never thought of that. . . ."

Pat was staring.

"I don't like the way this is going," he said slowly. "Are we still on the wrong track, even now? If three of the four of us repeat a pattern of dead time, what about the fourth? Douglass Campbell was married. Are we trapped in some ghastly repetition of history?"

"Campbell's wife died in childbirth," Ruth reminded him, "and there's no hint of another woman. No, Pat; I didn't feel myself—shadowed—ever. But I did feel, tonight, as if that confrontation had happened before. If Campbell found you a suitable host, what about Anthony Doyle and Bruce?"

"No," Bruce said, with a finality that surprised them all. "I'd have felt it, Ruth. If I'm sure of anything, I'm sure that Doyle is, in his own way, at rest."

"You didn't see yourself," Ruth insisted. "You didn't feel. . . ."

She knew then that she would never, ever, be able to tell anyone about the final collapse of the fabric of time, when she had smelled lilac that had withered two hundred springs before. "It had happened, another time," she said stubbornly. "You and Pat, Campbell and young Anthony. The same positions, the same emotions—"

She was expressing herself badly, she knew that; but Bruce seemed to catch something of what she was trying to say, and his response fascinated her. His jaw dropped, with a slow, mechanical movement, and his eyes opened so widely that they seemed to fill the upper part of his face. But before he could speak the girl sitting cross-legged before the fire lifted her head.

They had all chosen to forget that Sara needed no help in doing what she wanted to do. The rapport was established; her new-found pity, and her fear for the others, did the rest. While they argued and ignored her, she made her decision. The thing was done in silence, without struggle. But they knew, even before they turned to look, that what they saw was no longer Sara.

IV

"Sara. . . ." Bruce's voice was a groan.

"Not Sara. Gone." The dark head moved in negation, and Ruth went sick at the unfamiliarity of the gesture.

"Ammie," she said.

"Ammie . . ." the soft slurred voice agreed sweetly.

"Where is she?" Bruce demanded. He was so white that Ruth thought he was going to faint; but she could not move, not even to prevent him from falling. It was Pat who took charge; his hand on Bruce's shoulder pushed the boy back on the couch; his voice, professionally flat, took up the questioning.

"Forget that. Amanda, you come to Sara. Why do you come?"

"Help," the voice wailed, and Sara's body shook from shoulder to heels. "Help . . . Ammie. . . ."

"We will help," Pat said quickly. "Don't be afraid. You're safe here, safe with us. No one can hurt you. Whom do you fear? Is it Douglass Campbell? Is he the one who comes in the darkness?"

"Father."

"Your father, Douglass Campbell. Is he still there, in the house?"

"Still there," the soft voice whispered. "Still . . . hurting. Help . . . Ammie. . . ."

"What does he want?"

"Hurt . . . oh. . . ."

The voice was unbearably pitiful. Pat's face was as pale as Bruce's, but his voice retained the professional calm of the trained hypnotist's.

"He can't hurt you, Amanda. You are safe. Safe. I tell you that, and you know it is true. But you must help us, so that we can keep you safe. What does your father fear? Was he involved in the Plot—when they were trying to free the British soldiers in Georgetown?"

"George Town," said Ammie's voice; and Ruth heard, with a terrible thrill, that it broke the word into two parts. "Father helped. . . . Anthony knew. . . ."

"Anthony Doyle?"

"Anthony . . . knew father. . . ."

"I understand," Pat said, as the voice rose. "Anthony knew your father was a traitor. Anthony was a soldier, wasn't he? In the Continental army?"

"General's . . . aid. . . ." The voice had an echo of dead pride that struck Ruth more coldly than anything it had yet said.

"Why didn't he tell the General?" Pat asked. "About your father?"

"Told . . . father. . . ."

Ruth writhed with the ambiguity of it; she wanted to take Amanda by the shoulders and shake some sense into her. But she knew this would be dangerous, for Sara as well as for the dazed girl ghost. And Pat seemed intuitively to understand the incoherent words.

"He told your father he knew? Is that right? He wanted to warn him?"

"Told father. Fair. . . ." Sara's lips twisted in a spasm of silent laughter, and Ruth shrank back against the couch.

"Of course, that was the only fair thing to do," Pat agreed soothingly, though his forehead was shining with perspiration. "He was your father, and Doyle loved you. He came for you, didn't he? Now, Amanda, listen to me. You are safe; no one can hurt you here. Tell me what happened the day Captain Doyle came to take you away."

"Night," Amanda said strongly. Sara's eyes, and what lay behind them, grew glazed and fixed. "Came . . . night. . . ."

"At night," Pat agreed. "What happened, Amanda?"

"Night. Came . . . Father saw . . . Father. . . ."

The glazed eyes lifted, and for the first and only time Ruth saw the living face of Amanda Campbell, as it had looked on that night in April (oh, the lilacs!) of 1780. It was the same face she had seen in her dream.

"Father," the voice began again, with obvious strain; and then the last syllable lifted and soared into a scream that made Ruth's heart stop. "Not dead! Not dead!" the dead girl cried, and the body of the living girl wrung its hands and twisted as if in pain.

Pat's arm swept out just in time to heave Bruce back onto the couch. He dropped out of his chair onto one knee before Sara, and took her by the shoulders.

"Ammie, be still, stop, be quiet, everything is all right. . . ."

It was the tone rather than the words that did the job, the blend of firm confidence and cajolery. The screams died to a wild sobbing; and finally the mesmerist, now gray to the lips, was able to insinuate his final command.

"All right, Amanda, you're a good girl. . . . You

helped, you helped very much, it's all over now. . . . Forget. Safe. . . . You're safe. It's time for you to go now, time for Sara to come back. Time for Amanda to go home."

The sobbing was quieter and less endurable; it had a piteous quality that wrung the heart. The fading voice said, in tones of infinite desolation,

"Can't. Ammie can't . . . go home."

V

A single silver chime sounded. Ruth looked dazedly at the clock. Only an hour, for all that turmoil. . . . She turned back to Pat, putting the fat-bellied glass into his lax hand.

"Drink it, all of it. You need something."

"She's asleep?"

"Yes, finally. The sleeping pill worked."

"God, I hated to give it to her! I'm terrified of drugs in these abnormal states. But what could I do?"

"Nothing. You had to." Ruth sat down on the couch beside him. She was abnormally calm herself; seeing everyone break down all around her had strengthened her will. Resolutely she pushed to the back of her brain the memory of Sara after the invader had finally gone. Or had she? In the moments before the sleep of exhaustion and drugs had claimed her niece, she had not been at all sure what part was Sara and what the lingering remnant of Amanda Campbell, now firmly implanted in the channels of another girl's brain.

"I sent her away," Pat insisted, as if to convince himself. "I tried, Ruth."

"You did marvelously, I couldn't have spoken, let alone handled her as you did. Pat, it's all right! She'll be fine in the morning."

"Is Bruce still up there?" Pat gulped roughly two ounces of brandy and sat up a little straighter.

"Yes, I told him to lie down on the other bed. This is no time for the conventions."

"I don't give a damn about the conventions; the kid needs sleep himself. You'll have to sit up with her, Ruth. We can't risk it. I'd do it myself, only. . . ."

He hid his face in his hands with a painful groan, and Ruth rescued the brandy glass just before it baptized him.

"It was a crazy, touching thing for her to do," he said between his fingers.

"In a way I know how she felt—and I don't even have this fantastic empathy with Ammie. She's desperate to end it, Pat. We'll all go out of our minds from the strain, even if nothing worse happens."

"Bruce has an idea." Pat took the glass back and finished its contents. He gave a short, unpleasant laugh. "I never thought I'd see the day when I would hang breathless on the words of a young twerp like that."

"He's better able to handle this. More involved than you, brighter than I. And less hidebound than either. He was right about that, Pat; they all are, darn them. You do get petrified in your thinking as you grow older."

"Not in all your thinking." He gave her a feeble, sidelong smile, and then withdrew his hand from her touch. "Ruth, I'm afraid to touch you, and that's the truth. But you know—"

"Yes, I know. This can't last forever, Pat."

"Then the other ghosts are laid?"

"I think so. Yes."

"Then maybe some good has come out of this ghastly mess. I'd like to believe it. I'd like to believe something."

The low flames on the hearth sputtered, dying, and the stillness of late night gathered closer.

"My own beliefs are all jumbled up," Ruth said somewhat shyly. "But, Pat, I can see hints of things I never dared believe before. . . . Isn't this one of the great questions? Survival?"

"Yes, survival—but of what? We've been given no proof of Heaven, Ruth. Only of Hell."

Chapter Eleven

Sara picked up a fork and stared at it blankly; and Ruth's heart stopped. Her panic was only slightly lessened when Sara shrugged and plunged the fork into a piece of bacon. There had been too many such incidents already this morning, and it was not even eleven o'clock.

Ruth had not meant to sleep at all, but her body was too much for her; it demanded rest. She fell into a solid, dreamless sleep at dawn. Bruce had already eaten and left the house by the time the others stumbled downstairs, and there was no sign in the kitchen that he had any breakfast beyond a cup of coffee.

The doorbell rang as they were finishing breakfast, and Pat went to answer it. The ringer was Bruce, who ambled into the kitchen with something less than his usual grace. He looked like Death—a decadent, elegant Renaissance version, bearded and long-haired.

"I borrowed your car," he told Pat, and held out a bunch of keys on one forefinger. "Hope you don't mind."

Pat took the keys and looked at them stupidly for a moment before shrugging and putting them in his pocket. They were all stupid with weariness, Ruth thought; and felt a surge of hope. Maybe Sara's frightening moments of unresponsiveness meant no more than that.

"Where'd you go?" Pat asked, pouring more coffee.

"Huh? Oh. Hardware store."

"Did you have any breakfast?" Sara seemed more alert in Bruce's presence. "I'll cook you some eggs."

"No, thanks," Bruce said. A look of profound distaste curled his lips. "Not hungry."

"Well," Ruth said, with a bright air which even she found hideously inapropos, "let's get to work, shall we? The attic for me and Bruce—"

"Not the attic," Bruce cut in. "Have you got some slacks with you? Well, you can change after we get there."

"What do you—Bruce. What did you get at the hardware store?"

"Tools. Ax, crowbar, wrenches."

"The cellar door," Pat said. "Is that it, Bruce?"

The eyes of the two men met and a flash of understanding passed between them.

"We've a problem of tactics," Pat went on, while Ruth sat speechless. "Ruth isn't exactly bulging with muscle, and it's your right hand, isn't it, that's damaged. If I remember that door, you need a bulldozer. Or two strong right arms."

"Of all the people who shouldn't—" Bruce began.

"I couldn't agree more. But I don't see how you can do it otherwise."

Bruce said nothing, but his shoulders sagged visibly. His hands lay on the table, curled around his cup of coffee. The bandages on the right hand were amateurishly clumsy, bulky enough in themselves to make any effort awkward.

"You should have a doctor look at that hand," Ruth said, still groping. "I used half a bottle of iodine, but—"

"Time for that later," Bruce said. The implication hung

heavy in the air, but he did not voice it. "God. I wish I knew what to do."

"You can't call anyone else in to help," Pat continued, with hard insistence. "If what we suspect is true, this is going to be a hell of a mess. Don't forget, Bruce, we haven't seen Douglass materialize in the daytime yet."

"Yet," Bruce repeated witlessly.

"If we keep the women out. . . ."

"Sara, yes," Ruth said. "But I'm coming."

In the end it was decided that they should all go. Ruth knew that Bruce gave in to Sara's insistence only because he was equally afraid of leaving the girl alone. And as they prepared to leave the house he took Ruth aside for a moment, and she learned the other, principal reason for his surrender.

"I want you to have this," he said, and handed her a can, a fat aerosol spray container.

"What on earth. . . ."

"Sssh!" Bruce glanced over his shoulder. Pat's footsteps could be heard in the hall upstairs; Sara was finishing the breakfast dishes in the kitchen. "It's one of those chemical gas sprays they use in riots. You know how to operate it, don't you? Point it, like shaving cream—what else comes in these cans? Furniture polish? Then you've operated them before."

"But what—" Ruth was beginning to feel as if she had never been allowed to finish a sentence. Bruce interrupted, "You pick out a nice safe spot, out of the way, near the exit. Keep this thing handy, but out of sight, your finger on the nozzle. If you see the slightest sign of anything you don't like, from Pat or Sara—or me, for that matter—point the thing and let 'em have it. It's a new kind, works instantaneously. Remember to hold your breath; but since you'll be behind it—"

"I don't believe it," Ruth muttered. She eyed the harmless-looking can with repugnant incredulity.

"Ruth, I'm counting on you! I don't think we're in any danger at this time of day, otherwise I wouldn't dare risk it. But you're the reserves. I was planning to keep this can myself if Pat and I went down there together; I don't much enjoy the idea of meeting Douglass Campbell when he's armed with an ax. But this is better. You can keep it ready, and he won't know. . . . Sssh, here they come. It's important that he doesn't know you have it, stick it in your purse till we—"

He turned to give Sara a fairly convincing smile; and Ruth, her hands trembling, jammed the can into her bag.

II

The atmosphere of the cellar had not improved since their last visit; it was still dusty, damp, and grim. After the ominous, unused stillness that overlay the rest of the house, a stillness that seemed to Ruth to hum with ominous anticipation, the cellar was even worse.

With a meaningful glance at Ruth, Bruce turned on the electric lantern he had brought and ducked into the space behind the furnace. Pat followed without a word, heaving the heavier of the two crowbars onto his shoulder. He had shed coat and overcoat, as well as his tie, upstairs, and the muscles of his back and shoulders, visible through his thin shirt, were impressive. Ruth felt a shiver slide down her spine. She had never had a higher opinion of Bruce's courage. To be trapped in that dusty, confined space, with something armed for murder, something that still raged with an insane fury that had survived two centuries. . . .

"Sit here," she said to Sara, indicating a place on the

stair; and, rising, she went to stand near the wall in a spot
from which she could see the two men. She still wore her
coat, on the not invalid excuse that the basement was chilly,
and her right hand was in the large patch pocket.

Bruce glanced at her over his shoulder and Ruth smiled at
him, willing him all the strength she could give, by her
presence and her knowledge. He produced a rather strained
smile in response; and she thought, I've done him an
injustice. If Sara can catch him, she'll have a prize. This
isn't an intellectual game for him; he's risking his life for her
sanity. How many men would do that for a girl?

Then the ax in Pat's hands came down with a crash that
echoed through the close, dank air.

After all it took less than an hour to force the door. Pat's
strength made the difference. The solid planks had hardened
with age, the nails had rusted in place, and each piece of
wood had to be hacked to pieces before it could be
wrenched out. But finally only an inch of wood lay between
them and the hidden space beyond. Nothing could be seen;
there was not a trace of light from the inner cellar. But a
breath of dead, noisome air penetrated the cracks and made
both men back away.

"Why don't you rest for a minute?" Ruth suggested.

She was half sick herself with apprehension. It had gone
too smoothly; she could not believe that they would
accomplish their aim without interference. Unless, she
reminded herself, it was pointless. Perhaps their effort had
been for nothing, and the mysterious blocked-off space was
only an empty, abandoned cellar.

But in her innermost mind she did not believe it. The
tension could not be all imaginary; some of it, thickening as
the moments wore on, must come from the outer air. At one
point she had thought she felt a breath of the familiar,
deadly cold, and she had risked leaving her post just long
enough to dash up the stairs and close the door. Illogically,

she felt more secure with even that frail barrier between her and the ominously quiet living room. On her way down she had almost stumbled over an object which lay on the stairs beside Sara. She recognized it—the big Bible, which the girl had evidently carried down from the living room. Ruth approved the thought, but her glance at Sara did nothing to lighten her apprehension. Silent and withdrawn, the girl sat on the step staring into nothing, like a statue.

Now as the final barrier lay before them, ready to be breached, her fingers were so wet with perspiration that they slipped on the slick surface of the can in her pocket.

"Why don't you rest for a minute?" she repeated.

"Better not wait," Pat said briefly and significantly. He inserted his crowbar into the center boards. They gave, with a creak and a screech, and Pat stepped back, his hand before his face, as the unwholesome air gushed out.

"Whew," he said. "The place is like an ancient tomb. Wait a minute, Bruce, and let the air clear."

Bruce nodded. He was leaning frankly against the wall, his chest heaving in and out, his shirt clinging damply to his body. Ruth knew that his exhaustion was not solely the product of physical exertion. After a few minutes Pat said, "It's better now."

He picked up the ax and knocked out the remaining fragments of wood. Hoisting the lantern, he vanished into the hole, which brightened with wavering light.

Bruce gave Ruth a desperate, wordless look, and followed.

Ruth glanced from the rigid form of her niece to the dusty yellow-lit hole in the wall. She did not like Sara's look or Sara's position, so near the upper doorway; but she knew her presence was more badly needed elsewhere.

It would have taken some resolution to enter the condensed atmosphere of the hidden room under ordinary circumstances. But for Ruth, personal distaste was swallowed up by her fear for the others. She was afraid to let Pat out of her sight for an instant; and, under the other emotions that drove her, she was conscious of a feeble flicker of plain, ordinary curiosity.

At first glance the old cellar was a disappointment.

It had even fewer features of interest than the outer room. It had always been windowless. The walls, of heavy stone instead of cement, were covered with slimy lichen, of a sickly yellow-green, and they gleamed wetly in the light of the lantern. The floor was beaten earth, so hard that the dampness lay on its surface in oily-looking beads. In a corner, out of the direct lantern light, something shone with pale luminosity. The basement made a splendid nursery for mushrooms, very big, very white, and oddly swollen-looking.

Despite the seeming normalcy of the room, Bruce was not at ease. He had gotten his back up against the wall—or as close against it as he could get without actually touching the slimy surface—and he still held, with an attempt at casualness that was definitely unconvincing, one of the crowbars. Pat seemed comparatively unmoved. He looked up as Ruth hesitated fastidiously on the threshold.

"Hand me that shovel, Ruth, will you?"

Ruth obeyed, concealing her reluctance at stepping onto the nasty-looking floor. The space was larger than she had anticipated. It must lie under most of the long living room area, and—she shied back, uncontrollably, as the realization struck her—it must be, in actual fact, the original stone-built foundations of the first house. Douglass Campbell's house.

After a wordless consultation with Bruce, who only shrugged helplessly, Pat went to the far, back corner and shoved the spade into the earth. The floor was not as hard as it looked; Pat's big foot, placed firmly on the head of the spade, forced it several inches into the ground.

It was as if the shovel touched a spring buried deep in the earth, and set off the reaction. Ruth had turned to watch Pat. She was still puzzled as to his intent, though it seemed clear enough to Bruce, and for a moment she had forgotten nervous fears in curiosity. Bruce was the first to see it come, perhaps because he was expecting it. His mouth opened in a shout which never emerged; and Ruth's eyes followed the direction of his pointing hand.

She had actually expected to see Sara, once more in the grasp of her unwelcome visitant. But the other—no, she had always seen it in a certain spot, and never expected to see it elsewhere. The cloud of black was dim; it writhed as if in struggle. Douglass Campbell did not like the daylight. But his need, now, was more desperate than custom.

"Not here," Ruth said, hardly aware that she had spoken. "No . . . not here. . . ."

"This is where it comes from, this is the center," Bruce shot at her. "The spray, Ruth—get it. Pat. . . ."

Ruth obeyed, though with difficulty; her fingers were already numb with cold. Balancing the crowbar in unsteady hands, Bruce swung around to face Pat; and Ruth hesitated, because the field of her weapon included both men.

And because, this time, Douglass Campbell was not having it all his own way. Perhaps it was because he was weaker, between cockcrow and dusk; perhaps because Pat now was warned and reacting with all the strength of his will. From first to last he did not utter a sound, nor move beyond the first involuntary start of surprise that swung him back, away from the shovel. Somehow his immobility only made the struggle more apparent, and its ferocity more felt. Ruth watched the perspiration gather and stream down his face, saw the muscles tighten in the arms that still gripped the spade handle. His lips were drawn back in a spasm that bared his teeth. She stood waiting, her hand on the incongruous weapon, and as she watched the wavering column of darkness seemed to shrink.

Then the cry she had choked back rose up in her throat. In the doorway, behind the Thing, stood Sara. It was Sara, not the other girl, but a Sara who appeared to be walking in her sleep. In her arms she cradled the heavy Book as another woman might hold a baby.

Bruce lunged forward, raising the heavy steel bar. Ruth never knew what he intended to do with it, for as he moved his foot slipped and he skidded to his knees. Before he could rise, Sara spoke.

"It's no use." She spoke in a conversational tone, and Ruth's blood froze as she realized that Sara was not addressing any of the three human beings in the room. "It's over, can't you see that? You can't silence all of us."

She paused, her head tilted in an uncanny listening look.

"It was never any use," she went on, in the same reasonable voice. "Who were you trying to fool? He beholdeth all the sons of man."

Ruth wondered who "he" might be. Then she knew, and her breath caught painfully in her throat.

"'Behold, the eye of the Lord is upon them that fear him,'" Sara said. "It was all known, and the end determined, from the beginning. Now go, and seek the hope that even such as you were promised. Go . . . in peace."

The smoky column swayed and shrank. Then, with an absurd little pop, it was gone; and Ruth, running through the space it had occupied, caught Sara in her arms as the girl collapsed.

III

They found what they were seeking almost at once, in the very spot where Pat had begun to dig. Sara had recovered from her faint almost at once, and with only the vaguest memories of what she had said. Standing with her arm around the girl, Ruth looked down at the pitiful remnants of mortality. Some quality in the clayey soil had preserved them well.

"So he was here," she said. "Douglass Campbell."

"No." Bruce shook his head. "These bones have never been touched by fire. And Douglass's remains would have been gathered up with the debris of the upper stories of the house." He stooped, and with careful fingers pulled from the earth a twisted piece of corroded metal. "The buckle of the belt of a military uniform," he said, holding it up. "This wasn't Douglass, Ruth. It was Anthony Doyle."

The light shone steadily on the four white faces and motionless hands, but there was nothing in the foul air now beyond its own natural gases.

"He came that night for Ammie," Bruce went on, "but he never left. He's been here ever since—ever since Douglass Campbell murdered him and buried him in the cellar."

"And that was the secret Douglass Campbell tried to hide for two centuries," Ruth said; but she knew the truth, even before Bruce's head moved, again, in the slow gesture of negation.

"No. Douglass Campbell went mad that night, but not because of Doyle's murder. I can almost predict the spot where we'll find her—right under that certain area in the room above—the opposite corner from this, as far away from her lover as he could put her. Even in death he couldn't endure to have them lie together."

IV

It was like being born again, to come up the stairs into the thin sunlight of a winter day. Ruth went to change her clothes and found herself scrubbing her hands over and over, as if the miasma of the cellar and what it contained could be washed away. When the four gathered, in the kitchen, Ruth suggested lunch, like a good hostess; but it was unanimously and immediately refused. Her offer of wine was more acceptable and as she poured the sherry, Ruth remarked,

"If this hadn't ended we'd all have become alcoholics. I've never drunk so much, at such peculiar times of day, as I have lately."

"If this hadn't ended," Sara repeated, and stared rather blankly around the circle of pallid faces. "I can't believe it. This," she indicated, with a wave of her hand, the smug modern kitchen. "This is anticlimactic."

"But it is over," Ruth said. "He won't be back. I don't know why I'm so sure, but I am."

"Yes, he's gone. And how the hell Sara ever—" Ruth caught Pat's eye and shook her head in silent warning, but he had already stopped speaking. They all felt, somehow, that Sara's last seizure had better not be discussed, at least not then. Instead Pat turned to Bruce.

"He wasn't normal, was he? That was the terror we felt, his madness."

"He lived the last forty years of his life, and died, insane," Bruce said soberly. "That was the state in which his spirit lingered. Imagine those years, month after month, cooped up in this house, with what lay below in the cellar, rotting. . . ."

"Don't," Ruth said faintly.

"That wasn't the worst—not what was in the cellar but what still clung to the house and the old man's mad, decaying brain. He must have seen her in every room, heard her at every moment of his waking life—and in his dreams. . . ."

"He had to kill her, after he killed Doyle," Pat said, more prosaically. "She'd have destroyed him if he hadn't stopped her. She must have known; maybe she saw it done."

"Oh, yes, she saw it done," Ruth said; she was shaken by a sudden fit of shivering. "She saw it done. . . . Dear heaven, don't you remember? We heard her screaming, just as she must have done that night. . . ."

"'Not dead,'" Sara repeated. "She wasn't talking about herself when she said that. A phonograph record, cracked and caught, repeating—repeating the words she said when she saw Anthony Doyle fall, by her father's hand. 'He can't be dead—he's not dead. . . .'"

"At least she didn't have much time in which to suffer," Ruth said.

"Only an eternity." Bruce's face was pinched. "However the dead reckon time. . . . She never stopped suffering, she was caught in that one unendurable moment like a fly in a spider's web. Both of them, she and her father—murderer and victim. . . ."

"Maybe the first murder—Doyle's—was an accident," Ruth said. "Surely he wouldn't have had to kill the boy to keep Ammie from eloping."

Bruce shook his head.

"Part of it will always be conjecture; but—remember Ammie's own words. Doyle was the General's aide. I'll give you three guesses which general," he added.

"There were lots of 'em," Pat said practically. "Gates, Greene, von Steuben—"

"I know which General," Ruth said. "You be logical. I know."

"Me, too." Bruce smiled at her. "Hopeless romantics, both of us. Anyhow, the General, whoever he was, sent Doyle to this area. He fell in love with Ammie, and she with him; but he never had a chance with the old man. In the course of his duties Doyle came across the Plot. Imagine his feelings when he discovered that the old rat Campbell, who had thrown him out of the house, was up to his neck in treason! He had a perfect instrument of revenge—but he couldn't use it without destroying his fondest hopes. The other conspirators were hanged, if you recall. How could he expect to marry the girl after he had, in effect, killed her father? So he came that night to warn the old S.O.B. to give up his dangerous activities. Remember Ammie's own words; he wanted to be fair. I would guess that he had already recorded the names of the other conspirators, but he omitted Douglass Campbell's name. He came in good faith; but he underestimated Campbell's hate. He probably never even had a chance to defend himself."

"And yet you say he is at rest," Ruth said wonderingly.

"Ruth, I don't pretend to account for this world, let alone the next. But maybe . . . Doyle died in what you might call a state of grace. His intentions were honorable, his actions harmless; hell, he probably wasn't even mad at anybody. There was no guilt on his soul, to keep it from the peace his faith had taught him to expect. But Campbell—by the terms of his own creed he was damned! He expected to go straight to Hell, and he did. I can't think of any greater hell than to endlessly relive the act that destroyed you."

"And Ammie?"

Bruce's face assumed the curiously gentle expression it wore when Ammie's name was mentioned.

"Ammie. He wouldn't let her go, in life or in death. And she—she had time, before she died, not only for terror and the last extremity of fear, but for hate. How could she help but hate him, after what she had seen him do?"

"But how did you know?" Ruth demanded. "You did know—both of you. Pat even knew where to start digging."

"You, of all people, should have seen the truth," Bruce said. "Good Lord, you were the one who told me about your feeling, when you saw me and Pat squaring off, that it had all happened before. You even suggested that it must have been Douglass and Doyle who were the original antagonists. But if they had ever met in such an encounter— one so violent that it left an imprint on the very air of the house. . . . Doyle would have been as helpless as I was. He couldn't have killed her father, any more than I could slug Pat."

"I knew after that last talk with Ammie," Pat said. "It seemed so hellishly plain to me—maybe because I was still getting flashes of Douglass's memories. She tried so hard to tell us what happened. . . ."

"We should have suspected from the first," Bruce concluded. "All the clues were there. Ammie's terror and shock indicated a violent end in the house to which she was bound, not a peaceful death in Camden, New Jersey, at the ripe old age of eighty. And there was Douglass's behavior— shutting himself up, not even going to church—that suggested something stronger than grief. He was afraid to face his angry God with that black sin on his soul."

"His own daughter," Ruth murmured. "Infanticide. The worst possible sin. . . ."

"No." The boy's dark head moved in the now-familiar gesture. "It was bad enough, but it wasn't the worst. The thing that drove Douglass Campbell mad was not so much his crime as the reason for it. He didn't kill Ammie to keep her from betraying his other murder. No normal father could have done that. He killed her because—"

His eyes met Pat's; and the older man's head bowed.

"You felt it," Bruce said.

"I felt it," Pat agreed heavily. "But I didn't know what it was, not until we had the whole story. The ravenous desire, and the sick hatred of that same desire. . . . It's in here, somewhere. . . ." He pulled the Bible toward him; Ruth had carried it up from the basement. He began leafing through the pages.

"He never remarried," Bruce said. "Not in all those years, when other men acquired three and four wives. She was all he wanted, or needed. And then she tried to leave him. . . ."

He broke off, as something in the quality of Pat's silence struck him. Pat had found the reference he wanted; he sat staring down at the page, where a passage was savagely underlined in strokes of dark blue ink—the same ink which had obliterated Ammie's name.

"But I say unto you, that whosoever looketh on a woman to lust after her hath committed adultery with her already in his heart."

V

The words had all been said; but the final scene was not played until some weeks later. The famous oaks of St. Stephen's raised bare branches into a sky sagging with iron-gray clouds, and the somber green of the pines made a dark background for the white marble of crosses and headstones. When the first flakes of snow began to drift down, Father Bishko excused himself and went in. The others lingered, looking down at the simple stone with its paired names and dates.

"How did you ever get Anthony's birth date?" Ruth asked. "Oh—from the army records, of course. I'm amazed that they go back so far."

"Not only that, but they can be revised," Pat said with an air of modest triumph. "I told you about Doyle's being listed as a deserter."

"Yes. Final confirmation of the truth, if we needed confirmation. . . ."

"Hardly," Bruce said grimly. "I didn't know it was possible to tell so much, just from bones."

"Age, sex, manner of death," Pat said. "I took that course in physical anthropology twenty years ago, but a fractured skull and a broken neck aren't hard to spot. Campbell must have been a giant of a man. . . ." Ruth shivered. He put his arm around her, and went on more cheerfully, "Anyhow, Doyle has been reinstated. I don't know that he cares; but I feel better, somehow."

"How on earth did you accomplish that?" Ruth asked.

"I found a General with some imagination." Pat laughed, and gave Bruce a friendly slap on the back that almost sent the boy sprawling. "Bruce is still sulking. He hates to admit that any army officer can have a heart."

"He's an Irishman," Bruce said sourly. "As you might expect."

"And a friend of Pat's?" Sara guessed.

"Like Father Bishko," Ruth said. "Thanks to Pat's wide circle of acquaintances, we've managed to do this without publicity. I didn't think we could. Father Bishko was splendid."

"He's a master at tactful planning," Pat said. "And think how relieved he was to find out that all he needed to arrange was a memorial Mass and a cemetery plot. Not much com-

pared with a full-scale exorcism—and the distinct probabil-
ity of another encounter with evil incarnate.''

"How you can find it amusing, even now. . . .''

"It's been over a month," Pat said. "And not a sign.''

"Yes, I can put the house up for sale with a clear
conscience.''

Hands jammed in his pockets, black hair powdered with
snow, Bruce glanced at Ruth.

"You really intend to sell the house? After all the years
it's been in the family?''

"I offered it to you and Sara," Ruth said, and smiled, a
bit wryly, at the boy's involuntary gesture of rejection.
"Yes, well, you know how I feel, then. The place is purged,
I'm sure. But. . . .''

"Anyhow, family pride is the emptiest of vanities," Sara
said firmly. She bent over to straighten the sheaf of flowers
that lay against the stone.

"Where did you find lilac, at this time of year?" Ruth
asked.

"You can get anything anytime, if you pay enough for
it," Bruce said. "And we paid enough.''

"You're already starting to sound like a husband," Ruth
warned. Bruce gave her a sheepish smile.

"I was just kidding. Sara had this thing about lilac; she
kept insisting it's what Ammie would have liked.''

"Oh, yes," Ruth said. She looked at Sara. So she was
not the only one who had smelled the scent of lilac on a
night in November. "Yes, nothing could be more suitable.''

"I'm freezing," Bruce said crankily. "And I've already
missed one class today. Since I've got to get that damned
degree before Sara's mother will let us get married. . . .''

"It's easier than dragons," Ruth pointed out.

"One thing still bugs me," Pat remarked, as they started
to turn away from the quiet earth, now blanketed by the soft

white purity of the snow. "The voice. It must have been Douglass. But it sounded so pathetic. . . ."

"No," Ruth said. "Ha—beat you to it, Bruce. You know everything, so you must have an idea about this too. You never did think the voice was Douglass, did you?"

"No." Bruce drew lines in the snow with his toe, and studied them intently.

"Well?"

"It sounds so damned . . . sentimental," Bruce complained.

"What's wrong with being sentimental?" Pat asked.

"Well. . . ." Bruce added two more lines, making a rectangle. "He was safe," he said, addressing the tip of his shoe. "But how could he rest quietly, knowing that she was still lost?"

"Oh," Ruth said. "I see."

"He doesn't need to call her anymore." Bruce's eyes went to the sheaf of delicate purple flowers, sending their sharp perfume through the falling snow. "Because now, finally, Ammie has come home."

NGAIO MARSH

"She writes better than Christie."
—The New York Times

____ 07504-3	WHEN IN ROME	$2.95
____ 07503-5	DEATH OF A FOOL	$2.95
____ 08757-2	FINAL CURTAIN	$2.95
____ 08798-X	LAST DITCH	$2.95
____ 08775-0	CLUTCH OF CONSTABLES	$2.95
____ 08718-1	SPINSTERS IN JEOPARDY	$2.95
____ 07627-9	BLACK AS HE'S PAINTED	$2.95
____ 07507-8	NIGHT AT THE VULCAN	$2.95
____ 07440-3	DEAD WATER	$2.95
____ 07851-4	THE NURSING HOME MURDER	$2.95
____ 07501-9	A WREATH FOR RIVERA	$2.95
____ 07700-3	DEATH AT THE BAR	$2.95